MW01127250

Reviews of the *MacGregor Family Adventure Series*
Cayman Gold: Lost Treasure of Devils Grotto
Book One

VOYA • Journal for Librarians • August 2000
"Science fact and fiction based on folklore intertwine in this fast-paced story of pirate gold and adventure. In an increasingly rare story line, the family is intact, with parents who are intelligent and involved in the lives of their children....surely will appeal to older teens—mostly boys—looking for a blend of adventure and a bit of romance."—Pam Carlson

KLIATT • Journal for Librarians • May 2000
"In this quick-moving adventure story, teenagers who are expert scuba divers bump up against modern-day pirates....The author, an environmental biologist and college professor, shows his love and fierce protectiveness of natural resources and endangered species. This story is fun to read while making teens aware of environmental issues."—Sherri Forgash Ginsberg, Duke School for Children, Chapel Hill, NC

***Midwest Books Review* • "Children's Bookwatch"**
"...*Cayman Gold* is a well crafted adventure with meticulous attention to accuracy in detail and highly recommended reading for teens and young adults."
                    —James Cox, Editor-in-Chief

"Kids Books" • *Northwest Metro Times*
"This riveting story combines historical events, hurricanes, daring escapades and some nasty bad guys and puts them all together in a way that will keep you on the edge of your seat until the final page.—Dale Knowles

"Book Briefs" • *The Sunday Oklahoman* • Feb. 2000
"...Billed as a young adult-family novel, this adventure story offers suspense and some good lessons in conservation."—Kay Dyer

Elephant Tears: Mask of the Elephant
Book Two

"An action-packed journey for young adults through the trials and triumphs of wildlife conservation in the African bush."—Dr. Delia and Mark Owens, Zoologists, Authors of *Cry of the Kalahari, The Eye of the Elephant,* and National Geographic film, *African Odyssey.*

VOYA • **Journal for Librarians** • **December 2000**
...portrays the teens' relationships with each other and with their parents as wholesome but realistic...respectfully depicts the native Africans and their tradition without glossing over their problems...descriptive narration is admirable—family-friendly realistic wildlife adventure."—Leah Sparks

KLIATT • **Journal for Librarians** • **September 2000**
"...the author weaves an exciting adventure while stressing the importance of protecting the earth's dwindling resources and endangered animals. It is a powerful, enlightening novel that remains exciting without being didactic."—Sherri Forgash Ginsberg

Midwest Book Review • **"Children's Bookwatch"**
"*Elephant Tears* is a thriller adventure novel...superbly researched and written, *Elephant Tears* is one of those infrequent novels for young readers that are so easy to pick up, and so hard to put down! Also highly recommended is Trout's first adventure novel, *Cayman Gold.*"
—James Cox, Editor-in-Chief

"Kids Books" • *Northwest Metro Times* • **August 2000**
"This is an action-filled thriller set in the plains of East Africa that you will want to read for the excitement factor as well as gaining a lot of insight into the problems of wildlife survival. I certainly enjoyed it, and I think you will also.—Dale Knowles

Falcon of Abydos

Falcon of Abydos

Oracle of the Nile

Richard Trout

MacGregor Family Adventure Series

Book Three

Pelican Publishing Company
GRETNA 2005

First published by Langmarc Publishing, 2001
Published by arrangement with the author by
Pelican Publishing Company, Inc., 2005

Library of Congress Cataloging-in-Publication Data

Trout, Richard.
  Falcon of Abydos : oracle of the Nile / Richard Trout.
    p. cm. — (MacGregor Family adventure series ; bk. 3)
    Summary: While in Cairo for an international
environmental summit, the MacGregors discover ancient
artifacts in the shifting sands of the Sahara that could
lead to a major war and change the face of the Middle
East forever.
    ISBN 9781589803275 (alk. paper)
    [1. Egypt—Antiquities—Fiction. 2. Adventure and
adventurers—Fiction.] I. Title.

PZ7.T7545 Fal 2001
[Fic]—dc21   00-064858

Jacket illustration by Aundrea Hernandez

Printed in the United States of America
Published by Pelican Publishing Company, Inc.
1000 Burmaster Street, Gretna, Louisiana 70053

Dedication

for

Keely

who would have loved
living among the grandeur
and glory
of ancient Egypt

Contents

Introduction 1

Prologue: Bahariya Oasis 575 B.C 5

1 Sahara, August 2000 25

2 Dunes 33

3 The Sting of Pharaoh 43

4 Little Shop of Thoth 57

5 Wings Over Egypt 69

6 Never Eat Camel 81

7 Bears and Sand Fleas 99

8 The Well of Muhammed 107

9 Princess of the Nile 123

10 Khensu Eyuf 137

11 House of Thutmose 143

12 Hawks, Vultures, and Falcons 155

13 The Osirieon 169

14 Entombed 187

15 Ras Mohammed 203

16 114 Degrees 217

17 Sign of the Falcon 233

18 Oracle of the Nile 245

Epilogue: On the Mediterranean Sea 257

Disclaimer 269

Acknowledgments

A special thanks goes to Joe Zorger, Lynn Nored, and Kent Bogle for technical advice on aviation, satellites, uplink stations, and explosives. Thanks to Dr. Virgil Trout and Bill Knight for providing unique insight into ancient Egypt. And thanks to those who have continued to support this series with solid advice and encouragement. They are Margo Funk, Ann Hovda, Diann McKasson, Martha Nored, Dale Knowles, Carolyn Knowles, Judith Turner, and Donna Watson.

Introduction

World-famous Dr. Jack MacGregor is taking his family on an adventure around the world while he is writing a book on endangered species and conservation.

Book One of the MacGregor Family action/adventure series, *Cayman Gold: Lost Treasure of Devils Grotto*, deals with hurricanes, the safety of tropical reefs, and beautiful sea turtles while involving Chris, seventeen years old, Heather fourteen, and Ryan, age twelve, in a great mystery.

Book Two, *Elephant Tears: Mask of the Elephant*, deals with the difficult subject of elephant exploitation and the illegal ivory trade with the three MacGregors in a wonderful adventure in East Africa.

Book Three, *Falcon of Abydos: Oracle of the Nile*, touches upon the subject of the exotic and beautiful Nile River while at the same time takes the reader on an adventure involving terrorism, international espionage, and lost treasure of the Pharaohs.

The theme of each novel briefly touches on one or two environmental topics with a moderate viewpoint being expressed. I do not support environmental extremism and fully support hunting as a means of conservation. Building fences around wilderness areas makes no sense.

In 1968, the Aswan High Dam was completed with the purpose of controlling water flow down the Nile River toward the delta at the Mediterranean Sea. This environmental modification of water flow was achieved at a great cost in money and effort. What seemed to be a great idea decades ago now appears to be an environmental disaster looming on the horizon. Every effort to manipulate the natural course of this planet should be studied extensively before resources become unrecoverable and ecosystems are damaged forever.

In my novels, I portray the world as it is, a place where the forces of good and evil struggle to dominate. But in writing about good and evil, it should be noted that evil can only be portrayed as horrible and sinister. Writing about evil is just as uncomfortable as reading about it.

This novel deals with a part of our world where there are millions of good people struggling to gain their freedom. It is a struggle that has been going on for centuries and has had a great impact on the modern world, causing wars and generating internal strife and terrorism. When good nations have been oppressed long enough, they will always yearn for self-determination. The intrigue of this and other *MacGregor Family Adventure Series* novels is that Chris, Heather, and R.O. confront the realities of life with the tools their parents have provided. That is what we want for all kids—tough preparation for a tough world, wrapped in love and understanding.

One last note about spelling. In researching this novel, I discovered that there are three different ways to spell the name of an Egyptian Pharaoh, god, or city.

In the two dozen books I read about Egypt, I found

many glaring differences in spelling by very learned people. Writing about this complex ancient civilizationwas no easy task. I have made a valiant effort to be consistent in spelling and capitalizations. However, the spelling may change within the novel because of a variation that is part of the mystery of this novel and / or the mystery of ancient Egypt. Read and enjoy!

Richard E. Trout

Prologue

Bahariya Oasis
Eastern Sahara Desert
250 Miles Southwest of Cairo
575 B.C.

The sand was kicked high in the air behind the two white steeds. Their mouths were foaming from the lack of water. The chariot driver snapped the whip high over the horses. They continued to dig hard through the soft sand of the Sahara.

The driver looked over his shoulder and could see the cloud of dirt of his pursuers. His red and gold headdress flew freely in the wind and trailed behind him. His enemies were only a few miles behind him. He cracked the whip again and yelled at the horses, their hearts pounding from the chase. For them, it could have been just another race across the hot sand. They had no fear, no anxiety. They only wanted to please their master. So they galloped with every ounce of strength they could summon.

The gilded chariot reflected the rays of the bright sun that baked the dry sands. The side panels were decorated with reliefs that depicted a Pharaoh in a similar chase two hundred years ago. Five thousand years earlier the desert had been a lake. But with time, the earth's axis had changed and now the lake, once teeming with life, was nothing but a hot, dry forsaken land. It is the formidable Sahara Desert.

The whip was cracked again as the horses raced up a large dune. Sinking in the deep sand, the wide wheels of the chariot danced from side to side. As the driver pulled back on the reins, the horses stopped and heaved for air. The driver turned to look back across the rolling sea of sand and immediately spotted his pursuers only a mile or so away. They were all on horseback and were gaining on the gilded chariot.

The driver looked down at his precious cargo. It was safely packed in a wooden box that was brightly painted with hieroglyphics and inlaid with gold. He had no choice but to race toward the oasis at Bahariya. He prayed to Ra that his master would still be there and soldiers would be ready to fight. He cracked the whip once again as sweat rolled down the back of his neck on to his robe. The horses bolted forward.

He could see smoke rising above a row of dunes. He knew he was close to the oasis and the fortress. He wrapped the soft black leather reins around his aching left hand and reached down to the inside of the chariot with his right hand. There he found a brass horn. He yanked at the leather strap. The slip knot came loose, and he brought the horn to his lips. He took a deep breath and blew into it. There was no sound. Only the sputtering of his dry lips echoed through the fluted end. He tried again. The same sputtering noise came out. The hot dry air of the Sahara had sucked every drop of moisture from his mouth and lips. His left arm was cramping because of the pull of the mighty steeds. His shoulder ached. He checked on the enemy again. They were closing fast. A drop of sweat rolled into his right eye and burned.

Desperation engulfed his entire body. He knew the surprise attack would penetrate the fortress and the mighty Vizier Khensu Eyuf's oasis city would surely fall. He threw the strap of the horn around his neck and let it dangle there. With his right hand, he pulled a knife from his belt. Somehow he knew he had to warn the city or all would be lost in the Pharaoh's surprise attack. With a swift movement, he brought the knife's razor-sharp blade high and in a downward stroke slashed his left forearm. The sudden pain caused him to loosen his grip on the reins of the horse. He struggled to maintain control. As blood spurted from his open wound, he placed his mouth over the gash. He dropped his knife to the chariot's floor and retrieved the horn from his neck. On the first try, his blood-moistened lips held fast and noise blared from the horn. He blew again and again. He sucked on the wound and blew his horn with all his might.

As he topped the last dune, he saw his fellow soldiers scurrying about with their weapons. Archers had begun to line the top of the fortress wall. The points of their arrows gleamed in the noonday sun. Holding tightly to the long leather leads from the horses' bits, Zahi (za-hee) steadied his balance as the horses and chariot raced down the last long dune to the two-hundred year-old fort. Before the pursuers had cleared the same dune, the archers were hidden from view. In the sandy courtyard behind the massive walls, infantrymen and horsemen were busily gathering. The defense was beginning to take shape. The surprise attack was fast becoming a deadly trap for the pursuers.

Two mighty wooden gates swung open as Zahi and the two white steeds raced inside the stone fortress. In a few seconds the horses were sliding to a halt. Two young boys jumped on the horses' backs and pulled on the reins. As Zahi leapt from the chariot, another young boy jumped in, bent over, and picked up the gilded box. He leaned over the side and gently handed it to Zahi. Then with a whistle the three boys drove the trusty steeds to a stable near the back of the fortress. Sufficiently trained and disciplined, the boys completed their task in less than a minute.

Zahi turned around and was face to face with his general.

"Is this it?"

"Yes, General."

"Good. Follow me. Khensu Eyuf awaits." The general then turned to another officer. "Let the enemy reach the gate. Then kill them all."

"Yes, sir." The young officer ran toward the horsemen who were waiting anxiously behind the gate.

Zahi followed the general toward the palace located in the middle of the fortress. Walking rapidly they climbed the twelve stairs in unison. Their hard-soled sandals slipped on the sand that lightly dusted the stone. Four soldiers, spears in hand, raced by them. Soon Zahi and the general were inside the palace where the light reflected on the polished stone floors. Comfortable furniture was placed around the room. Tables with platters of fruit and meat were convenient to whomever lounged there. Across the long room, eight men huddled around a stone table with maps spread across the top. They looked up as Zahi and the general neared.

"Zahi, the son of my sister. You have done well. Hand me our prize," Khensu Eyuf said.

He took the gilded box from Zahi's hands.

"Well, it is heavy indeed. My eyes are impatient to see that which the Pharaoh prized so much." Eyuf, the Vizier and supreme ruler of the Bahariya Oasis and its surrounding cities, set the gold-inlaid box on the table.

Eyuf noticed the dried blood that was splattered on the box. He looked up at Zahi.

"Let me see your wound, my nephew."

Zahi held up his arm showing the mighty ruler the clean slice he had made in his arm with his dagger.

"Did the enemy do this? You are very brave."

"Yes, he is," was the consensus of several of the men standing there.

Zahi blushed and looked to the floor.

"What is it, my nephew?" Eyuf noticed his embarrassment.

"The enemy didn't do this, my uncle. When my mouth was too dry to blow the horn to warn the fortress, I used my dagger to cut my arm so the blood could moisten my lips."

All the men grew quiet. Eyuf stepped forward toward Zahi.

"My nephew is much braver than I imagined. I will let him open the Pharaoh's box in honor of saving us from the surprise attack. Break the seal."

Eyuf's general stepped forward and, with the butt of his sword, he crashed down on the gold latch. It broke in half and fell to the top of the table. Zahi walked over and placed both hands on the sides of the lid. Gently he pulled upward. There was no movement. All the men looked at each other. Zahi pulled again. It was still not moving. Eyuf pulled his dagger and handed it to Zahi.

Beads of sweat rolled across Zahi's dirty face. Dried blood was caked around his mouth. He placed the sharp blade of the dagger into the seam between the lid and the bottom half of the exquisite box. With one prying movement, the lid began to move. But the suction of the tightly-sealed box would not release the lid easily.

Suddenly, footsteps could be heard coming up the steps and into the palace. A young soldier raced the length of the room, a quiver of arrows tightly held in one hand and a magnificent bow in the other.

He bowed quickly and then stood up.

"Sire, there is a storm coming in from the desert."

"How far away is it?"

"It is here now."

"Now, but how did we not know this?"

"Sire, just when the battle started with the invaders did we notice the storm on the horizon. But it moved quickly. The winds are mighty."

"How many of the enemy are left?"

"We don't know, sire. They approached the gates but turned and fled before the archers could kill very many of them. The others are sitting on the top of the dune waiting."

"Waiting?"

"Yes, sire. Just waiting."

Suddenly a horn blast could be heard outside. It was a defense call to arms on the wall. Then another echoed across the courtyard and into the palace. The eight men, all officers, began running through the palace. But before they had reached the door, a wall of wind and sand met them and blew them to their knees. Each grabbed for his eyes to shield them from the blinding sand. Grains of sand stung their skin.

The mighty Vizier and Mayor of the Bahariya Oasis and his nephew Zahi watched in alarm as each man struggled to his feet. They pushed their way to the doorway. When all were outside, they realized that the visibility was only fifty feet. They couldn't see the fortress wall. Then another horn sounded from the desert side of the fortress. Then another horn from the north.

"Uncle, what does this all mean?" Zahi asked holding his cloak over his nose and mouth.

"I am afraid Pharaoh is using the cover of the storm to attack us on all sides. He was only using you to distract us so that his troops could surround the oasis."

Khensu Eyuf reached out to his top general and grabbed him by the arm.

"Sound an alarm for all men to hold their stations. No retreat! No surrender! This is a fast-moving storm, and we will have clear skies soon. I know it. If we pull back, then the enemy will penetrate the walls and we all will die. Do you understand?" Eyuf shouted over the noise of the storm. The sand stung his skin like a hundred lotus flower bees.

"I understand."

The general turned and soon disappeared into the sandy netherworld that surrounded the elegant palace. In a few minutes more horns could be heard through the shrill wailing of the storm.

"Zahi, come with me."

Zahi followed Khensu Eyuf back into the palace. They walked swiftly toward the stone table where the gold-inlaid box was still sitting. Eyuf clapped his hands and a young woman appeared from a hallway near a scarlet curtain.

"Zahi, you know Ona."

"Yes," he replied.

"She is the most trusted servant of this house. I want you to take the box with whatever treasures lie within and follow Ona. She will lead you to a place where you will leave the box and return. When it is safe, I will see what is so important to the Pharaoh that he would send his army to kill us."

"Yes, my Uncle."

As Zahi and Ona began to walk away, Eyuf called his name.

"Zahi. I must know one last thing."

"Yes, Uncle."

"From where did you steal this box?"

"Our spies led me to the tomb of Seti I, one of the greatest Pharaohs of all. The tomb had been opened and closed many times and was used to store great treasures of the Pharaoh and the Pharaohs before him. Our spies revealed that the box held the secrets of the great alliances the Pharaoh had made. But most of all, in it is the eye of a god that allows its owner to see the future."

Khensu Eyuf stepped closer to Zahi and touched the box with both hands.

"To see the future would make me the most powerful man on earth. Maybe even more powerful than the gods. Hurry Zahi. Hide the box and come back to me, and we will kill the enemy together."

With adrenaline coursing through his veins, the
mighty leader of the oasis ran through the palace toward the storm and the battle that was violently raging
outside.

"Quickly, follow me," Ona said.

Zahi followed her to a small hallway that led to an
immense wall covered with hieroglyphics. With her
petite hands, Ona pushed on a block of stone on the
wall. It moved a few inches and then slid back into place
blending in with the hundred other stones on the wall.
The perfectly balanced wall shifted slightly. Then she
pushed with all her might. The wall moved and then
slid back into place a second time.

"Zahi, help me push."

Zahi leaned against the wall, and it began to slide on
a bed of smooth sand. Soon the wall had rotated and
revealed a small room with an entrance from the other
side. There they found a dark stairway leading downward. Ona reached into a chiseled indentation in the
wall and pulled out an oil lamp. A stick with a flint on
the end was hanging from the handle. She grabbed the
stick and dragged along the stone wall. Sparks flew. She
tried again but this time she placed the oil-soaked wick
of the lamp next to it. The sparks ignited the wick, and
the lamp began to illuminate the downward spiraling
stairs.

"This way," Ona said.

Zahi held onto the box and followed her. They
continued downward for quite some time. Zahi lost
count at seventy-four steps. The hot dusty air of the
palace was now replaced with a cool breeze that seemed
to rise from the depths below. Suddenly the stairway
ended and they were in a long dark tunnel. The lamp
only lit the path on each side for about ten feet. It was as
if they were traveling in a lighted bubble along a narrow
tube. They could hear a hissing sound in the distance.

"How much further?" Zahi asked. He was feeling

refreshed from his long hot ride across the Sahara.

"We'll be there soon," Ona replied.

They walked in silence for another ten minutes through the long tunnel. Words were not spoken. Each knew the gravity of their responsibility.

The hissing sound gradually changed to a rushing noise. And the rushing noise became a light roar. And the light roar became a deafening noise. The light from the lamp finally exposed a rushing river before them. The water vapor in the air had soaked their clothes and the moisture had refreshed their skin and lungs.

"I have never felt so good," Zahi shouted over the noise of the river below them.

"I love it here," Ona replied. "I have been allowed to come only twice before. I pray to the gods every day that I could return here."

They stood on a stone precipice that exited the long tunnel and looked over the mighty underground river, the source of the water at the oasis.

"Did my Uncle Khensu Eyuf carve this tunnel?"

"No. I was told that he discovered the tunnel. It once was a spring that rose to the surface, but the water now follows a different path. Your uncle's servants spent three years building the stone pathway in the tunnel to reach this spot."

"But why would he want me to leave the box down here?"

"Follow me. You'll see."

Ona walked over to the edge of the precipice and then turned to her right against the rock ledge. She disappeared into the side of the wall. Zahi, puzzled, followed her path. When he reached the edge and turned to his right, he could see a shadow in the wall. He knew it had to be another tunnel, but he couldn't see the light of Ona's lamp. As he stepped toward the wall, he could see a light flicker. He was in the crevice that led to another tunnel. Following the dim light, but not seeing

Ona, he followed another stairway downward. After twenty steps, the tunnel leveled out. It had water six inches deep over the pathway. Ona stood ten feet away and smiled. The water reflected the light and made it brighter.

"Don't worry. The river is now above us. The water is only a few inches deep. Follow me, we are almost there. Zahi treaded into the water; it was cool and felt good on his burning feet. He held the box tightly. As he reached Ona, he watched her climb even more steps and walk through an opening into a large room. He followed her. The room brightened dramatically even though Ona still held the small lamp. Zahi realized that the walls were covered with gold.

As he looked around, he could see gold images, gold furniture. Everything was covered or made of gold. Ona kept on walking and entered another room.

When Zahi caught up with her, he asked, "What is this place?"

She turned to face him. The lamp lit up her face. She had brown eyes and a beautifully painted face. Her eyes and lips were exaggerated with the make-up, but even in the dim light she was a stunning beauty.

"All I have been told is that this is a place of safekeeping. Khensu Eyuf can protect us as long as he has the riches to do so. This is where he keeps them. There are four rooms here. Each has something of value in it. There is a room for gold, one for iron ore, one for precious gems, and one for the gods. It is in the room for the gods that we will place the Pharaoh's box. It's over here."

Zahi followed her across the room with the gold and into a smaller room that was painted with bright hieroglyphics and lined with images of the many gods of Egypt. There was an altar of some sort in the middle of the room. Zahi walked toward it. He placed the gilded box on it and stepped back. He turned and looked at Ona standing at the doorway. Her dark skin was beautifully silhouetted by her wet yellow gown. He looked back at the box. He took out his uncle's knife and placed the glistening blade into the seam of the wooden box.

"What are you doing?" Ona asked as she hurried across the room toward him.

"I'm going to finish what I started in the palace."

"But you can't. Khensu Eyuf will be angry."

"I'm his nephew. I stole it from the Pharaoh Apries. How angry can he get?"

Zahi pushed on the dagger and could feel the lid beginning to move. In a couple of seconds the lid would pop free. Zahi laid the dagger on the stone altar and looked into Ona's beautiful eyes.

The earth rumbled under their feet and the walls began to move.

"We must go," Ona shouted and ran toward the door.

Zahi stood in darkness and let go of the box. He looked into the darkness at the box and then toward the lighted doorway. His decision was easy.

Soon Ona and Zahi were running across the room of gold and down the steps to the tunnel underneath the river. But the water in the tunnel was now waist deep and rising. Zahi grabbed Ona by the hand and shouted for her to hold the lamp high above their heads. Struggling through the tunnel they made it to the other side and climbed quickly up the steps. In a minute they reached the precipice overlooking the river. But now the river had risen and was rushing by them just inches away from their feet. In a few seconds they would be swept away.

Suddenly a giant wave created by an earthquake could be heard roaring through the underground labyrinth.

"Look. We'll be swept away. We've got to go back."

"But we'll die!" a terrified Ona shouted.

"We have no choice. In a few seconds the tunnel to the palace will be under water. We stand a better chance in the rooms above the river," Zahi argued.

Ona finally nodded her head in agreement, and they both started back down the steps to the tunnel under the river. The tunnel was now full of water up to their shoulders. Quickly they pushed through the rising water. As they reached the gold room, the water rose and flooded the entire tunnel. They both looked down in horror as their passageway turned into part of the underground river. The water began to creep into the room of gold. The ancient wooden furniture floated around the room.

Zahi and Ona rushed across the room and into the room of the gods. The oil lamp faithfully burned and provided the source of their only hope. If darkness engulfed them, it was doubtful they could survive. Water followed them and crept up to their knees. Zahi lifted Ona up on the altar and then climbed up himself. They both just stood there and looked into each other's eyes. Any other time, they might have found each other attractive and pursued one another. But now, they held on only with hope to live. The oil lamp continued to burn. They took turns holding it, hoping that at any moment the water would begin to recede so they could follow their tunnel back to the surface.

But the water didn't recede. Soon it reached the top of the altar. Zahi saw the water rush toward the gilded box. He bent over and grabbed the box. He had risked too much to see it wash away as a piece of gold-plated driftwood. Ona, about a foot shorter than Zahi, looked up into his face again. She noticed a shadow on the ceiling above.

"Look. Hold the lamp up high."

Zahi took the lamp and held it high over his head. What they had thought was a darkly painted hieroglyphic was actually a hole in the ceiling. Zahi gave Ona the box and with both hands reached up to the ceiling. The black smoke from the lamp was now trailing toward the ceiling and venting through the hole.

"Hold on to the box. I'll lift you to my shoulders. It's our only escape."

Without hesitation, Zahi bent down, wrapped his arms around Ona's legs, and lifted her toward the hole. Holding the box high with the lamp precariously balanced on top, Ona's hands disappeared into another chamber. Soon she was pulling her whole body through the hole. The light flickered from above, but Zahi was left in darkness. Water was now up to his knees. He jumped, but couldn't reach the opening. His heart pounded in his chest. He would have much preferred death by the sword of an enemy than drowning in the bowels of the earth.

Then he felt a soft cloth across his face. It was Ona's robe.

"Grab it and pull yourself up. I'm braced against a column. Trust me!"

He had no choice. He leapt high to free his legs from the suction of the water and with one hand over the other, he pulled himself toward the chamber above. His arms ached from the race across the dunes and the pull of the steeds. He knew he would surely die if he stopped now. With one last surge of energy and disregarding his pain, he reached out for the opening and found a grip with his right hand. In another minute he was untying the threads of the robe from Ona's tiny waist. She was gasping for breath.

The oil lamp was only minutes away from burning out. They could hear the rushing of the water below them, but the noise was muffled. Zahi stood up and held the lamp high in all directions. It was a small room, but yes, there was another door.

He pulled Ona to her feet, and for the first time, they

embraced. He then handed her the lamp while he retrieved the gilded box of the Pharaoh. They entered the
next room together. It was an apartment filled with
furniture. But it was from a different period of Egypt.
The fabrics were still bright with exotic hieroglyphics
woven into them. As they stood in awe, the earth began
to shake again. Dust particles danced around the room,
having been liberated for the first time in centuries.

"Ona, we've got to keep moving. The next room…"

"But our lamp is nearly out."

"We can only hope," Zahi said as he clutched the
Pharaoh's box with one arm.

Suddenly a wall shifted and the black, red, and blue
paintings of ancient Egypt began to crumble and fall
around them. A small piece of stone just missed Ona as
she darted through the doorway into the room behind
Zahi. The rumbling didn't stop this time. They raced
forward in their bubble of light, not knowing whether
they were going to ram into a wall, a closed hallway, or
drop into an abyssal pit deep into the bowels of the
earth. Their hearts were pounding. Already wet from
the river, the sweat that now drenched their bodies
made no mark on their robes or leather sandals.

They entered a long hall that began to slope toward
the surface. There were small and elongated steps that
eventually turned into stairs.

"We're going up. Zahi, we're going up!" Ona
shouted with glee and new hope.

The walls shook again and the stairs seemed to
move beneath their feet.

"Oh, no." Ona watched the flames begin to flicker .

"Look, another doorway." Zahi pointed as they ran
up the steps, their legs feeling like massive tree trunks
they could barely control.

"Run, hurry!" Zahi let go of Ona's hand so he could
maneuver up the crumbling steps. "Don't look back!"
he shouted.

The stairway disappeared behind them, falling backward into the remains of the ancient palace.

Zahi leapt as the step in front of him dropped two feet and a large crevice was formed. He reached the other side. He set the Pharaoh's gilded box in the doorway and reached back to Ona, who had stopped. She had a horrified expression on her face.

"Go on, Zahi! Save yourself!" She yelled over the rock grinding against rock.

"No. I won't leave you. Jump!"

The crevice was getting wider.

"Put down the lamp and jump," he pleaded.

Her eyes became wider. Finally in a last act of desperation, she set down the lamp, pulled her robe up to her knees, and took a long step backwards. Just as she began to move forward, the last of the oil burned from the wick and total darkness wrapped its cloak around them. Zahi's last sight of Ona was her tear-filled eyes as the lamp burned out. There was a horrendous rumble and the earth shifted its massive crustal plates. In that instant all time seemed to stop. The thought of imminent death had engulfed every thought of both Zahi and Ona. Their bodies cried out to survive; their minds were not willing to give in yet.

Then Ona's diminutive 100-pound frame collided with Zahi's outstretched arms in the darkness of the stairway, and he frantically pulled her to his chest. He smelled her perfume as their faces touched.

"We're alive," he said.

Zahi leaned over and felt through the darkness toward the Pharaoh's box. It was still there. He picked it up and tucked it under one of his muscular arms. He grabbed Ona's hand and told her to hang on to his arm, which was wrapped around the box. With his free hand, he led them through another passageway of the long lost desert palace.

"Wait. Steps. More steps to the right."

Together they climbed the steps in total darkness. Moving as fast as they could, they scraped their arms against the sharp walls of the stairway until they reached a landing. The rumbling of the earth seemed far away now. The cool air of the subterranean passageways and palace were replaced by the musty smell of the Sahara.

"I think we are in a room. I can't touch the ceiling."

"Oh, Zahi. We are doomed."

"No, I won't accept that. We are not going to die. The gods didn't lead us this far to dash our hopes now. I refuse to give in."

Zahi felt along the wall until he crashed into a large chair. Feeling their way around the chair, Zahi found the table.

"Let's move across the middle of this room. I'm letting go of the wall."

Ona held on tightly. Their wildest fears danced in their heads in the darkness. They imagined a crazy animal jumping from the darkness to consume them. Or a demon would appear and carry them away. Or even worse, a hole in the floor would materialize and they would drop into an abyssal pit forever. Their eyes strained to see, but there was nothing to see. There was only blackness.

Then suddenly, Zahi stopped.

"Ona. Stand beside me and look straight ahead. Then raise your chin a little and tell me if you see something."

"But it is totally dark in here."

"Try it."

Ona felt around until she was right next to Zahi. Slowly she adjusted her head until it was pointed in the right direction.

"A small white circle. A pin dot. It is faint but when I close my eyes and open them again, it reappears," she said.

"Light!" Zahi shouted.

With renewed hope they stumbled through the great hall of the palace bumping into furniture. First it was a chair, then a table. Twice they both nearly fell but managed to stay on their feet.

The pin dot began to grow. Soon they were standing under it. There was enough light to dimly see each other's face. It was a beam of light the size of one's hand piercing through the top of a window that was filled with sand. Without saying a word, Zahi handed Ona the box and climbed the sandy dune under the window. He dug at the sand as if he were a madman. It suddenly gave way and he slid down to the floor of the room. More sand entered through the window. The light was blocked and darkness fell inside.

"No..." Zahi yelled.

As if by command, the sand shifted and an even bigger beam of light reappeared. Zahi again climbed to the top of the window and began to dig. Ona set the box down and climbed up next to him. Together they dug with their hands, struggling each time the sand would move to engulf their bodies. Twice Zahi had to pull Ona out of the sand. Then without warning, the massive dune shifted and tons of sand began pouring through the window.

Caught in an avalanche of the Sahara, Zahi and Ona plummeted down the steep dune inside the palace and were quickly becoming consumed by the desert.

"Ona!"

"Zahi!"

They frantically grasped for each other but missed. The hissing sound of the moving sand filled the room. In a few minutes it was all over.

Zahi was buried to the waist. He looked around but couldn't find Ona. He frantically crawled out of the sand and ran up and down the newly-formed dune. The bright light of the Sahara was beaming into the room for the first time in centuries. Zahi shouted her name.

"Ona! Ona!"

He ran across the dune and began digging frantically like a dog after a bone. Then there it was. The
yellow corner of Ona's robe sticking out of the sand.
Zahi began to dig and pull as more robe was revealed.
Then he saw a hand. He clawed at the sand until he saw
the top of her head and then her face. Frantically he
pulled her from the grip of the fine sand and breathed in
her face.

He shook her. Then slapped her.

"Ona, listen to me. You can't die."

He shook her again and this time he heard a faint
cough. Pulling her up to his chest, he pounded hard on
her back. She coughed again. Then again. Her eyes
opened, and she choked and violently coughed. The dry
dust of the Sahara billowed from her lungs. Zahi held
her tightly, and she began to cry.

"Ona, you're alive."

Zahi steadied himself in the sand and picked her up
in his massive arms. She appeared as a doll against his
chest. Zahi marched steadily up the dune toward the
now open window and stepped out of the buried palace
into the bright light and burning sun. Ona lay in his
arms, now able to breathe normally.

"Zahi, I set the Pharaoh's box on the table."

"It's not important now."

"Oh, yes it is. It could mean everything to my
people."

Zahi carefully laid Ona on the sand and entered the
palace once again. The dune shifted a little below the
window. Sliding down the steep slope of the sand, Zahi
reached the bottom and could see that all of the furniture was buried under the sand. Retrieving the box
seemed like a hopeless task, so he began to climb when
something caught his eye.

It was a yellow-white glow in the sand near the
bottom. He edged his way over to it. He put his hand on

the sand over the glow and felt its warmth. Cautiously he began to dig until he could see the top of the Pharaoh's box. He pulled it free from the sand. What magic did he just witness? Maybe it was just an illusion. The Sahara was full of illusions. In a few minutes the box was in his arms. As he crawled up the sand toward the small window, the dune shifted again and tons of sand began to pour through the hole. Suddenly it was totally dark.

Zahi was soon buried up to his waist. He tried to dig, but with only one hand it was futile. In a few minutes he was back at the bottom of the mound of sand in the room of the ancient palace. The box emitted a glow that lit the room.

"I am not going to die in here!" He yelled as he wiped the sandy sweat off his face.

Looking at the Pharaoh's gilded box and then back toward the closed window, he made his decision. He made his way toward a table and set the box down. He began to crawl through the sand toward the closed window. As he neared the top, the sand began to shift again under his weight. He dug a hole and soon there was a glint of light. More sand moved and the hole was bigger. He saw two petite hands digging from the out-side. It was Ona searching for him. He dug faster. He had new hope.

With a desperate leap, he began to crawl through the small opening just as the sand caved in around him. He sucked sand up his nose and gasped for breath. He couldn't close his eyes because of sand under his eye-lids. The pain was intense but he dug ferociously with his hands and pushed with his cramping legs.

Suddenly Zahi felt Ona's hand and grabbed it. She pulled with all her might as he pushed with his legs and dug with his left hand. His head popped out of the hole. But more sand rushed down the dune toward him and filled the hole behind him. He kicked harder. Ona struggled and pulled. Finally Zahi was free from the death grip of the Sahara. The window was gone and only the top of a dune remained. The palace lay buried once again with the gilded box of the Pharaoh safe inside.

Ona and Zahi sat at the top of the enormous dune looking south toward the Bahariya Oasis. The fortress was on fire and massive plumes of black smoke billowed into the sky.

"My uncle is waging a valiant battle." He shed no tear; he had no lump in his throat. The struggle to survive had stripped him of all of these emotions.

"My people live at the Farafra Oasis one hundred miles to the south. They are good people, and I have not seen them in a long time. It will be good to go home. Zahi," she said. She turned to look at him. "Will you go with me? If your uncle survives, you can always return home and tell him where you left the Pharaoh's box. With a hundred men you can dig it free."

He looked into her big eyes and reached out and dusted the sand off her forehead.

"Yes, I will go with you. I can't help Khensu Eyuf if I'm dead, and I will surely die if I enter the battle now. Someday we'll see what the Pharaoh valued so much." He forced a weary smile.

As they walked down the long dune toward the Farafra Oasis, Zahi thought about the box that glowed and gave forth heat. A warrior by birth and a prince by birthright, he had no idea of the power and wealth that he had carried and now left behind for another day and another dynasty.

But Zahi's gods were smiling as the Nile beetle once again pushed the solar disc across the sky, and the secrets of Ra would lie protected for another twenty-five centuries.

1

Sahara

West of Cairo, Egypt
August, 2000

—————————◖▬◗—————————

"Mom, hang on!" R.O. yelled over the howling of the storm. "I've got you. Can you see Chris and Heather?"

"Yes. Chris is holding on to my belt," Mavis frantically replied doing her best to stay calm.

The hot sand pelted their bodies like small bee stings. Mavis tried to tie her bright red silk scarf over her eyes, but the wind kept yanking one end from her hands. She finally gave up and tucked it into the right front pocket of her khaki cargo shorts. The roar of the fast moving desert storm was deafening.

Mavis pulled R.O., her twelve-year-old-son, into her arms and sat down on the dune. Chris and Heather fell to the ground near to her. They crawled on all fours and were soon huddled together. Chris yanked at the seams on his right sleeve of the light weight khaki shirt and ripped the threads loose. He pulled off the sleeve and leaned over to tie it around his mother's head to protect her nose and eyes. He ripped off the other sleeve and handed it to Heather. She did the same for R.O., her younger brother. He then took off what was left of his shirt and handed it to Heather, leaving only his bright orange T-shirt to protect him.

The sand shifted and covered part of their legs as they huddled together.

"Chris! Are we going to be buried alive?" R.O. yelled over the wind noise.

"Mom, Heather, and I aren't. But you might be, little brother!" Chris smiled but only briefly as the sand flew into his mouth. He could feel it grinding between his teeth.

"Hey, don't yank me around, Chris. I mean it. Can this big dune cover us up?"

"No, I don't think so. The wind's blowing too hard," Chris yelled back.

At that moment, the forty-foot wall of the dune below them collapsed. All four of the MacGregors began to free fall down the shifting dune. Quickly losing their grip from each other, they began to roll like barrels down the slope.

"Ryan!" Mavis yelled as she tumbled head over heels.

Heather reached out and tried to grab her mother, but she couldn't see her with the shirt tied around her head. The storm had darkened the sky.

The wind howled louder and the sand continued to pepper her body. Heather's long blond hair seemed to suck up sand with each roll. Her yellow scrunchie was long lost in the desert. She rolled and rolled until finally she reached the bottom of the dune and collided with a small rise of sand. Then, without warning, a body landed on top of her.

"Ouch! Oh man! Who is this?"

Mavis groped around until she felt Heather's head. She crawled up to her until they were nearly face to face. She coughed out some dirt and sand.

"It's your Mum," Mavis said in her British accent. "And thank you for stopping me. I was growing rather weary of rolling down the hill, you see."

They hugged and then lay face down in the sand

with their arms supporting their heads while trying to block out the wind and sand. The storm raged on for nearly an hour. Heather and Mavis held each other's hands and prayed that R.O. and Chris were OK. R.O., the name her twelve-year-old son preferred, was short for Ryan O'Keef MacGregor.

Peeking periodically under the fabric of Chris' shirt-sleeve, Mavis was noticing a change in the light. Then just as quickly as the storm had interrupted their picnic lunch in the desert, it was gone. The howling wind stopped. The sun jumped from behind the clouds and showered the earth with heat-producing photons.

"It's passed. Let's find Chris and R.O." Mavis pulled the sleeve off her head and struggled to her feet.

She reached down and pulled Heather to her feet. It was a hard lift since Heather, a former competitive swimmer back home in Texas, was solid muscle.

"I'll lead the way, Mom."

Heather scanned the area and noticed that they were inside a reverse cone with a wall of sand all around them. There was no sign of anyone.

"Up is our only choice," Heather said and spit more sand out of her mouth.

She began the climb, shaking her head trying to loosen some of the sand that she was carrying in her thick hair. Mavis was right behind her. She had noticed the new courage that Heather had developed after the long trek across the Serengeti a few weeks earlier. Even though she was just a fourteen-year-old city girl from Texas, she had survived hurricane Keely in the Cayman Islands and the evil ivory poachers in Africa. She had grown up so much in just two months and her "Mum" was proud of her. Now Heather was following her up a giant sand dune in the eastern Sahara desert.

When they reached the top, Chris and R.O. were nowhere in sight. To the east, toward Cairo, was the blackened sky of the storm that had consumed them so quickly and wrecked their day trip into the Sahara. After three days of being stuck in a hotel in downtown Cairo, the three MacGregor kids and their mom had finally agreed upon a plan of action concerning their expected three-week stay in Egypt. The top priority was to get out of the musty old hotel that the convention had arranged for them and move to an enchanted resort on the Nile. While their bags and gear were being moved, Mavis had suggested a drive into the desert. A picnic lunch was prepared. What a good way to restart their Egyptian adventure!

Cooped up in a hotel room for three days had been trying for this adventuresome lot. But the stress and physical duress of their African trek had taken a toll. Their time was well spent just resting in the air-conditioned rooms, sitting in a hot tub, or watching satellite TV from around the world. Room service knew the well-traveled path to the MacGregor's rooms and for a time they thought perhaps the family was royalty.

Heather turned toward her Mom with a serious expression on her face.

"Mom, we need to move quickly! The boys might be buried under the sand."

Mavis was pale and short of breath.

"Chris!" she yelled as she began to run across the crest of the dune. "Ryan! Where are you?"

"Chris! Ryan!"

Heather began running in the opposite direction. She reached the edge of the dune and looked down the long slope to the other side and spied an orange T-shirt with a head attached to it.

"Mom, there's Chris!"

Heather began running down the slope and then dropped to her seat and started to slide. Mavis was right behind her. Before they got there, Chris was digging around in the sand.

"Where's Ryan?" Mavis shouted as she came to a stop next to Chris.

"I had his hand. He was here, but now he's not. I don't think he's buried. I mean, I didn't get buried and we were tumbling together." Chris again reached out and tore into the sand with both hands and then looked up at Mavis and Heather. Soon all three were frantically digging in the sand.

"Oh, Ryan O'Keef MacGregor. Where are you?" Mavis hollered as she created a rather large indention in the sand.

"I'm right behind you."

Chris, Heather, and Mavis jerked around to see R.O. standing there smiling. Mavis jumped to her feet and ran over to him. But at the last minute she resisted doing the motherly thing of embracing or crying. She simply leaned over to face him.

"Mr. MacGregor, R.O." She paused. "Are you OK?" Mavis stood up and put both hands on her hips.

"Yes, I am," was his simple reply.

Mavis shook her head up and down several times contemplating how to avoid being the over-protective mother that her kids disliked. Finally she spoke.

"That's cool."

Chris and Heather were trying not to laugh while at the same time grinding the sand between their teeth. They slowly got up and walked over to her, concealing their amusement with very sober expressions.

"Hey, R.O.," Chris said as he reached out with a high five.

"Hey back, big brother. Wasn't that really cool? I mean the wind lifted me up off the ground. I thought I was flying. Then I landed on the edge of the dune and turned into a human sled. It was awesome! I kept seeing your orange shirt pass by and then I would catch up. What a ride!"

"Oh yeah, thanks for the shirt, Chris," Heather said and handed it back to him.

"I'm glad you were thoroughly entertained, R.O.," Mavis said.

"It was so awesome, Mom. Dad won't believe it. Do you think if we got back to the car we could catch up with the storm and…."

"Absolutely not, young man." Mavis's steel blue eyes could have drilled a hole through him. "We could have all been buried alive."

Mavis turned toward the desert and tried to locate the rental car they had driven on the old caravan track out into the Sahara. Chris looked down to his right arm and the compass that was attached to his diving watch. Making some observations about the terrain and the sky, he looked toward the three motley members of his family.

"I think we are about a quarter of a mile from the track. I made some compass checks as we came out and a mental note of the directions." He turned and looked across the outstretched dunes to the west. "We didn't come from that direction. We wandered in the storm for an hour before the dune collapsed. If we hike around the dune and travel northeast, we should find the car."

Everyone felt better when Chris was around. Chris was a superb outdoorsman and marksman who had been well trained by his father, Dr. Jack MacGregor. He knew how to take charge in a crisis and his leadership had protected his family in both the Cayman Islands and East Africa.

"Mom, I need to ask a favor of everyone." Heather looked around making eye contact with everyone.

"What is it, sweetie?" Mavis stepped closer.

"I need for the boys to turn around and stay turned around for a few minutes."

"Oh, you need to…."

"No! I have sand in my shorts and I would like to shake it out."

"Honey, I have sand in my shorts, too."

"You don't get it, Mom." Heather looked perturbed.

"Oh, those shorts. Boys. About face and if you turn

around I'll yank your ears off."

"How gross, Mom. Who would want to turn around?" R.O. spouted off.

Chris laughed and started knocking the sand out of his thick dark hair. From past desert experience, he knew it would take several days and several shampoos to rid the Sahara from his wavy hair.

Within a few minutes they were all walking single file behind Chris around the giant dune that nearly buried them alive. When they were on top of the dune and walking the crest during the storm, it had been only a twenty-minute trip. Now the journey was approaching an hour before they finally reached the old caravan route that led out of the desert into modern Cairo.

"Wow," Heather said as she stopped.

"That is so cool," R.O. said as he walked over and stood on the top of the rental car that was buried in the sand. It was a BMW sedan.

"Well, let's get digging kids. I want my purse and then there's Chris's camera bag."

"And my backpack," R.O. added.

"And your backpack." Mavis smiled.

They began to dig with their hands. Heather took off one of her desert field boots to pour out the sand. She decided it made a pretty useful tool. Soon they had reached the assortment of things that had been left in the seat. They stepped away from the rental car.

"Mom, did you get the insurance?" Chris looked at her.

Frantically opening her purse, which was full of sand, she located the rental receipt and scanned it quickly.

"Yes. Yes!" She smiled and slapped a high five with Chris. They all began laughing.

"Why are we laughing?" R.O. said, a big smile still on his face.

"This is called "walk away" insurance. If Mom wrecks the car, which she technically did, we simply walk away and the car is paid for. That simple."

"Cool. But where do we walk?"

"Ryan," Heather said.

"Honey, we walk back to Cairo," Mavis said and looked at Chris.

"Mom, you didn't bring Dad's new Globalstar telephone, did you?"

"No, hon. I left it in my bag at the hotel. I thought we were just going on a picnic, not crossing the Sahara to Gad or Mali."

They couldn't help but laugh.

"It's two o'clock. I suggest we start moving," Chris said ominously. He began to walk down the old track.

Each one fell in behind the other with Heather picking up the spare water bottle they had dug out of the car next to R.O.'s backpack.

The sun god Ra had reached the point in the sky where his heat was showering the earth to replenish the energy that was lost to darkness each day. But before Ra would appear the next morning, the MacGregor's journey in the Sahara would indeed be a high anxiety beginning to their long-awaited Egyptian vacation.

2

Dunes

Digging through the shifting sand took more time than they had expected. The searing heat of the day punished them as they trudged down the old caravan track toward Cairo. The heat penetrated the soles of their desert boots. Their discussion was focused on how long Mavis had driven into the desert and the estimate was finally set at two hours.

All four had been awed by the austere beauty of the rolling dunes. The dunes had created a panorama so vastly different from the other exotic locales they had visited. Time passed slowly; so did the miles. Chris had calculated that they were somewhere between seventy-five and one hundred miles into the desert. Even worse, no one knew where they were. They hadn't bothered to tell Jack or anyone about their outing.

With only one bottle of water to share, Chris worried about how far they could go. He had filled the expandable water bottle to the limit. But since there was only one, the lack of water and the heat of the day could be crippling. Such prospects always seemed to domino toward the negative making the outlook rather bleak.

Mavis knew she had goofed. Taking the kids on a brief outing that turned into another life-threatening trek was not her plan. But crying over spilled milk was not her style either. Teaching her kids to cope with reality and learn from it was her goal. For Dr. Mavis O'Keef MacGregor, this wasn't a problem; it was just an inconvenience. It was one she could deal with and one that would make her close-knit family even stronger.

By five o'clock, the tired desert adventurers had stopped to rest on a small outcropping of rocks. R.O. managed to climb up the fifteen-foot slope of the largest boulder and enthusiastically point out his superiority to the rest. Each took a swallow of water from the bottle. This was the third round for everyone. By the time it reached Mavis there were only a few drops left. Chris noticed and after Mavis swallowed the last of it, he took his field knife and cut the bottle from one end to the other. He gently folded the bottle inside out and handed it to his mother.

"Lick the bottle, quick, before it evaporates."

Mavis took the two halves and quickly licked the plastic. A smile came on her face.

"There was more water there than I thought," she said.

"The microscopic particles were clinging to the plastic. There was at least a teaspoon left," Chris replied.

Mavis took her right hand and touched his cheek as mothers affectionately do to their children. Placing the cut container into R.O.'s backpack, Chris hiked up the large boulder and sat down next to R.O.

"Anything exciting up here?"

"Nope. Just been watching that camel over there. He seems lost like us," R.O. replied.

"Camel!" Chris said. He jumped up and balanced himself precariously on the giant remnant of an ancient seashore. "Where?"

R.O. stood next to him and pointed across the barren

landscape toward the camel.

"Over there." He pointed the index finger on his outstretched left hand.

Chris spotted the lonely camel walking between the dunes. He bolted down the large boulder, crashed to the sandy desert floor, and jumped to his feet.

"Camel! R.O. spotted a camel." Chris took off in a run. He could feel his legs trying to cramp from too much heat and not enough water. But he ran full speed nonetheless.

Mavis, Heather, and R.O. were not far behind him. In about three minutes he slowed down next to the large dune and began ascending to the crest on his hands and knees. Reaching the top, he remained quiet as he peered at the solitary camel walking casually by the dune. He noticed it had a bridle around its face with the lead dragging on the ground. A saddle blanket was hanging from its back but the saddle was missing.

Mavis was the first to crawl up next to Chris. Her purse was dragging in the sand. R.O. and Heather arrived a few seconds later, panting.

"Mom, how did you beat us?" Heather asked, gasping between words.

"Shh! Now listen," Chris whispered. "Heather and I will work our way down the right side of the dune and face the camel head on. Mom, you and R.O. go down the left side and calmly walk up to him. If he runs, Heather and I will stop him."

"And how do you plan to do that?" Mavis asked with her eyebrows raised.

"Heather will grab the leads and hike up on his back," Chris replied.

"I'll what?" Heather spoke too loud and the camel stopped walking and looked their direction.

"Shh. We'll figure out something. Let's go!"

Chris started sliding down the dune and working his way around in a vector to intercept the camel. Heather was right behind him. They watched the camel begin walking in their direction. Soon they could see Mavis and R.O. coming from the rear of the camel.

"Slow down," Chris said to Mavis even though he knew she couldn't hear him.

But it was too late. The camel had sensed Mavis and R.O. behind him and was now walking faster.

"Let's go," Chris said.

He stood up and began walking toward the camel. The camel seemed to ignore the two humans in front of him. He walked quickly toward Chris and Heather and was almost at a trot when Chris stepped into his presumed path. The camel was now only twenty yards away and closing. Chris turned to the left side and got ready to grab the lead. Heather moved in beside him.

"Remember what I told you," Chris said.

"Got it," she replied.

As the camel plunged into them, Chris jumped forward and grabbed the leather lead that was dragging in the sand. The camel immediately resisted and came to a halt. It jerked its head to the right as it felt Chris' resistance on the left. Chris pulled hard. The camel's body swung closer.

"Now!" Chris yelled.

Heather took the cue and with three large steps, she sprinted toward the hairy beast. With one big leap she jumped high. Her right desert boot landed in the middle of Chris' back. Her left boot found his left shoulder.

Suddenly she was vaulted high in the air. Her whole body lunged toward the back of the camel. In an instant she was there, wedged between the hairy humps. She grimaced at the pungent odor of the hair. She swung around and threw her right leg over the back hump and sat upright. Before she had completely adjusted her position, Chris had thrown the leather leads up to her. One of the old leather straps slapped her in the face and she winced.

Grabbing through the air, she found the other lead just as the camel bolted forward. It sensed that Chris no longer anchored it in place. The first gallop dislodged Heather and she bounced high in the air. Frantically pulling on the reins, she reached out to grasp the thick hair on the front hump.

By the second gallop, she was "back in the saddle" and hanging on for dear life. The camel was now in a run. Heather arched forward, as far as she could with the hump in front of her. She looked like an accomplished camel racer. Chris, R.O., and Heather had each mastered riding an animal that had a strong will of its own. It was just another part of growing up for them. "No big deal," as their Mother would say.

Heather was now in full stride with the camel. Glancing quickly over her shoulder, she spotted Chris' orange shirt. R.O. and Mavis were standing next to him.

"She is awesome. Never knew she could ride a camel like that!" R.O. said.

"She probably didn't know she could ride a camel like that either," Mavis said.

"But she is doing fantastic. Yeha!" Chris shouted letting out a cowboy yell and giving R.O. a high five.

Heather was experimenting with the leather reins. At first, the camel didn't respond. But each time she tried it, the tall hairy beast would begin to slow down a little, until finally on the fourth try, the camel came to a complete stop.

"That's good. Good boy...or girl...." Heather had the urge to lean over and look but figured she would fall off. "Now we are going to turn around and go get my family."

Heather gently pulled the reins to the hand-braided bridle. Beads and woven fabrics typical of Bedouin tribes decorated the harness. She managed to adjust the saddle blanket between the humps and was now nestled in fairly comfortably. Each time she gently pulled, the camel just kept on chewing and ignored her.

"All right. What if I promised you your favorite food? I would do that but I can't recall what camels eat." She was getting impatient and talking out loud just to stave off her nervousness.

"Let's see. A quadruped mammal, hoofed. Yes, it's got to be grass, grain, stuff like that."

Heather tried another gentle nudge and got the same annoying response. Nothing. Looking around she guessed she had traveled between the dunes about a mile or maybe two. Every sand dune looked the same. Finally she gave a hard tug on the reins to the left and kicked her heels into the sides of the camel. He moved instantly and turned around pointing the opposite direction.

"That worked. That worked." A big smile jumped across her face. "I have a stubborn little brother just like you. It takes a big stick to get his attention, too. OK, Heather. Let's do it."

Looking back from where she had come, she could see the camel's tracks in the sand.

"Heather, you better hurry before those disappear," she said to herself.

With a pop of the leather lead against the neck of the camel and a hard kick to its ribs, the camel jumped forward in a sudden bolt. This time Heather was ready and leaned into the motion. She whipped the leather again and in three strides, the camel was in a full gallop.

With each long stride, the camel leaned its long neck forward and its long legs were power-driving into the soft sand. Retracing the tracks, Heather and her camel were soon around a big dune and once again she spotted Chris's orange shirt.

"Here she comes. Go Heather!" R.O. shouted.

"Oh my! Come on, girl. You are doing great." Mavis smiled with pride.

In a few seconds, Heather was pulling hard on the

reins. The camel responded to its new master. Its hooves dug into the sand and began to slow to a halt. Guiding the camel up to her two brothers and her mother was a victorious moment for this young lady who had endured so much in East Africa. She tried hard not to smile and to appear that this was completely normal for Heather O'Keef MacGregor. Sand was clinging to her face and clothes.

"Anyone need a lift?" Heather yanked back hard on the lead and the camel began to sit.

"Very impressive," Mavis said.

In a couple of minutes, all four were jammed together on the camel's back. R.O. was up front, then Heather, Mavis, and Chris hanging on the end.

"Well, let's go to Cairo," Mavis said.

Heather gently kicked the camel and jerked on the leather rein and the beast rocked forward and began to stand up. Everyone held on until the clumsy beast was steady on all fours. Soon they were following the old caravan track to the northeast, toward Cairo.

"Ouch!" R.O. yelled and squirmed.

"Ryan, be still," Heather chided.

"Sorry, but something just bit me."

"What bit you?" Mavis asked as she leaned around Heather and touched R.O. on his shoulder.

"Here on the back of my leg," R. O. said and rubbed the supposed attack site.

"I don't see anything, hon," Mavis replied.

"Well, I sure felt it," R. O. said. He turned and faced the trail ahead. The moment had maxed out for him and the Sahara had gotten his attention once again.

The foursome tried talking but they were all exhausted from the storm, the dig for the car, and catching the camel. They sat like four Bedouins who had traveled this caravan route a hundred times. Mavis hummed some of her old favorite tunes from England, the tunes she had heard as a child. Chris kept checking his compass and watch and scanning the horizon. Heather's new found sense of accomplishment was still riding high. She was in control, and she liked that feeling for a change.

Suddenly, R.O. leaned forward and began to fall.

"Ryan!" Heather screamed. She reached out and frantically grabbed his shirt, nearly pulling it off his back. He was unconscious.

"Mom!" she screamed.

Mavis was already practically standing on the camel's back and reaching across Heather.

"Make the camel sit down, Heather," Mavis said calmly as she grabbed R.O.'s shirt.

Chris bounded off the back of the camel and was already standing under R.O., lowering him to the ground. In a couple of minutes the big beast was sitting on the desert sand appearing to be slightly annoyed at all the commotion. Mavis and Chris had laid R.O. on the sand.

"Ryan. Ryan. Wake up," Mavis said and patted his cheeks. "Ryan."

"R.O., wake up," Chris said.

Heather stood next to the camel's head and clutched the leather leads.

"Mom. He's not sleeping. He's lost consciousness." Chris looked into his mother's face.

Mavis immediately started checking his vital signs. Heart rate. Breathing.

"He's burning up. A fever that would come on so fast, what could it be?" She kept her composure and approached the crisis as the scientist that she was.

"Let's check for bug bites. Couldn't be anything he ate or drank. We all ate the same food and drank from the same bottle.

They began to roll R.O. gently around looking in his shirt and on his legs. Chris started to take off his boots.

"Chris. Look here." Heather pointed to the back of his leg.

"Wow! That's not a bug sting. Looks more like a scorpion. See the two welts and how the redness radiates away from the center," Chris said. "I've seen that before in West Texas."

"A scorpion. Egypt is famous for its nasty scorpions. We've got to get him to a hospital fast," Mavis said.

"It will be dark in two hours. I estimate we are about five camel hours from Cairo. If we get lucky, another tourist vehicle might come along," Chris said.

"No one would be as careless as we have been," Mavis observed.

Everyone was keeping their heads. Chris loaded R.O. into Mavis' lap and jumped on behind. Heather was up front and guiding the camel to a standing position. No one spoke. All knew how dangerous the sting was and how urgent it was to get R.O. to Cairo.

Once again, the protector of the gods, the scorpion, had reached out from the Pharaoh's tomb and unleashed its lethal venom on invaders from the north. Which curse was this? Only time would tell. But for Ryan O'Keef MacGregor, his twelfth year could very well be his last.

3

The Sting of Pharaoh

Heather worked tirelessly to hold the camel to a steady walk. But the camel would either go too fast and bounce R.O. around or would slow to a lope, which cost them valuable time. R.O.'s fever climbed steadily. He had become dehydrated from the heat of the day, struggling through the storm, digging out the car, and chasing the camel. Each had contributed to his heat load because of little or no water. The fever only made it worse.

Mavis' shirt was soaking wet from holding R.O. close to her, even though R.O. was feverishly dry. She was mentally kicking herself for being so cavalier about the desert. She should have known better. Accompanying British scholars into wastelands on paleontology digs had taught her the basics of field research and work in tropical deserts. The three most important items were water, shade, and more water.

"Chris, how far have we gone?" she asked.

"Only about five miles, Mom," came his solemn reply.

The sun fell behind the mountain-like dunes to the west. The sky was getting dark. On any other day she would have wished that her husband Jack was nearby to enjoy the lovely display that nature provided, a romantic desert sunset. But this beautiful Egyptian evening would have to be enjoyed by other people in love and not by those who were stranded in the Sahara.

"What's that?" Heather asked.

"Shh," Chris said quickly.

"What is it?" Mavis said.

"Quiet! Listen!" shouted Chris. "I know that sound. I would recognize it anywhere," Chris said looking up.

"Me, too. It's a Bell Jet Ranger," Heather said.

But before she had finished the sentence, Chris had bounded off the back of the camel and was stripping off his orange T-shirt. He frantically waved it in the air, even though he had yet to spot the chopper. In a sudden rush of wind and noise, the Bell Jet Ranger cruised over the top of the nearest dune, zooming over their heads. It happened so fast that Chris couldn't imagine how they could have been seen. But just as his heart, and his hope with it, had fallen, the helicopter pulled off to the north. In an amazing display of aeronautical ability, the helicopter pilot seemed to literally reverse the aircraft and arced wide to return to the stranded victims.

"It's coming back!" Heather screamed.

"Oh, thank God," Mavis said as she stroked R.O.'s hot face.

Chris waved his shirt wildly in the air. The helicopter returned to them in a few seconds and began hovering about fifty yards away. The fast turning rotary blade kicked up loose sand, creating a miniature replica of a Sahara desert storm. Finally the engines could be heard winding down and the prop slowed to a stop.

Mavis was handing R.O. down to Chris as the pilot's door swung open on the helicopter. The pilot bounded out and ran toward them. In a few seconds she was standing next to Mavis and reaching out to R.O.

"What's wrong?" the pilot asked.

Chris put his shirt back on and stood staring at the pilot. She was about five feet five inches tall, dark shoulder length hair pulled under a dirty khaki cap. She wore an army green tank top and khaki field shorts. With her sultry dark tan, she looked Arabic.

"We think he's been stung by a scorpion. You sound like an American," Chris replied.

"I am. I'm Dr. Jennifer January. Help me carry him to the helicopter," the pilot replied.

Without much being said, Mavis and Chris carried R.O. to the Jet Ranger. Heather held the camel by the lead and walked the beast over to the group. Opening the side passenger door, the pilot flipped down a full seat inside the cabin across the back passenger area. Mavis and Chris laid R.O. on it.

"Step back." The pilot spoke and retrieved a red plastic box from another seat. She pulled out a stethoscope and started unbuttoning R.O.'s shirt. She spoke to Mavis without looking up.

"Are you his mother?"

"Yes, I am."

"I'm a medical doctor. May I treat him?"

"Oh yes. Yes."

Chris looked away as tears formed in his eyes. He used the tail on his T-shirt to wipe them away before anyone could see him. Heather walked up, the camel right behind her like an overgrown puppy dog.

"What's happening?" Heather asked, a solemn look on her face.

"The pilot's a doctor," Chris said.

"No way," Heather replied.

"Yes, she is...."

"I am so relieved." Heather dropped the lead to the camel and walked over to Mavis. Mavis turned and they embraced.

The doctor checked all of R.O.'s vitals and then reached into the red kit. In a matter of minutes she had started an intravenous drip and hung the saline solution from a hook dangling from the roof of the compartment. She then took a syringe and opened the sterile bag that surrounded it.

"I'm going to inject an anti-venom into your son. It's definitely a scorpion sting."

The doctor took the syringe and injected the anti-venom into the I.V. tube. She checked R.O.'s pupils and looked up at Mavis.

"He should start to come around in a few minutes. He's very dehydrated from the sudden fever, and the toxin does have some lingering neurological effects. But he should be fine once we get him to the hospital."

She took the syringe and placed it in a small red box with a biohazard label on it inside the red medical kit. She turned to Mavis.

"Now. What in the heck are you guys doing out here?" Dr. January asked.

Mavis looked to Chris and Chris to Heather. Heather shrugged her shoulders and said, "We were on a picnic."

For the first time in hours they all smiled. The young doctor looked at them and smiled back.

"Let's get this young man to Cairo. We'll visit along the way."

"What about the camel?" Heather asked.

"It's a Bedouin camel that probably got loose in a storm. He'll wander home."

"OK. Let's go," Chris said.

In a few minutes, everyone had buckled in with Mavis next to R.O. Heather was just across from Mavis. The doctor had instructed Chris to sit up front with her. The long rotor blades began to turn. Being experienced with helicopters, Chris, Heather, and Mavis put on headsets and plugged the cords into the Jet Ranger's intercom/radio system. Darkness was creeping quickly across Arabia toward the Sahara when the Jet Ranger lifted off the desert floor. The hawk god Horus had flown across the sand to greet Ra, the morning sun. Four more souls had been saved.

****

The tall blond-haired man crossed the expansive lobby of the Nile Hilton. He walked over to a beautiful fountain dedicated to the goddess Isis with her out-stretched wings. Standing there for a few minutes he looked around the marble-shrouded lobby until he spotted an Arab of medium height with a *USA Today* tucked under his right arm. In his left hand was a black brief-case.

That was his mark. Carefully the blond man walked across the lobby, dodging luggage and tourists until he was face to face with the Arab.

"Senswosret III"

"Amenhotep sends his greetings."

"Let's talk," the tall blond-haired man said.

"Follow me," the Arab replied.

"It better be public."

"Don't worry. You will be safe. If what I tell you is not worth your time, then you don't have to pay me."

The two men left the hotel lobby and walked down the black stone walkway toward the Nile River. A color-ful felucca sailed by reflecting the last rays of the sun. A young boy about ten waved to a group of tourists who were busy snapping the shutters on their expensive cameras.

"Such infidels," the Arab spoke with acid in both words.

"Why do you curse them? Without them this coun-try would fall back in time a thousand years."

"Yes, but it would be our country again. We wouldn't be owned by America, the Russians, or the Japanese."

"Fine. I'm already weary of your politics. All I want is what I've paid you to find out. Nothing more. Keep your third world political garbage to yourself," the blond-haired man said.

"That's the problem with you Westerners. You think you can buy anything with money. I'll give you the information, but first you pay me," the Arab said.

The blond-haired man looked around and then reached into his right front pocket. He pulled out an envelope and handed it to the Arab. The Arab opened it and thumbed through the fresh US one hundred dollar bills.

"Five thousand dollars. A lot of money just to know where a family of five is staying and their itinerary for a couple of weeks. Here it is. Dr. Jack MacGregor, Dr. Mavis MacGregor, Christopher 17, Heather 14, Ryan 12. A nice American family by all my reports. Two famous parents. Three smart kids."

"Give it to me," the man said gruffly.

The Arab set the briefcase down on the wrought iron bench and opened it. From it, he retrieved a large folder that had a security string and button on one side. He handed it to the Westerner.

As the blond-haired man leaned over and reached for the envelope, he noticed the stainless steel frame of a CZ75 9mm automatic pistol nestled in the briefcase. The Westerner looked up into the glistening dark eyes of the Arab who now had a broad smile.

"You prefer the Czech 9mm over the newer style weapons?" the Westerner asked.

"How can you argue with quality? And it has great sentimental value. A gift from an old KGB friend of mine. From a time when good guys and bad guys could be easily recognized and sometimes shared a fine dinner before they tried to kill each other." The Arab never took his eyes off of the Westerner. "I gave my son a newer model."

Taking the envelope, the Westerner opened it quickly and pulled out the contents. The folder contained two sheets of paper with the hotel assignment, rental car description, speaking schedule for Dr. Jack MacGregor, and the airline departure schedule of the entire family.

"You must hate this family quite a bit," the Arab said.

"You'll never know. Now haven't you forgotten something?" the Westerner suggested.

"Oh, yes. My aging memory fails me.".

The Arab reached into the top pocket of the briefcase and pulled out a bulky envelope. He handed it to the Westerner. The tall blond-haired man opened it on one end and peered inside. Tucked securely in the padded envelope was a Browning 9mm automatic pistol. The Westerner smiled.

"Spare magazines?"

"There are two clips, fourteen rounds each plus fourteen more in the pistol. If you can't hit your targets with this many bullets, then you should consider hiring an old lady to do it for you. Shall I call my mother? She is eighty-four and a very good shot."

"Our business is finished," the Westerner snapped back.

The Arab closed the briefcase and picked it up. He turned to walk away when the Westerner spoke to him.

"This information better be correct."

The Arab turned back and stepped close to him and spoke.

"Since we have just conducted business, I will take your comment as a clarification of your point of view. The next time we meet, you will simply be another infidel who pollutes our culture and I will not hesitate to kill you."

The Arab turned and walked away. The Westerner looked down at the document. It gave the following information.

"Hotel Assignment: Jack MacGregor and Family— Nassar Hotel & Convention Center. Cairo Rental Car Service—BMW sedan." As he reviewed the data and his

sinister plan, little did he know that the MacGregor
family had already moved from the assigned hotel and
their rental car was buried in the Sahara one hundred
miles southwest of Cairo. But more importantly, just
one mile down the river at the luxurious Cleopatra's
Palace Resort, Dr. Jack MacGregor had just received
word about his family's ill-fated picnic.

"Are you Dr. MacGregor?" the short man in the
white suit and red fez asked.

"Yes, I'm Dr. MacGregor."

The man handed Jack a note on hotel stationery.

Jack looked up with a combination of panic and
concern.

"What's this about my family? Where's the hospital? Can you get me a taxi?"

"Sir, your family was picked up somewhere in the
Sahara about one hundred miles southwest of Cairo."

"The Sahara? What were they doing out there?"

"We hoped you could tell us, Doctor MacGregor. I
am Inspector Samut with the Cairo Police. I have been
assigned to the security force for the Nile River Environmental Conference. I was dispatched here to find you
and take you to the hospital where your family is being
delivered by a medical helicopter."

"Who is injured?" Jack asked calmly.

"I don't know, Dr. MacGregor. But if you will come
with me, we can be there in about fifteen minutes. That
is the estimated time of arrival for the aircraft."

Jack followed the short detective out the majestic
entryway of the hotel to the waiting police car. The sun
had set beyond the desert and the world's noisiest city
had come alive. The city was much like a desert lizard
that had been hiding from the sun all day, anxiously
awaiting the splendor of a cool night.

"Cairo tower, this is November One Four Seven
Seven. Roger. Transporting a patient to G.A. Nassar
Medical Center. Have already advised Cairo Police on
their frequency."

"November One Four Seven Seven, maintain your current heading and go to one nine hundred feet on your approach to the hospital."

"Roger," Dr. January replied.

She turned to Chris and smiled.

"We should be there in about twelve minutes."

"Good! Thank you. You know, we got your name, but we don't know who you are. I mean, I understand with the treatment you gave my brother and flying the helicopter, there was no time."

"You're right! My apologies. My name is Jennifer January. I'm an archaeologist from Stanford University. We've been excavating the Bahariya Oasis ruins and the tombs at Farafra. We've found evidence of a cache of lost treasure, possibly from the ruler of the oasis or a Pharaoh."

"Anything really exciting?" Chris asked.

"It's all exciting. But we've been chasing leads about a lost box with great secrets locked inside."

"That is exciting. But I thought you said you were a medical doctor," Chris said with a puzzled look on his face.

"I am. UCLA Medical School class of 1994."

"And you can fly a Jet Ranger. I'm impressed. But...."

"I'm impressed, too," piped in Mavis over the intercom.

Chris glanced over his shoulder at Mavis. She was nestled tightly against R.O., who was becoming a little restless. It was a good sign.

"I know. I have to explain all the time. I love medicine, but my grandfather was an archaeologist. Before I went to medical school, I earned my first degree in archaeology. After I finished my ER and pediatric training, I signed on as the medical officer on these expeditions. When I am back home in California, I'm an emergency room pediatrician. That way I'm not tied down to a medical practice."

"And the flying?" Chris asked.

"Well, my father was an Army Warrant Officer in Viet Nam. He flew helicopters and I grew up around them. Army brat, you know. Couldn't resist the allure. Guess it runs in the family. Hang on. Got to talk to Cairo tower again. My radar is picking up some small aircraft on the west side of Cairo."

While Dr. Jennifer January talked on the radio in Arabic, Chris couldn't help but notice her tanned skin, smooth complexion, and muscular physique. He felt a tap on his shoulder. He turned around to see Mavis and Heather grinning. R.O. was awake and drinking water from a plastic water bottle that Heather had retrieved from a built-in ice chest. Chris was all smiles and took another bottle of water that was handed to him.

"Ryan's fever is gone. The I.V. and the anti-venom have worked," Heather said to her mom.

"Doctor," Mavis said over the intercom.

"Yes."

"My son is awake," Mavis replied.

"Excellent. I knew he be would all right. Dehydration and scorpion stings are pretty common place around these parts."

Mavis turned back to R. O. and Dr. January spoke to Chris.

"Now, your turn. Explain why you all were out in the Sahara on a picnic."

"It's a long story."

"Make it eight minutes max. We'll be at the hospital by then," Jennifer smiled.

"My dad is Dr. Jack MacGregor. He is a zoologist who's on a year-long sabbatical. He is writing a book on the current status of endangered species and some rare habitats. We started in the Caribbean about two months ago, the Cayman Islands."

"The Caymans. Been there. Loved diving 'the wall'," Dr. January said. " Did you get to dive the wall while you were there?"

"Oh, yes. But that's another story. Well, after we left the Caymans we traveled to Kenya where my dad was researching the increase in elephant poaching. From there we came to Cairo."

"Sounds like fun, " Dr. January said.

"You could say that," Chris replied, briefly pondering the hurricane in the Caymans and the trek in East Africa.

"So, what's the story on the family?" Dr. January asked.

"My name is Chris. I'm seventeen, almost eighteen. My sister is Heather, she is fourteen, and your patient is my brother Ryan. He prefers to be called R.O. and he's twelve."

"Your mom is British? I picked up on a British accent that's been diluted a little with something, but I couldn't pin it down."

"That's British with a Texas twang. She's a paleontologist from London. Met my dad at Cambridge and moved to Texas where, you know, the rest is history."

"And a good one, too. What a neat family! But what about this picnic in the Sahara?" Jennifer asked.

Chris blushed and then looked over at the big blue eyes of Dr. January, who was staring at him. She glanced back to the fast-approaching lights of Cairo.

"You might say that four very accomplished outdoorsmen got a little careless and overconfident."

Seeing his embarrassment, Jennifer came to his rescue.

"But you are safe now!"

"Yes, thanks to you. Without you, R.O. might be dead. We all might be dead."

"But you're not and there's the hospital at two o'clock."

"Cairo tower, this is November One Four Seven Seven making final approach to Nassar Medical Center. We'll be down for about twenty minutes. Thank you."

Chris looked through the giant Plexiglas windows to see the massive medical complex below them. As they descended toward the helipad, he could see his Dad standing next to a short man in a white suit with a red fez on his head. With the last rotation of the rotor blade, Mavis opened the door and stepped out. Two nurses helped load R.O. onto a waiting gurney. Jack ran over to Mavis and they embraced.

"Jack, I have never been so stupid."

"Hush," Jack said trying to comfort her.

"Hi, Dad." Heather gave Jack a hug.

"Hi, Dad." Chris walked up and watched his dad holding his mom and sister.

Jack reached out and pulled Chris into the three of them.

"What am I going to do with the four of you?" Jack said as he forced a smile.

Dr. January was talking in Arabic to a doctor who had just arrived to escort R.O. into the hospital. She then turned to the MacGregors.

"R.O. is going to be fine. He needs to stay overnight to get some fluids from the I.V.'s. After a couple of days rest he'll be like new."

A nurse handed Dr. January some papers to sign. Chris walked over to her. When she had finished, she turned to Chris. Chris was a little taller and looked down into her tanned face framed by her long dark brown hair. Her blue eyes and wide smile made for a perfect face, especially to this seventeen-year-old young man. Chris took a deep breath and spoke.

"Dr. January, thanks for everything."

"Oh, I'm just glad I saw your orange shirt. It's not a color the Bedouins fancy so I knew it had to be an oil company worker or tourists. When I saw only a camel and no vehicle, I knew there was a problem."

"Can we repay you in any way?"

"Oh no. I was coming to Cairo to pick up supplies and a couple of archaeologists who were flying in from Greece. The mummies we found at Bahariya and Farafra were neoclassical Greek and Roman. Alexander the Great era."

"That's amazing," Chris replied.

"Say, I just thought of something," Dr. January said as she walked slowly back to the Bell Jet Ranger. Chris walked by her side. "If you're going to be in Egypt very long, maybe you would like to visit our dig?"

"That would be awesome," Chris said as he tried to calm his teenage enthusiasm in the presence of Dr. Jennifer January, aviator, doctor, archaeologist, and beautiful woman.

"Good." Dr. January reached into her left cargo pocket and pulled out a leather cardholder. It had the sign of Ka embossed on the cover. As she peeled out a card, sand trickled from inside.

"Once in the Sahara, always in the Sahara. The sand never leaves you." She smiled and handed the card to Chris. "These are the numbers where I can be reached. The first is a cell phone, the second is the camp phone. If I'm not there, leave a message where I can reach you."

"Thanks," Chris replied.

"Got to go. Later Chris!" The pretty young doctor opened the door to the helicopter, buckled in, and put on her headset.

In a couple of minutes the helicopter was lifting off in the darkness quickly to become just another blinking light over Cairo. R.O. had already disappeared into the labyrinths of the massive hospital complex. Jack and Mavis were at his side listening to his barrage of questions.

Heather walked over to Chris and stood next to him watching the helicopter disappear in the sky.

"What a neat person," Heather said.

"You can say that again."

"What a neat person."

"Get out of here," Chris said and they both started laughing.

In the distance, a giant spotlight focused on the great sphinx as a narrator began to tell the enchanted story of Egypt and a people who worshipped life and lived it to the max. The narrator began to reveal the secrets of the Pharaohs and their constant search for life after death. As the laser lights flashed about, the crowd let out "oohs" and "aahs." But amidst the magic and illusions of the revealed secrets of the Pharaohs, the narrator couldn't tell the one secret he did not know. It is a secret so powerful that it could once again allow the ka of the Pharaohs to live again.

4

The Little Shop of Thoth

Time passed quickly and the three kids grew tired of room service and the hotel swimming pool. R.O. had regained his strength and was once again the primary source of irritation for Heather and Chris.

"Chris, have you seen my curling iron?" an impatient Heather shouted from the bathroom of the expansive hotel suite.

"Nope," came the reply as he continued to read the English Literature assignment given to him by his mom. Even though on a year-long vacation from school classrooms, school did carry on. Today's assignment was a continuation of the Shakespearean unit he had begun in Grand Cayman, but didn't have time to work on in East Africa. Following Shakespeare, it would be physics.

Heather walked down the short hall and into the kitchen.

"Ryan! Give that to me now!" she shouted.

R.O. looked up quickly and then back at the curling iron and his small tool kit. He had begun to disassemble the appliance. Heather hurried over and jerked it from his hands.

"Ow! You could have cut me," R.O. whined.

"Find something else to tear up, but leave my stuff alone!" Heather marched from the room.

Chris walked over to the table and sat down. He glanced at the forlorn twelve year old.

"I guess we need to go shopping today, don't we little brother?"

R.O. looked up.

"You mean it?"

"Sure I do. I mean, you haven't put anything together since Roger in Nairobi," Chris said, referring to R.O.'s penchant toward building mechanical gizmos that make noises, flashed lights, but did nothing else. R.O. was, indeed, a young mechanical wizard.

"We'll find an electronics store in downtown Cairo and get some supplies that you can work on. That way Heather's curling iron, my radio, and Mom's hair dryer will be safe. What do you say?"

"Too late for the radio, Chris. Sorry. I used it for part of my spider."

Chris held his temper and thought about it a second.

"OK. All the more reason to go."

"You're the best, Chris. When can we go?"

"How about now?"

R.O. jumped up and ran down the hall to get dressed. He passed Heather coming the opposite direction.

"What's that all about?" she asked.

"We're going to find an electronics store and pick up some stuff for young Thomas Edison to work on before he tears the electrical lines out of the walls. Want to go?"

"Sure. I'm tired of room service and if I hear another tourist down at the pool talking about some lame adventure they've been on, I'll just puke."

"Get dressed. We'll leave in about fifteen."

Shuffling through their assortment of beachwear

from the Caymans and safari clothes from East Africa, the boys managed to locate a clean pair of jeans and their favorite T-shirts. Heather picked out a cute pink top to go with her white capri pants. In about twenty minutes they were on the street adjacent to the expansive and busy Nile.

"Chris, did you leave a note for Mom?" Heather asked .

"Yes, I put it on the dinette table. We're set," Chris replied as he flagged down a taxi that was waiting at the curb just outside the resort.

Once inside the 1985 Chevrolet Caprice, Chris instructed the driver to take them to an electronics store. The driver replied in English. They quickly entered into the rush of traffic running parallel to the river, a river that once saw Pharaoh's royal ships full of grain and mighty Roman battleships cruising her waters. Within a few minutes the kids were well into the heart of Cairo with taxis, buses, and cars honking at every turn.

"There is so much noise," Heather said as she peered out the dusty window.

"I once read that Cairo is the noisiest city in the world," R.O. said.

"You did?" Chris said.

"Sure did, and Mexico City is the most polluted city."

There was a pause.

"OK. I'll ask. And the most polluted country is…?" Heather said.

"Poland," R.O. replied.

"Poland?" Chris and Heather said at the same time.

"Well, I think I'll take the noise over the pollution any day," Heather said and pointed to a merchant pulling a camel behind him.

"I wonder if our camel found its way home," R.O. asked.

"I'm sure it did. You heard Dr. January. She said it

looked like a Bedouin camel that is accustomed to roaming the desert," Chris said.

Not much else was said as the taxi swerved in and out of traffic finally reaching a retail district that mirrored the old bazaars found throughout northern Africa. Coasting to a stop on a small street, the cab driver leaned over and put out his hand.

"That will be twenty dollars U.S."

"Twenty dollars for a fifteen-minute ride?" R.O. shot back.

"That's about right, R.O. Maybe a little steep, but for three people, three kids with no parents around, one of which is a girl, that's about what a thief would charge," Chris glared back at the driver.

"Who are you calling a thief?" the taxi driver angrily replied.

"You, sir. Your card on the dash says it is £2.5 Egyptian pounds per mile, plus ten pounds for the first mile. Then you add two passengers at two piastres each and convert that to U.S. dollars. That figures to about £41.5 Egyptian pounds or $10.56 U.S. for a seven-mile trip. Here's $11 U.S. No tip for trying to cheat us." Chris handed him the money.

The driver snapped the bills out of his hand as the three teenagers piled out of the car quickly.

As the taxi sped away, R.O. jumped in close to Chris.

"That was so cool, Chris. How do you know all that?"

"I've been reading it in the welcome guide for the last few days since we have been imprisoned at the resort waiting for you to get better. That's how."

"I'm impressed." Heather patted Chris on the back.

"OK," Heather looked around at the streets of old Cairo, the colorful bazaar with bright fabrics swaying in the breeze, fruit and vegetable merchants, and brass and metalware tents. "This doesn't exactly look like the electronics district to me."

"Ditto that," R.O. mumbled.

"Well, I don't see any more taxis, so we'll have to walk anyway. Besides, I love these old buildings. Imagine being here thousands of years ago. The excitement of the ancient civilization, the caravans from Ethiopia and Persia, the grand bazaars with wild animals..."

"And no toilets, no running water, no electricity, and no restaurants. You can have your imaginary moment, but I prefer the here and now-but not necessarily here." Heather crossed her arms in disgust.

"Well, let's get walking anyway," Chris replied. He tugged at R.O., who was gawking at a toothless woman selling rugs.

"Yuk. She just spit something brown on the ground," R.O. said with a grimace on his face.

"Fairly gross to me." Heather began walking between the variety of tents and merchants' carts until she found a leather dealer. "Cute billfolds."

Chris was examining a belt when he heard R.O. holler at him. He realized that R.O. had wandered about twenty yards away from them.

"Chris, Heather. Look!"

Chris dropped the belt and walked quickly to R.O. Heather, not wanting to be left alone, set down the billfold, smiled at the merchant, and quickly joined them.

"Look up there on the sign," R.O. pointed at the facade of one of the old buildings.

The sign read: "The Little Shop of Thoth—Old Cairo's Communication Experts." The Ibis-headed god Thoth was painted on the sign.

"So what's the communication part have to do...wait I got it. Good, Heather," Heather said as she pointed to her head. "Communications, radios, electronics."

"Why Thoth, Chris?" R.O. asked.

"Thoth was the god of writing and scribes and even wisdom. Writing was the oldest form of communication other than speech. So it makes a good image for the business."

Before Chris had finished his sentence, R.O. had headed at a fast pace toward the old front door. Next to the heavy cedar door was a window with a variety of writing instruments, radios, cell phones, palm-size computer date books, and a small satellite dish.

"Jackpot! I just rolled a seven!" R.O. shouted as he pulled open the door and bounded inside.

"Where did he get that?" Heather asked.

"Got me. Too much TV, I'd wager," Chris said.

"Get out of here. You two make me sick," Heather said but couldn't help but laugh with Chris.

The centuries-old mud brick walls were lined with glass shelves covered with every electronic device imaginable. One wall was covered with metal detectors while an entire case was dedicated to remote listening devices.

"I have never seen any store like this before." R.O.'s mouth was agape.

"Me either," joined in Heather.

"Me, too," Chris said. "I bet some of this stuff is illegal back in the states."

"And right you are young man," spoke an Arab dressed in a traditional caftan of purple and yellow.

"Sorry. I didn't mean to startle you," the Arab said as he brushed his fingers through his long gray beard. "But I still have many American customers who purchase this fine equipment. Where they take it is their concern. Not mine."

"I apologize if I insulted you," Chris said.

"How polite you are, young man. Such a rare trait for your generation. But you didn't offend me. Only if you come into my shop and leave without buying something will I be offended," the Arab said. Then he laughed so loud everyone in the busy shop stopped to look his direction.

"We were looking for something for my brother to buy. He likes to build things, put batteries in them, get them to move or whatever, and then tear them apart."

"Let me get one of my girls to help you while I return to my business clients. Akila!" he shouted across the shop.

A young Arab girl, about twenty, walked over to them.

"Yes, Father?"

"These fine American children want to buy something. Will you help take their money?" The Arab laughed loudly again and walked away toward a circle of three men in suits. These were the only suited men that the MacGregor kids had seen in old Cairo.

"What do you want to look at?" the Arab girl asked.

"I want to see some robotic heat wires that I can power up with anything from a two volt to nine volt battery. If you have a timing circuit with a 555 chip, then I can add lights and arrange the sequence for the movement of the wires. I need the smallest motor you have. Maybe two of those." R.O. grinned when he finished.

"Why do you need all of that?" Heather asked with a bewildered look on her face.

"For my spider. You'll see," R.O. replied.

"Follow me, I have what you want over here," Akila replied.

The young woman led the trio across the shop to a case that was jammed with all kinds of gear, wiring, circuit boards, and an assortment of microchips in sealed glass boxes.

"What's this?" R.O. asked as he picked up a very small amplifier connected to a high tech transmitter.

"It belongs to a satellite system that we sold and the customer returned. We have separated the parts to try to sell them faster. This is part of the amplifier-transmitter for the satellite."

"Cool, I'll take it, too," R.O. said

For the next hour, Chris, Heather, and R.O. wandered around the large interior of the shop with each focusing on something different. The young Arab woman stayed glued to R.O. since he was the primary customer who would decide on what to purchase. The three men in suits and the Arab shop owner had disappeared through blue silk curtains into a back room. It was filled with cardboard boxes with Hong Kong, Singapore, and Japan stenciled on them.

"I am only going to make the offer one time," a tall man in a dark gray suit said in Russian.

"You already made the offer when you asked me to acquire it for you. I am sorry my comrades feel this way. For many years we have carried on a comfortable business. Whenever western electronics secrets came into my shop, The Little Shop of Thoth was always ready to share them with our friends. Not once did the CIA, British MI6, or Israeli Mossad learn about my side business. Not once. Now that Russia is engaged in a free market, you should have money to burn. Even the Americans are giving you free money! The Americans give you money to dismantle your missile silos, and you spend it to refurbish your nuclear submarines. What a racket you have going," the Arab said as he stroked his beard.

"Yes. All that is true. But the competition for, shall we say, high quality electronics is very high. Iraq, North Korea, India, Pakistan, and even Iran, all have become bidders for missile and satellite technology. There are only so many systems for sale and too many buyers," the tall Russian said as he raised his eyebrows. The other two men in suits, one Russian and one Arab, nodded their heads in agreement.

"Then I will show you. Excuse me one moment." The Arab shop owner lifted the front of his caftan and walked quickly across the back room to an staircase leading to a higher level over the main shop. Once at the top of the stairs, he stepped into a large room that resembled a modern office with plush carpet, bright overhead lighting, mahogany furniture and bookshelves. As he walked across the room, there were several chirping noises that emanated from the bookcases.

"Seven, twenty-nine, fourteen, ninety-four, Hamilton, Bermuda, Tutmosis II," the large Arab said softly. As he reached his desk, a 12-inch by 12-inch section opened up like the top of a toy jack-in-the-box. It was a palm scanner. The beam danced quickly across the palm of his left hand, then his right hand.

"The Pharaoh's bark is purple, the queen is Nefertiti."

A series of red lights flashed until finally a green one appeared and a panel on the bookshelf opened slowly. He walked over to the panel, leaned forward, and rested his chin on a rubber ledge as the infrared camera scanned his retina. Only then did a panel behind the desk begin to open, revealing a large walk-in closet.

Finally a third panel inside the closet opened. He stepped up and reached inside. There he retrieved the small circuit board, dropped it into a velvet pouch, put it into his pocket, and closed the panel. As he walked through the office, all of the secret compartments closed simultaneously. He bounded down the stairs to find the three men talking softly among themselves.

"My good friends. I apologize for being so tardy. But the nature of what I am to show you requires the utmost security."

The men crowded around as he pulled the miniature piece of electronics out of his pocket and cradled it as if it were made of gold and precious gems. Just at that moment, loud voices and a great deal of commotion emanated from the front of the retail shop. A woman shrieked. The three men reached inside their coat pockets and pulled out semi-automatic pistols.

The Arab shopkeeper slipped the priceless piece of

electronics back into his pocket and stepped through the blue silk curtain into the sudden chaos. Two small children ran across the room chasing a battery-powered car. A solar-powered steam engine was tooting like a teakettle under a halogen lamp. Two magnetometers were beeping loudly and personal alarms were sounding off.

"What is going on here?" yelled the owner just as the two kids being chased by the cars ran by him .

"R.O., put that remote down now!" Heather shouted.

"Look at these go! Did you see that steam engine blow?" R.O. shouted as he chased the kids with the cars and carried a sack full of electronic gear in his left hand.

Chris was practically on his knees laughing as he watched R.O. going from counter to counter engaging every device possible that could move, toot, or talk. R.O. was definitely in heaven and, after being stung by the scorpion, Chris didn't want to spoil his fun.

Suddenly the Arab shopkeeper turned and stepped on one of the cars and lost his balance. R.O. tripped on the other car. It shot out from under him and crashed into the big Arab. Becoming entangled together, R.O. and the Arab fell to the hard stone floor just as the two kids ran by again. The bag of circuit boards, batteries, and wiring hit the floor and burst open. The Arab landed flat on his back and lost his wind with R.O. crashing on top.

"Sorry, mister," R.O. said, but the shop owner was wheezing and out of breath.

Crawling off of him, R.O. stood back as two shop employees rushed over to tend to the Arab.

"Hurry. Let's get your stuff picked up and get out of here. Chris has already paid for everything," Heather said.

Heather started shoving the parts into the torn bag. She reached behind the counter and retrieved another bag. Soon everything was picked up and the three

MacGregors were making a mad dash toward the front door.

They didn't stop running until they were three blocks away where Chris hailed a passing taxi. Once inside the taxi, destination given, Chris, Heather, and R.O. breathed a sigh of relief.

"What did you buy?" Chris said to R.O.

"Just some stuff," R.O. replied.

"A hundred and fifty dollars worth of stuff. I wasn't going to get it but the place started falling apart and we needed to leave quick. You are going to be my slave for a long time," Chris said with a grimace on his face.

As the shop owner regained his breath, the three men in the suits were gathering around him.

"Are you all right, my old friend?" the Russian said.

"Just a little winded," the Arab replied as he put his hand into his pocket to retrieve the circuit board.

"It's gone! I had it right here. It's gone!"

"Gone? How could that be?" the Russian said.

The Arab shopkeeper glanced around the store at all of the customers who stared down at him.

"Those three kids. They took it. How could I have been so careless!"

As the old Mercedes taxi sped down the highway adjacent to the beautiful Nile, little did R.O. know that the sack full of electronics gear he had just purchased contained the most valuable single piece of electronic hardware in the world today. From the ancient writing instrument of the god of Thoth now arrives the instrument that will either breathe new life into a tired planet— or completely destroy it.

5

Wings Over Egypt

———————◁▭▷———————

Chris adjusted the fiberglass helmet. A trickle of sweat ran down his forehead. Another one raced down the back of his neck and was quickly absorbed by the cotton khaki shirt he was wearing. The climb to the top of the bluff on the Cairo side of the Giza plateau, adjacent to the pyramid of Khufu, had been exhausting. The weight of the hang glider was the biggest burden. The breeze that clipped the top of the bluff quickly evaporated the water droplets on his shirt even though the sun had yet to clear the horizon.

Another ten minutes and the unbearable Sahara desert heat would be back. August in Egypt was not the most accommodating time of year to be a visitor, nor a camel, nor even a scorpion.

The weatherman had predicted that the day would be a cool day with a high of only 99 degrees. It would be a relief from the life-sucking heat of 110 and 112 of the past few weeks with an occasional spike to 120. Four tourists had died of heatstroke at Luxor and Abu Simbel in the past week. Chris couldn't imagine that kind of heat. Even the summer temperatures he had experienced the past two months never reached this level of discomfort.

"Chris, adjust my shoulder strap," Heather said.

Chris leaned forward and yanked at the nylon fabric and steel buckle.

"How's that?"

"Good. Are we ready yet? "

"We haven't gotten the signal from Mom and R.O."

"Chris, I can't believe you talked Mom into this. I mean this is the coup of the year. Who would have thought Mom would have ever permitted this, even fly with us?"

Heather smiled and looked across the short expanse toward the other bluffs. Perched high atop were Mavis and R.O. Dirty and stinky Cairo lay in front of them.

At exactly 5 A.M., Mavis, Heather, R.O., and Chris had been met by six men. Each of them had carried a large pack and led them up the bluffs before dawn. Even though security around the pyramids was always tight, the MacGregors were allowed in with an Indian religious order that had arranged for a sunrise ceremony near the pyramids. Considered by police as just more strange tourists, the entourage of Mavis, the kids, and the six men proceeded at will after gratuities exchanged hands and the packs were thoroughly searched. At that early time of day, the police didn't recognize the contents as anything more than tent material, poles, and cord.

"Ryan O'Keef MacGregor, I can't believe I let you guys talk me into this. Your dad will skin us all when he finds out."

"Mom, it's going to be great. You've never flinched before. I mean climbing in Colorado, kayaking off of Baja, diving in Cayman—you were never left behind. You always encouraged us to safely challenge our limits." The twelve year old presented a formidable argument.

Mavis reached over and touched his sweaty cheek. The sun was peeking over the horizon and shining on the ancient pyramids.

"You're right. Well, let's have a go of it," she said. Her perky British accent penetrated the steady howl of the winds buzzing across the plateau of Giza.

Nearby, perched as a guardian, was the eroded and very ancient Sphinx. From this angle and height, it blended into the sand as if it were but a shadow.

"Misses," the Arab spoke. "They signal from other side. The wind is changing. It is time. They ready!"

Mavis thought she could see Heather and Chris waving from the top of the bluff. But the flashing red lens of the flashlight was the signal that the Arab had been waiting for in the predawn darkness. The leading edge of the sun began to peak over the horizon. The Indians, nearby at the base of Khufu, began to chant and fall to the ground only to rise up and fall again.

"Let's go, Mom." R.O was confident. "They trained us well. We learned perfectly. Now we can go do it," he coaxed, using the same words she always uttered. He could tell his mother was anxious.

"Right," Mavis said nervously. "I'm ready, I think? Oh, Jack, I wish you were here right now," she said to herself.

The two Arabs lifted the hang glider high enough for Mavis and R.O. to connect their harnesses. Mavis had a glider of bright orange and white fabric. R.O.'s was blue and white. On the other massive bluff about five hundred feet away, Chris was fastened to his green and black glider, while Heather had picked the yellow one.

Without hesitation Chris ran across the flat surface at the top and into the wind blowing south from the Mediterranean Sea. Before he had reached the edge, the glider lifted up and sailed into the air.

"Ryan," Mavis said. But he was already airborne as

well. Mavis could see Heather lifting off. Her heart
pounded as she could see all three of her children
gaining altitude over the three pyramids. As she ran
across the top of the dune, she said a quick prayer. She
also hoped that the ten hours of lessons were helpful.

Before Mavis could say amen, her feet lifted off the
ground and she was airborne. The harness held her in
the perfect position. Slightly adjusting her weight left or
right could turn the glider. If she caught a gust of wind
and pushed the horizontal bar forward, she could gain
altitude.

"Relax, be graceful, and don't stall!" She lectured
aloud to herself.

A crowd of tourists stepping off a bus on their first
stop of the day began to gather at the base of the Khufu
pyramid. Cameras were clicking and everyone was
enjoying the beautiful display of color and aeronautics.
An aggressive food vendor pushed his cart up to the
crowd and started selling coffee and pastries. He was
soon followed by street merchants selling beads, fabric,
and some of King Tut's artifacts—guaranteed! The circus atmosphere soon attracted four more tourist groups
that had been unloaded in the parking lot. While Mavis,
Chris, Heather, and Ryan sailed overhead, a crowd of
nearly five hundred people watched in awe from below.

Suddenly Heather's bright yellow glider crossed
quickly in front of Mavis, causing her to jump in her
harness.

"Go, Mom!" Heather yelled.

"Heather, you are in big trouble," Mavis said nervously and then laughed. "No, if I don't pay attention, I
am in big trouble. Mavis O'Keef MacGregor, what are
you doing up here, lass?"

Mavis scanned the sky and counted her brood. But
she started to worry when she couldn't locate Chris in
his black and green hang glider. Maneuvering her glider
in a wide turn over some apartment buildings on the

edge of the pyramid plateau, she searched the sky in all directions. She finally spotted him.

Chris gained another five hundred feet in altitude and sailed nearly a half mile to the west and was still going in that direction. Mavis could feel the tug of the winds from the Mediterranean and fought to keep the glider over the pyramids. R.O. and Heather were doing the same. But Chris moved further and further away into the Sahara before he turned back east toward the Nile River.

The carnival atmosphere around the pyramids had attracted the authorities. Four police cars and a truck full of soldiers had arrived. The Arabs who owned the hang gliders were hurried together and arrested for trespassing. Chris began closing in around his family and pointed below. Mavis, Heather, and R.O. all looked down at the commotion around the pyramids.

"They said it was legal to do this. That makes me so mad. Being arrested in Cairo just won't do," Mavis said out loud, but no one could hear her. She noticed Chris motioning them to fly closer. Within a few minutes Heather, Chris, and Mavis had all moved to within a few yards of Chris. Each was careful to keep a distance to avoid a collision. Chris was pointing down and then east toward the Nile. R.O. acted like he didn't understand and engaged another large circle.

"Good idea, Chris," Mavis shouted. "Let's land where we won't be arrested and have to spend the day in a nasty Cairo jail. Oh, my. Jack will kill me for certain for this."

Finally R.O. finished the circle and whizzed underneath Heather, laughing heartily. Chris got his attention and gave him the look that usually brought his younger brother under control. It worked again this time and R.O. stopped showing off. Chris motioned for all to follow as he turned to the east and flew away from the pyramids. The police and army troops below just watched in amazement while the tourists enjoyed the added entertainment of Egypt's most visited shrine.

Within a few minutes the MacGregors were enjoying a good tailwind and drifted southeast toward the Nile. The beautiful blue ribbon snaked along from south to north between the Sahara, centuries-old buildings, and modern resort hotels. It is the only major river in the world that flows south to north but yet the wind blows regularly from north to south. Boats can travel down river, north, with the current or upriver, south, with the help of sails.

Soon Chris spotted the string of resorts and the Nile Hilton where they had been staying. Pointing down, he knew the only place to land would be in the hotel parking lot or, in an emergency, the Nile. Heather, R.O., and Mavis watched anxiously as Chris descended toward the hotel resort. Within a few minutes, while the others circled above, Chris soared across the parking lot and found a fifty-foot stretch of clear asphalt. With his feet touching on the run, he let the weight of the glider drag to a halt while he was still on his feet. Unsnapping his harness he stepped out from under the right wing and waved them all down.

Soon Heather was on the ground with R.O. right behind.

"I wasn't ready to come down yet, Chris!" R.O. yelled as his feet touched the ground.

"Too bad. Now pull your glider out of the way so Mom has plenty of space to land.

Mavis, her palms sweating, made her last half circle and started descending toward the massive resort. The sun was well over the horizon and glaring in her face when she decided she would bring the glider in from the east. Making a quick weight adjustment and pushing the horizontal bar forward, she gained altitude and swung around to the southeast. One more body shift and she was lined up with the parking lot.

"Mom, I hope you know what your doing," Chris murmured. "Get ready to grab her if she comes in high!" he shouted to R.O. and Heather. R.O. and Heather moved over next to Chris as they watched their mom sail in from the east. She just barely cleared a row of telephone poles, which was why Chris chose to land from the west.

"You did it, lass!" Mavis shouted and pulled back on the horizontal bar. She was now only forty feet off the ground and whizzed over the road next to the hotel. But suddenly a gust of wind off the Nile caught the expansive wings of the gilder, and she gained ten feet in altitude. It was too late to correct as she zoomed over the heads of her kids and across the parking lot toward the Nile.

"Oh my gosh. She's going into the river!" Heather shouted.

All three kids sprinted across the asphalt lot and jumped the stone fence that lined the scenic pathway down to the river.

"There they are," the young Arab said to Kevin Turner. Turner had been watching the hotel for two days after he realized that the information he had paid for was bogus. The Arab jumped out of the boat onto the sandy shore and ran away. Now he was positioned in a boat about two hundred yards up river from the hotel. His contact in the hotel had told him the MacGregors had departed around 5:00 A.M. The message they had left for Dr. MacGregor read that they would return before 9:00 A.M. Dr. MacGregor had been in Alexandria and was expected back by air around 8:30 A.M.

Watching the three kids clear the wall on the run chasing after someone in a low-flying hang glider brought a smile to Turner's face. He had searched long and hard in the Cayman Islands, East Africa, and now Egypt. He was here to avenge the death of his brother James Turner. The MacGregors weren't going to get away from him this time. He turned the ignition switch on the motor and pulled the anchor from over the side.

"Mom, pull down on the horizontal bar! Pull down on the bar!" Chris shouted as he led the chase down the pathway closer and closer toward the Nile.

"Oh, Mavis, what have you done. Chris, what? I can't hear you." Then she noticed Heather holding her fists out in front of her and pulling back. "I've got it. Pull the horizontal bar back when going into a headwind to land."

Mavis took a deep breath and jerked the bar backward toward her. But it was too hard. The nose of the glider suddenly dipped and she quickly lost twenty feet of her fifty foot altitude. Panicked by the sudden plunge she pushed it forward quickly, but it was too late. She had created a stall. The forward motion of the glider was now being slowed by the headwind. The glider seemed to slide to the right and made a fast plunge the last thirty feet toward the blue Nile.

Turner's boat was circling in from the far side of the river. He reached into his briefcase, pulled out the Browning 9mm pistol, pulled the exchange, and loaded a round into the firing chamber.

"Fourteen rounds ought to take care of three kids and whomever is flying that glider into the river."

Mavis hit the water with such speed the aluminum frame of the glider collapsed around her. Chris had just reached the water's edge. He ripped off his desert boots and dove into the river. Heather was right behind him. R.O. stopped at the wall anxiously looking on. He heard a voice behind him.

"R.O., R.O. What's happening?"

R.O. turned around and to his astonishment found Natalie Crosswhite running toward him. He hadn't seen Natalie since he had left the Cayman Islands several weeks ago.

"Natalie. What…"

"R.O., is that Chris out there?"

"Yes. He and Heather went in after Mom. She crashed her hang glider into the Nile. What are you doing here?"

"Later." Natalie snapped back. She stood on top of the wall looking toward the rescue.

"Mom!" Chris yelled as he surfaced and swam frantically toward the sinking glider.

Mavis struggled with the harness, yanking at it as hard as she could while trying to keep her head above the water. The current began to pull the glider northward away from the hotel. Chris and Heather swam as hard as they could. With the style of a competitive freestyle swimmer, Heather soon caught and passed Chris.

Mavis finally found the buckle and pulled the quick release, freeing her from the weight of the glider. She yanked at the fabric when suddenly she heard a pop and whiz. The 9mm bullet ripped through the fabric and severed one of the aluminum wing supports.

"Gunshots, Natalie!" R.O. shouted.

"From there. That boat," Natalie pointed.

Chris and Heather hadn't noticed anything because of their frantic swim. They were almost to the half-submerged glider when another shot came from the swiftly moving boat.

Natalie took off in a run toward the hotel dock where three wave runners were parked. R.O. was on her heels with the same thought in mind. There was a pop and another bullet tore through the glider's fabric.

"Chris! Heather! Someone is shooting at us. There." Mavis shouted pointing to the approaching boat. She then ducked under water for a second to pull the wing out of her way. When she surfaced, Chris and Heather had finally reached her.

"Gunshots," Mavis said.

"I heard you. We've got to go under and swim toward the bank. Spread out so he can't shoot all of us at once," Chris instructed, now breathing hard.

Heather didn't say anything while trying to catch

her breath. A fourth bullet suddenly ricocheted off another aluminum support.

"Down, now!" Chris shouted. They all took as much
of a breath as they could and dove below the drifting
glider.

"OK, where did you go? If I run out of bullets, I will
just cut you in half with the prop of the boat. I owe you
big time!" Kevin Turner muttered.

Natalie had reached the wave runners and untied
two of them. R.O. jumped on one and turned the ignition. It fired up right away. Natalie's did the same.
Quickly they pushed away from the dock and reached
full speed in a few seconds. The glider and the
MacGregors had drifted about two hundred yards north
of the resort. The driver of the speedboat was circling
the downed glider, looking for a shot.

Natalie pointed for R.O. to hang back. She headed
straight for the boat. The driver had not seen her or R.O.
Mavis, Chris, and Heather finally surfaced for air. Turner
fired three more rounds at them just missing them as
they dove again into the Nile. Natalie's wave runner
finally caught up with the speedboat. Accelerating to
full throttle the wave runner picked up speed.

"You're going to ram him! Go, Natalie!" R.O.
shouted.

Natalie's wave runner was pointed toward the outboard motor of Turner's boat. She knew she would have
to ride the runner into the boat as far as she could
because the second she moved from the seat and let go
of the throttle, the motor would kick off. She quickly
changed her mind and decided to drive in front of the
speedboat from his blind side. In a few seconds she had
changed her course.

Turner never saw her coming when, at the last
second, she dove off the wave runner. It drifted into the
path of the speedboat. The noise of the crashing fiberglass was horrendous followed by the grinding of the

prop over the top of the wave runner. Then the outboard went dead.

R.O. maneuvered next to Natalie and helped her aboard. Turner, surprised at the sudden collision, had dropped the gun onto the floor of the boat. Without power, he was frantically searching for the gun to get off a few last shots.

Chris, Mavis, and Heather surfaced again.

"I can't breathe," Mavis panted.

"Hang on, Mom," Chris calmly assured her.

"Look! There's Ryan with someone coming after us," Heather shouted.

"Where's the guy with the gun?" Mavis said.

"He's drifting away. He's lost power."

R.O. turned the wave runner to make a short circle around his family. Turner had located the Browning and was now firing. At that distance, his accuracy was poor, but one bullet pierced the fiberglass side of the wave runner just above Natalie's foot.

Chris saw Natalie but didn't say anything as he pulled Heather and Mavis toward the runner. Soon everyone was jammed on top of the three seater. R.O. gave it all the power he could, and it sluggishly moved forward gaining speed.

"Take us away from our hotel!" Chris yelled to R.O.

"That's a roger, Chris!" R.O. shouted back.

In the distance they could see the attacker fire one more bullet and heard the pop. But it was off mark.

A mile down the river was the Marriott. As they reached the dock, the dock manager ran over to them and started asking who they were. In a few minutes they were all standing on the dock as two hotel policemen approached. Soon three more police were there and all felt secure once again.

Chris turned to Natalie and their eyes met. Without saying a word, they moved together and embraced in a kiss. Mavis, Heather, and R.O. smiled. Chris and

Natalie's brief encounter in the Caymans had brought them close together.

The young Arab pulled up next to Turner's damaged boat and helped him into the small dingy. Neither man spoke. The Arab sensed his life would be worthless if he made a comment. Turner just kept looking down river. He finally spoke.

"Round one goes to the MacGregors. Next time they won't know what hit them. Enjoy your last week of life, kids." Kevin Turner smiled grimly and sailed away.

6

Never Eat Camel

"Mom, where's Chris?" R.O. asked as he pulled the turquoise Miami Dolphins T-shirt over his head and combed his hair with his fingers.

"He left about an hour ago to meet Natalie at the convention center. They're going to meet us at the restaurant in Old Cairo. Weren't you just thrilled to see Natalie yesterday? I mean, landing the internship at the Environmental Summit was a sweet deal for her," Mavis said.

"And for Chris, too. Why are we meeting in Old Cairo?" R.O. inquired.

"That's where your father is going to meet us and some important dignitaries for lunch."

"Dad always has to meet someone for lunch or dinner," R.O. said. He plopped down on the bed in Mavis's room as she picked up a bottle of perfume and sprayed it behind her ears.

"You always smell so good, Mom."

Mavis turned, leaned down to him and placed her hands on his cheeks, framing his face. She knew he didn't like that but that's what she wanted to do.

"Thanks, sweetie," she said and kissed him on the forehead.

"And aren't we in a sweet mood?" Heather said to R.O. as she walked into the room.

"Shove it, Heather," R.O. said and gave her an ugly face.

"Ryan," Mavis said sternly as she glared at him.

He got the message and stood up quickly. Mavis greeted Heather with a light hug. Heather was wearing her khaki capri pants, a yellow spaghetti strap top, and a pair of black flip-flops.

"Cute, hon," Mavis observed and slipped on her Rolex Explorer watch, which she wore religiously since the adventure in East Africa.

The telephone rang.

"Yes," Mavis answered.

"Madam, your taxi is here," the bellhop said.

"Thank you."

In a couple of minutes Mavis, Heather, and R.O. were in the elevator and going down to the main lobby of the Cleopatra Resort. As the doors opened, the smell of Cairo hit them in the face. It was really foul, a combination of dirt, smog, cooking smoke, and millions of people. In the brief time they had been in Egypt, the MacGregors had grown accustomed to the odor and hardly noticed it unless they were downwind of a camel.

The beautiful hotel was fashioned with marble floors, Corinthian columns, gorgeous Arabic rugs, and greenery everywhere. It was an oasis in the new hotel district. The new and modern resorts lined the ancient river as if welcoming a host of gods back from the river of the dead. They were colorful, shining, clean, and almost sterile when compared to the rest of Egypt. The resorts were tributes to the western world and seemed an intrusion on the old, mud brick homes that had occupied Egypt for six thousand years.

The taxi driver was standing next to the old Mercedes

300D with the doors already opened. He stood well over six feet tall, which was extremely rare for an Arab. He wore a traditional caftan that was red, purple, and gold. Three rows of gold chains made up his necklace and matched the braiding in the earrings that dangled from his large earlobes.

"Good morning, Madam," he said as he bowed and pointed to the open door in the back where he wanted Mavis to be seated. As he gently closed her door, Heather climbed in the back on the other side. R.O. hopped in the front passenger side and buckled his seat belt.

"Good idea," the driver said to R.O. "Driving in Cairo is not like driving anywhere else in the world," he said proudly. "It is an adventure. A challenge of one's courage and in your case, manhood! So we shall begin our journey to where?"

"We are going to the old district. I believe the name of the restaurant is Arabesque," Mavis said.

"I know it well. I have dined there many times myself with beautiful women and powerful clients," the cab driver boasted.

As he smiled, Heather noticed the two gold front teeth and giggled at his humorous nature.

"Where is your home?" the driver asked.

"Texas," they all replied simultaneously.

"Ah, Texas. Texans are the only people I meet that when I ask them where their home is they say Texas. The Japanese always say Japan. The Germans always say Germany. The Spaniards always say Spain. Occasionally a New Yorker will say New York instead of the United States. But Texans are like some Russians I have met. I ask them where they are from and they say Moscow, not Russia, unless of course they are from St. Petersburg or Minsk. But Texans and Moscovites, I like them because of their pride."

"And where is your home?" R.O. asked.

"My home is Luxor," the Arab said proudly. "It is

the burial place of the Pharaohs and the most honored city in Egypt. My ancestors carved the tombs out of the face of the mountains and then decorated them with the ancient language."

"Hieroglyphics!" R.O. shouted.

"Yes, hieroglyphics. You are very smart. And what do they call you?" the cab driver asked.

"R.O., and this is my mom, Mavis, and my stuck-up sister, Heather. She thinks she is really hot." R.O. laughed at Heather. Heather returned the laugh with an annoyed stare.

"What's your name?" R.O. asked.

"My name is El Serapis bin Khety Qakare Merananum bin Babu al Sadat." R.O. looked at him.

"El Sahara, Qatar Muhammad Baby al sady?"

"Very close. It is El Serapis bin Khety Qakare Merananum bin Babu al Sadat."

"El Quatara, Shikara, Kaheen Muhamanum Al Sadat," R.O. said.

"Very close again, R.O."

"Look, my full name is Ryan O'Keef MacGregor. But to help out my family," Heather rolled her eyes knowing the embellishment that was about to occur, "I let them call me R.O. So why don't I call you E.S.B.K.Q. M.B.A.S. Esbcumbas."

"I've got a better idea," Heather spoke. "Let's just call him 'E'."

"Great idea, Heather," Mavis said.

Suddenly E swerved in traffic, just missing an overloaded tourist bus. He pressed down hard on the horn. He then dodged three more taxis and nearly clipped the end of a police car before he turned off the main highway and onto the side streets of old Cairo.

"Reminds me of Mexico City," Heather observed as she looked out the window at the contrasting buildings of bright pastels and brown mud brick.

"Yes, crazy like Mexico City but fast like Atlanta

when we were there to visit your father's sister and attend the Olympics," Mavis said.

"And don't forget noisy," R.O. said.

"Yes, Cairo has the reputation of being the noisiest city in the world," E said.

Swerving quickly around pedestrians, both local and tourists, E guided the old Mercedes, as it belched blue and white smoke, through the narrow streets. Soon they could see Chris and Natalie standing on the old stone street straight ahead. E rolled to a stop.

Jack walked up behind them and waited as Mavis, R.O., and Heather climbed out of the taxi. Mavis kissed Jack on the mouth and R.O. looked away. Chris and Natalie hugged Mavis, Heather, and Jack while R.O. just wandered down the street looking around.

"Did you come straight from Grand Cayman or did you get to go home to Oklahoma first?" Mavis asked Natalie.

"The delegation met at Oklahoma State for a couple of days first. So I got to go home for a week. It was great to see everyone," Natalie replied. "But I'm going back to the hotel camera shop in Georgetown, Grand Cayman, for three weeks before the fall term starts. I can use the extra money for school and a few days on the beach won't hurt either."

"It won't ever be the same," Mavis said.

"It already isn't the same. Every time I put on diving gear or a storm blows in, I get goose bumps thinking about what we went through. I mean sharks, Hurricane Keely, and those two nasty bad guys. I don't want that to ever happen again."

"It won't, dear. It's just smooth sailing ahead for you and all the MacGregors," Mavis said and kissed her on the cheek.

Jack turned to E and paid the fare and tipped him with a U.S. five dollar bill.

"Thank you, sir. Will the family be needing a ride

back to the hotel?" E asked.

"Yes, but it will probably be a couple of hours or so," Jack replied.

"Then I shall be happy to wait and transport them back later."

"You don't have to do that," Jack replied.

"It is no problem. I need to do some business in old Cairo and then I will return to collect you," E said using the British vernacular he had learned. Mavis sensed a slight British accent. But that was normal for many educated Egyptians who had attended university in England. It puzzled her nonetheless since E was a taxi driver. She had never met a university educated taxi driver, except of course, in New York City. But the thought quickly passed as the family required her attention.

"Thank you," Jack replied.

Just as Dr. MacGregor turned toward the family, he felt a tap on his shoulder. Before him stood a short, stout man in a white suit and a red fez that matched his blood red tie.

"Dr. Jack MacGregor?"

"Yes, I'm Jack MacGregor."

"I am Inspector Samut, Cairo Police. We met at the hospital a few days ago."

"Oh, yes, Inspector. I never got a chance to really thank you," Jack replied.

"You are very welcome, sir. But it seems, Dr. MacGregor, that your family has a penchant for attracting the worst elements in our exotic land," the Inspector said.

He reached for a small pad and pen in the inside pocket of his suit jacket.

"You mean the incident yesterday in the Nile?" Jack asked. Everyone was now quiet and listening.

"Yes, but of course, Dr. MacGregor. Unless there is something else you would like to report to the police?"

"No," Jack said and looked around at Mavis, Chris, Heather, Natalie, and R.O., who was currently distracted by a snow white pigeon that had landed a few feet away. The others shook their heads indicating no. "Then, Doctor, I must ask you a few questions. It seems that the police report that was filed about the incident was incomplete."

"I can't talk this very minute, Inspector. I have a very important luncheon that begins in ten minutes. Maybe later this afternoon," Jack asked.

"I understand, Dr. MacGregor. But I don't want you to think that the Cairo Police takes this incident lightly. When a visitor is assaulted, especially such a high profile visitor as the famous Dr. Jack MacGregor, then we want to know everything about the incident. We are concerned for the safety of Egypt's guests," the short stout Inspector said.

"I am pleased to hear that, Inspector. But the truth is that we don't know anything about who might be so angry at us. Who would want to shoot at my kids and wife? I can only assume it was a random mugging by someone who had planned to rob a tourist and just happen to seize on the opportunity when my family was in a very precarious position."

"I would not call shooting at someone who has just landed a hang glider in the Nile as a random mugging, Doctor," the Inspector said and turned toward the family. "In fact, Dr. MacGregor, I believe that there is more to this than you are telling me. What is your family concealing?"

"Now wait a minute, Inspector," Jack shot back.

"We will pursue this later, Doctor. Say around 4:00 P.M. at the Cleopatra Hotel? I will be there ten minutes early. Good day." The inspector said and walked away quickly before Jack could say another word.

"Presumptuous little man," Mavis said as she stepped closer to Jack.

"What do you think, hon?" Jack said to Mavis.

"I don't know, Jack. I mean we were flying in unannounced. No one knew we were to be there at that time. Gosh sakes, we didn't even know. It wasn't in our plan."

"Flight plan, Mom," R.O. chimed in. Chris gave him the look to be quiet.

"I stand corrected. Flight Plan."

"And that is yet a whole other discussion," Jack said staring at each one, except for Natalie. "Random is still my choice. We've run into some pretty shady characters the last two months in the Cayman Islands and East Africa. But this would be a real stretch to say anything was connected. I just don't believe it."

"Nor I," Mavis said instilling confidence in everyone.

"Yeah, Dad. But don't you think it would be really weird if there were some sort of conspiracy that linked us to terrorist activity around the world? I mean the really bad guys that bomb embassies, factories, highjack airplanes, and smuggle guns and drugs into third world countries to promote revolutions...."

"Ryan. I hope it is not that way and I would advise you that another word of this will only limit your television and movie watching that much more. Do I get an affirmative on that young man?" Mavis said while never losing eye contact. "It's not cool to watch people die!"

"Yes, Mom," R.O. said staring back at her.

Trying to regroup, Jack reached out to everyone with a pat on the shoulder or light hug and herded them toward the massive doors of the restaurant. Soon the talk turned toward the Giza pyramids and the Egyptian Museum. As they walked into the main dining area, R.O. spoke up first.

"Where are the chairs?"

"They don't have chairs, silly," Heather replied. "We get to lounge on big pillows with the little square table in the middle. That's the way it's done in the Middle East."

"That's weird, but I like it," R.O. replied and followed along behind the maitre d'.

There were two large square tables with a group of four men and two women. Three men were dressed in business suits and one was dressed in military style khaki shirt and pants. One of the women was dressed in a stylish navy pants suit replete with jewelry and a very contemporary hairstyle. The other wore a traditional Egyptian caftan with matching slacks but, unlike most Moslem women, she did not have her hair or face covered. Instead she wore bright red lipstick and pearl earrings. As the MacGregors approached, the maitre d' shuffled the kids to another table close by and seated Jack and Mavis.

"Ah, Dr. MacGregor," a very dark-skinned Arab in a western suit smiled and offered his hand. "It is good to see you again and to finally meet the lovely Dr. Mavis."

"Good to see you again, Khalid," Jack said and shook his hand. He then turned to the man on his right.

"Drs. MacGregor. I finally get to meet this famous team of scientists," the man said.

"And it's good to meet you as well, Mr. Secretary." Mavis reached out and shook the hand of Kofi Annan, the Secretary General of the United Nations. "I must admit I am surprised at the lack of security," Mavis said.

"Oh, but don't be concerned, Dr. MacGregor. Every customer you see in this lovely restaurant and half of the citizens on the street and on every roof in three blocks are United Nations Security personnel," the Secretary General said.

"I'm impressed, but I half expected it." Mavis sat down on a large red satin pillow. She was glad she wore pants instead of a skirt. She glanced at Jack as if to tell him that he should have warned her where they were going to eat. But he didn't catch the silent message and only raised his eyebrows.

After the introductions had taken place, the eight scientists and world leaders began to discuss politics and situations that usually put most kids to sleep. But the MacGregor kids were not most kids. However, they were at an adjacent table and weren't able to join the discussion. Takany al-Aman, Economic Minister of Egypt, was the first to speak.

"Dr. MacGregor, the reason we asked you to come today, rather than meet with you at the convention, is to convey the seriousness of the economic and environmental problems we are facing in Egypt. As you are aware, the Nile River has become devoid of the silt that for thousands of years has nourished our land and provided the foundation for our economy. But since the High Aswan Dam was completed in 1968, silt from the Ethiopian highlands has backed up behind the dam.

"Lake Nassar is quickly becoming a muddy lake and the agriculture of the region may be facing a decline because of the use of chemicals. Before the dam, the silt provided all the nutrients our farmers needed. The fishing fleets in the Nile delta have reported a drop in the numbers of fish caught because of a lack of nutrients that flow to the Mediterranean Sea to support their growth."

"Yes, our economy has boomed for nearly thirty years. Boomed by Middle East standards, of course. Electricity is cheaper. Better flood control. More land to farm. More agriculture jobs for the poorer class. But that all may change if we unleash the Nile. In short, Doctor, our current situation may prove challenging in the near future."

"Our dilemma is this. We lack the international support to act alone. We need a spokesman of your reputation, a famous scientist, one who is known around the world and respected for a common-sense approach to conservation rather than being an environmental extremist. We need your help. If you supported the destruction of the High Aswan Dam in order to save the ecosystem of the Nile and to provide the nutrients this great river needs, then other scientists from the west would follow your lead," Menes al-Qatar, an economist, said. "We can't do it alone. It is too expensive and without western money we would fail."

"And then," Takani interrupted, "nothing would have been gained by building the dam nor tearing it down. It would have all been an act of futility."

Everyone around the table became silent and all eyes turned toward Jack. Mavis smiled, looked at him and raised her eyebrows. Jack glanced back knowing it was his turn to speak.

"I have reviewed the problem. The entire scientific community is aware of it and many papers have been written about it. But how do you undo forty years of environmental damage overnight? That's the question. I am sure there is a solution, but, if it takes too long to find it, the problem only grows worse and makes it even tougher to solve. You just can't tear down the dam and expect everything to be OK. It just won't work that way. The repercussions would be monumental throughout the Middle East."

"Dr. MacGregor. One of the more conservative, even radical political parties, suggests that a single F-16 fighter jet carrying a 500-megaton bomb could release the water from Aswan in just a few seconds. Their argument is that it would purify the Nile of all western influence. A rebirth of some kind would follow. It would be the beginning of Jihad. Of course, the sudden rush of water and flooding will devastate the population of Egypt and the Cairo community. But to have that even suggested should be a warning to all of us that sooner or later a fanatic will bomb Aswan."

A pall of silence fell around the table and everyone stopped eating the stuffed duck and potatoes.

"Then I guess a solid plan needs to be developed to

release the silt while at the same time saving the ecosystem of the Nile," Mavis said to break the silence.

"Mom," Chris whispered in Mavis' ear. "Can we leave and take a walk through the district? We can meet you back at the hotel later," Chris suggested.

"Sure, hon. This will get more involved, I am sure," Mavis replied and kissed him on the cheek. Chris blushed and turned around.

"Lovely children," Kesi Onan, wife of the Secretary General, said.

"Thank you," Mavis replied. "Two fine boys, if I may boast, and a lovely young lady."

At that moment Chris, Heather, Natalie, and R.O. stepped from the dark restaurant in old Cairo. Before their eyes had adjusted, they heard patting feet on the street and a shrill voice.

"MacGregors. I am back and not too soon I see. How was your meal? I bet it was just exquisite," E said towering over them as a silhouette against the midday sun.

"We didn't eat," R.O. said quickly. "It looked funny. Egyptian ducks don't look like Texas ducks."

"I am sure it was good food, but just not our choice," Chris said.

"I see," E said. "Then you all must be very hungry? I will show you my favorite place to eat in this district. You will love it."

"Good, I'm starved," Natalie said as she reached out and took Chris's hand in hers. For a second their eyes locked and a brief message of affection was exchanged without saying a word. Heather smiled and then looked away. R.O. was already crawling into the front seat of the old Mercedes taxi and buckling his seat belt. In a minute they were in and cruising through the narrow streets of Cairo. It took about ten minutes in bumper to bumper traffic. There was a snarl around a donkey cart that had dumped a load of melons in the street. Two taxis had collided and the drivers stood in the street yelling at each other.

As the entourage arrived at the restaurant, they noticed a small neon sign that hung over a single arched doorway with an iron gate. An old man in a long white shirt called a thobe and wearing a fez sat in an old chair with peeling blue paint.

E parked the Mercedes, put his "free parking" sign on the dash, and led the way toward the doorway. He flashed a card he had retrieved from his billfold and the old man smiled and waved him past. All the kids followed him through the doorway into a dark hall that had descending steps.

Going down exactly forty-two steps through the dark hallway, they entered a dark room where a young man in a red jacket, white shirt, black slacks, and a bow tie presented himself. He spoke to E in Arabic and then said, "This way" in English. They walked down another dark hallway. The kids noticed several small dining rooms on each side with the aroma of cooked meats filling the air and being sucked into their nostrils.

"What smells so good?" Heather said.

"Ditto, that," R.O. added.

As they continued down the hallway of this dungeon-like restaurant, they stopped in front of an elevator door.

"Who would have thought?" Chris smiled at Natalie.

In a second they were all aboard and the elevator climbed rapidly. The young boy in the red jacket had pushed a button that only E could read. In less than a minute the doors opened and they all stepped out.

"Oh my gosh," Natalie spoke revealing the impression of all of them. Before them on the rooftop cafe was a beautiful panoramic view of Cairo with the plateau of Giza and the three pyramids serving as the backdrop a couple miles away.

"This is awesome," Chris said.

"And the food is even better," E replied as he herded them to a table where a waiter was standing. Ordering quickly in Arabic, E turned to the kids. "This restaurant is owned by my uncle, and it is my treat to you on your first visit to Cairo."

"Thanks, E," R.O. said. He stood next to the table and leaned over the wall to look down. But he quickly looked up and around because the view down was only of another rooftop.

The meal began with an appetizer of hummus and a special Egyptian bread called aysh shami. It resembled pita bread. They were so hungry that very little conversation took place. Each MacGregor kid and Natalie savaged the bread by tearing it and dipping it into the hummus.

"What is this great stuff?" R.O. asked E.

"It is hummus. A wheat dip," he replied.

Just as they had finished eating all of the hummus in the large ceramic bowl, the main course arrived.

"That really smells good," Natalie said as she leaned over the new dish.

"It is called bamya," E said. "It is stewed beef with onions, garlic, tomatoes, mint, many different spices, lemon juice, and the secret ingredient."

"Which is?" Heather asked and smiled.

"Okra!"

"Okra?" they all asked together.

"I've eaten fried okra and pickled okra, but never cooked like this," Natalie said.

"Well, let's try it," Chris added.

In a few minutes the kids were filling up on bamya and loving every bite. R.O. stopped and looked up with a spoonful of bamya a few inches from his mouth.

"E."

"Yes, R.O.?".

"You said this was beef, didn't you?" R.O. asked.

"Yes, beef," E said.

"No camel," R.O. said.

Everyone looked up quickly and stared at E.

"No camel. One never eats a camel. They are tough, chewy, and they taste really bad. No camel."

"Good. Thanks," R.O. said and put the spoon of bamya into his mouth.

"That's a relief," Natalie said and took another bite.

"I am getting so full." Heather leaned back from the table.

"How long have you been a taxi driver?" Natalie asked.

"About five years. I had been working for another uncle in his leather shop when this opportunity presented itself. I meet interesting people and the job is never boring." E took a drink of the Egyptian coffee called aiwa.

"I think it would be interesting. And if you are happy, then that's all that matters," Natalie said.

"I agree with that," Chris added.

"What did the inspector want with your father?" E asked, quickly changing the subject.

"When we were at the end of our hang gliding two days ago, someone in a speedboat shot at us and then tried to run over us while we were in the Nile," Chris said.

"Shot at you? How horrible!" E replied and pretended to shiver, acting like a wimp. Of course, the kids didn't know whether he was acting or was for real. "That is absolutely frightening."

"If it weren't for Natalie and her quick thinking, who knows how it would have turned out," Chris said.

"Probably on CNN or Fox News as the incident of the day where U.S. tourists were killed by terrorists," R.O. added and took another bite of bamya and aysh shami.

"I really don't want to talk about it anymore," Heather said. They all looked at her. "I just want to enjoy

our trip to Egypt, see the pyramids again, travel down
the Nile to Luxor. We do have that Egypt unit Mom
assigned. We have to learn the cartouche of ten Pharaohs, outline the history of the three kingdoms, and
know the importance of Saqqara, Abydos, Elephantine
Island, Luxor, and the Bahariya Oasis."

"I am impressed. I would wager that half of Egypt
can't do that," E said as he ate a piece of bread.

"Can half of Egypt read?" Natalie asked, not meaning to poke fun.

"Probably not the way you are thinking. Most everyone can read Arabic characters, but other types of
reading, well, I doubt it. But that is a major goal of our
new president."

"We take far too much for granted, guys," Chris
said.

"True," Natalie added. "Back in Stillwater, the main
concerns of the students are grades, parties, class projects,
parties, graduation, and more parties."

"From my experience with American culture, that
is fairly common, isn't it?" E said.

"Yes, I imagine it would be," Chris said. "But not
everyone is like that."

Natalie nodded her head in agreement.

"Where are we going tomorrow?" R.O. asked.

"I have an idea," E spoke up. "I have the next two
days off. Why don't I take you on a tour of Cairo and the
outlying temples?"

"Awesome," R.O. said.

Chris thought for a second, then nodded in agreement.

"That would be great. Day after tomorrow, we are
scheduled to sail up the Nile to Luxor with my parents.
We'll be gone for two days. So a tour around Cairo
would be awesome. We'll be here for just two weeks,
until the environmental summit is complete. Then we'll
be off again for another country.

Natalie looked sad. "I've seen you for only two days and you are already talking about leaving. Where will you go?"

"I'm not for sure, but I heard Mom and Dad talking about India, China, and Australia. Who knows? It depends on the environmental problem and which is the most urgent, I suppose," Chris replied.

"Let's don't even discuss that right now, Chris. I still want to see the Valley of the Kings so I can do the report that is part of our homework assignment," Heather said.

"Why the concern for the homework, papers, and projects?" E asked with a frown on his forehead.

"If we don't do our school work during the trip, then we get sent back to the U.S. to live with our Aunt Marcia in Georgia for the remainder of the year," Heather replied quickly.

"And you don't want to do that!" R.O. said

"The famous Drs. MacGregor would actually do that?"

Chris, Heather, and Ryan all nodded simultaneously.

"Oh, my! Then we better get going so we can see everything and give you time to do homework as well," E said.

As they were leaving, each teenager looked out across ancient Cairo. The history and the culture were magnificent, but the smog and noise were horrible. Cairo had become a modern city, only after being dragged into the twentieth century kicking and screaming. This rich culture was still heavily consumed with poverty, dirt, and pollution. If the ancient Egyptians had been living today, they would have prayed to Bastet, the cat god of war, to carry out vengeance on those who had kept their people in poverty and disease.

But for now, deep in the ancient tombs of the Pharaohs, engulfed in the heat of the burning sun, the oracle of the Nile lay waiting for the time of vengeance to come. And soon it would.

7

Bears and Sand Fleas

---○---

Just eight blocks away from the rooftop restaurant where the MacGregor kids were dining, three men sat at a small round table sipping a cup of thick ahwa. The Egyptian coffee was very hot. The two Russians wore caftans that bore the bold purple and reds of the Russian Czars and were common as lounging garments in the nineteenth century. The older Arab, however, wore a more traditional caftan that was white with a trim of burgundy and black. Seated on large fluffy pillows, each man enjoyed the dates, pomegranates, figs, and smoked meats laid out before them. If one didn't know the date, August 2000, one would have thought it was a meal for an ancient Egyptian family from Thebes or Heliopolis.

"What progress have you made on finding the lost hardware?" Sergei asked. He took a big bite out of the beef rib that was dripping in pepper sauce. The sauce smeared across his gray beard and coated his hands and burned his lips.

"My technicians told me not to worry. The piece, as I call it, is still in Cairo. Our instruments have narrowed

it to twenty square miles," the large Arab said as he
popped a fig into his mouth. "Lucky for you, I attached
a small homing device to it."

"Twenty square miles. Ziyad, you ruthless old camel
trader, that is seventies technology. This is 2000. We can
read the cancer warning on a package of American
cigarettes from a satellite over a hundred miles up in
space," Alexander Raiken said and slammed his hand
down on the table.

All sat in silence for a minute. The two Russians,
former KGB agents Alexander Raiken and Sergei
Andropov, stared at Ziyad without blinking an eye. The
old Arab, who had survived the cold war between the
USSR and the United States, didn't even flinch. He tore
off a piece of bread from the loaf in front of him. He took
a silver-plated knife, gently wiped some goat's butter
on the bread, and took a huge bite. Some of the butter
stuck to the whiskers of his big moustache. He looked
up slowly toward the Russians as he chewed.

"My dear comrades. When I arranged to acquire
special night vision equipment for the periscope of your
Delta class submarines in 1968, you had faith that for
one million dollars I would deliver. I did deliver and
your submarines could see as good as the British and the
Americans.

"When I arranged to acquire the special naviga-
tional guidance systems from the American F4 Phan-
tom fighter bombers flying in Viet Nam, you had faith
that for two million dollars I would deliver. I did deliver
and your MIGS soon could target and deliver a bomb
load with as much accuracy as the Americans.

"When your communist system was falling down
all around you and you needed arms for your rebels in
the Balkans, Eastern Europe, Indonesia, and Ecuador, I
again, for three million dollars, delivered. And my
dear communist comrades, when you needed to transport weapons grade plutonium from Turkmenistan, an

all Arab, all Muslim nation, back to safety in Moscow, I delivered for the sum of four million dollars. And I did so without the American CIA, British MI6, French Secret Service, or Israeli Mossad knowing that it had been done. And that part was free. No charge. My compliments."

"Ziyad," Alexander started to speak.

"I am not finished, Comrade Raiken." The Russian shut up and lifted his cup of thick coffee.

"You see, gentlemen, my father fought the British, then the Nazis, then the British again, then the Israelis, then the Americans, but now," he paused and took another bite of the bread, "I don't know who to fight anymore!" Ziyad grinned with the bread showing through part of his mouth. The Russians looked steely eyed at the old sly Arab who had been their ally. They knew that, like a Nile cobra, he could turn and devour them both. He was never to be totally trusted.

"So when I tell you that I will retrieve the satellite device, then that means that I will get it back. And that means that our deal is still good, and you will pay me the ten million dollars that you owe me," Ziyad said.

"We owe you?" Sergei shot back. "You don't even have the device. And we frankly don't think you can find it soon enough. The master circuit board will be put into the control panel in Alice Springs, Australia, in just one more week. If we don't have the CD and the circuit board to install in our own control panel, we will miss the window of opportunity." Sergei looked at Alexander and then they both nodded.

"What we are about to tell you, you must not tell anyone," Alexander said in a whisper.

At that moment, a young woman walked up with a fresh tray of meats, steamed vegetables, and sliced melons. All were quiet while she placed the food on the table and removed the used dishes.

"Thank you, Kesi. She is so sweet. She is the wife of

my grandson Uni, just nineteen. My nine sons and daughters have brought me great joy with nearly forty grandchildren. All but five work for my enterprises in Cairo."

The Russians seemed annoyed at the interruption. As soon as Kesi left, Alexander began talking.

"The circuit board that we asked you to acquire is a copy of one that is in the master control computer at Alice Springs, Australia. At a prescribed moment, the computer will go off line for two hours while routine annual maintenance is performed on the system. At that time, our agent will replace the circuit board with our copy."

"My copy," Ziyad said. "It was I who found the scientist who developed it, paid her a million dollars to copy it, and make the small changes you requested. I took your order and like a good businessman I filled the order. I have not offered it to the North Koreans, Iraq, the Libyans, or any terrorist group. I ask no questions and expect no answers. So what you are telling me is at your own risk."

"Whatever you say, you old Arab. But you will know because, if it fails, we will have another meeting very soon," Sergei said and took a bite out of the rib.

"In seven days," Alexander continued, "our agent will put the circuit board in the computer. When the system is restarted, our special CD will be downloaded containing the software that is compatible with the new circuit board."

"And what new magic will it perform?" Ziyad asked quietly, not really wanting to know. He had learned that knowing too much in the spy business could be dangerous.

"The computer will communicate with most of the defense satellites of the United States, Great Britain, France, Canada, Australia...in short, all the western nations and NATO." Alexander smiled. "We will have a link to the computer."

"But there is more," Sergei added. "Do you remember that from 1994 to last year, the Americans were a little too careless about sharing technology with China and North Korea?"

"Of course they were," Ziyad replied. "The Americans are always giving secrets to their enemies. A good Arab would never do this." He took a bite of the pomegranate.

"That is another argument. But in regards to our piece of electronics, the Americans didn't know what they were sharing." Both looked at each other. "We had agents in every electronics shop in every satellite manufacturing facility around the world. Every satellite that was constructed for five years was fitted with hardware and software that could receive instructions from the master computer in Alice Springs.

"What the Americans didn't know was that each time they shared information with any nation, they were delivering our system to them. Each computer installed in a satellite had a slight adjustment, one that would allow us to control the satellite. This had been planned for twenty years, but not until the Americans developed the technology and then gave it away could it have happened. Never in our wildest dreams did we expect this to take place without war, aggressive action, covert espionage, or your brand of terrorism."

The old Arab scratched his chin and smiled.

"When your little circuit board is activated, it will send a very powerful message into space. The satellites we control will look wherever you want them to. You can see what your enemies see. When the gods of Egypt made a wise and infallible statement, we would call it an oracle. It was a divine revelation to the people. The message that your little device will send around the earth will indeed be such a revelation."

"Yes, Ziyad. It will be the key to returning Mother

Russia to her former greatness. When we have this
advantage, many nations will rejoin us to stand against
the Americans and British once again. The Soviet Union
will rise from its ashes and a new power will be born.
And we will do it without firing one shot," Alexander
said.

"But we still have a problem, Ziyad," Sergei said.

"But, of course. I will acquire the device before your
deadline. I have never failed," Ziyad replied.

"We know that, my old friend. But to be sure that
you will find it in time, we have taken out an insurance
policy. One of our agents has taken your daughter,
Zalika."

Ziyad lunged across the table. Coffee spilled everywhere and dates and figs rolled off the table. A young
man lunged from behind a curtain with a long steel
sword and held it at the neck of Sergei.

"What do you mean, you have taken Zalika?" Ziyad
said, only five inches from Sergei's face. Ziyad's face
was red with rage.

Alexander leaned back and got to his feet.

"Resorting to violence will only make matters
worse," he said.

Ziyad let go of the Russian's caftan and rose slowly
to his feet. When he had finally stood up, all three men
took one step backward and the young man with the
sword lowered the razor-sharp blade.

"All of these years, no one has ever threatened my
family. You realize that when this is over, Ziyad and the
Little Shop of Thoth will no longer be a business partner
of Mother Russia," he said.

"But Ziyad, you know this is not personal. It is only
business. A little insurance to be sure you move swiftly."

"No. This is typical Russian-style negotiations. You
are the bear, a bully, an animal not to be trusted even for
a moment. You have yet to learn that it is better to be a
sand flea. It is a small creature that hides until it is

hungry and then it takes its blood meal. But it never kills its host. It never becomes too aggressive to cause the dog or the camel to reject it. In the end the flea will survive, but the bear will force its own demise."

"Your clever riddles still don't change the facts. The circuit board is missing. We need to get it to our agent in Australia in five days. Get it back, Ziyad."

The two Russians pulled the caftans over their shoulders revealing their western street clothes. They threw the caftans to the floor. Soon they were downstairs and walking toward their rental car, a new Peugeot.

A young man was running through the expansive house as the Russians were leaving. He met Ziyad walking down the old stairway.

"Grandfather, we have great news. The surveillance camera in the shop showed that the young man paid for the items with a credit card. My sister remembers the items purchased, and we have matched the ticket with the card. It belongs to a Mr. Chris MacGregor."

"Excellent, Menes. Call your Uncle Setep at Central Bank and have him find the owner's home address and telephone number. The young man may be traveling with an adult who is in Cairo as well. After you get the name, then call your Aunt Dedi at the Egyptian Travel Service and find where they are staying. Hurry, we don't have much time."

As Ziyad walked through the old stucco house with its twelve-foot ceilings and archways everywhere, he ignored the large fountain that splashed carelessly in the atrium. He had passed it thousands of times and many times he would stop and watch the water splash on the blue and black marble tiles. But he was still full of anger. However, this new break gave him the glimmer of hope that he needed. He thought for a brief moment that this would be his last venture into international espionage. He had grown old and weary and had many grandchildren to enjoy. His family had become wealthy with several businesses funded by American dollars and Russian rubles. He had developed an elaborate Arab crime syndicate. While the rest of the world fought over whose ideology would rule, Ziyad had grown fat and rich in Egypt. Many innocent lives had been sacrificed to make him wealthy. He knew that the Pharaohs would be proud of him. But for now, time was short and the task was still very huge.

8

The Well of Muhammed

———————◻———————

The mini time warp was complete, as the old Mercedes taxi was passed by a sleek new Jaguar. A brand new fighter jet of the Egyptian Air Force was flying overhead. A Bedouin leading three camels and a donkey blocked the busy intersection.

"I guess if I saw a Pharaoh driving a chariot down the street, I would feel complete," Heather said, really bored with the traffic and the noise.

"There is a chariot race on Saturday in the north side of Cairo, if you would like to attend," E said.

"Well, I just think my calendar is too full, E. I would have just been thrilled to see that," Heather replied in a snotty manner.

"Heather," Chris said softly and glanced at her.

She refused to look at him.

"As for me, I would like to see the Egyptian Museum and the harbor at Alexandria where they are digging up Cleopatra's Palace," R.O. said.

Suddenly E slammed on his breaks and swerved to the right. All the kids were forced against their seat belts. Too stunned, they were silent. There was a loud

bang and the sound of metal grinding against metal and
the pavement. E gunned the Mercedes and jumped the
curb as a city bus just missed his left rear fender and
crashed violently into the car in front of them. People
were screaming.

"Oh, my gosh," Heather shouted as E sped the
Mercedes past the crash, down the sidewalk, just missing a large fruit stand full of melons.

"Hang on!" Natalie shouted and braced R.O. sitting
next to her.

"Those poor people," Heather said.

"Wow! Did you see that?" R. O. chimed in.

Chris pointed to the overturned donkey cart that
had started the chain reaction. Hundreds of oranges
were scattered all over the street.

"It is a dangerous thing to do, to drive in Cairo," E
said.

"No kidding. We've seen four accidents just today,
not counting the one we were nearly in. How did you
learn to drive like that? I mean, one second we were
sliding to a dead stop and another second we were
catapulting onto the sidewalk at fifty miles per hour,"
Chris said.

"No, you mean sixty kilometers per hours," E corrected.

"Yeah, I said that," Chris replied smiling. He looked
over his shoulder at Natalie.

"One of my uncles owns a small racetrack in the
delta. When the United Nations forces were stationed
there, he made lots of money letting the soldiers drive
his cars for fun and money. I was a boy and would clean
the cars, change the oil, and then when all was done, I
would get to drive them. It was great fun!" E said. "Here
we are. Out of the jam and back into the flow of smooth
traffic."

All four kids looked in astonishment that smooth
flowing traffic was still bumper to bumper, car horns

blaring, drivers yelling at each other, and smog so thick you could cut it.

"I've got an idea," E said. "Instead of the museum today, why don't I take you to Saqqara. It's on the southeast side of Cairo past the Pyramids of Giza."

"What's Saqqara?" R. O. asked.

"It is the home of the famous step pyramid. But it is also the ancient shrine of the holy bulls and other animals of the Pharaohs. It has the temples of Djoser and King Wadj. Ah, but wait. Look ahead. It is the Shrine of Muhammad Ali, one of the greatest spiritual leaders of Islam," E said.

"Awesome. I thought he was a great boxer. I had no clue that he had a shrine that big in Egypt," R.O. said in wonderment as they approached the massive mosque.

Everyone laughed but the humor wasn't caught by R.O. He would catch on soon enough that it wasn't a shrine to the greatest boxer of all time, Muhammad Ali, a.k.a. Cassius Clay of Houston, Texas.

As E parked the old Mercedes between two tourist buses, he didn't bother to roll up the windows or lock the car. He just placed a little placard written in Arabic on the front dash. Chris and Heather just shrugged their shoulders and followed the tall Arab toward the front entry. Ryan was already a good fifty feet ahead of them. The dry heat of Egypt was beginning to bear down on them with a vengeance.

"Are you hot, Chris?" Heather asked.

"Yes, very," Chris replied.

"And I am burning up in these linen pants," Natalie said.

She pulled her long auburn hair and twisted it into a knot on the back of her head. Retrieving a pencil from her purse, she pushed it through the makeshift knot to hold it in place.

"E," Heather said.

"Yes?"

"E, I am very hot. See those ladies selling the light cotton caftans. Can you get a good deal for me so I can get rid of this belt and stuff?" Heather almost pleaded.

"If you do, I want a good deal, too," chimed in Natalie.

"Yes. It will be my pleasure." He reversed his course and walked over to the host of merchants who lined the street next to the shrine. In a few minutes he was jabbering away, waving his hands in all directions and pointing back to Heather who now was only a few feet away.

"What color do you want Miss Heather and Miss Natalie?" E asked.

"I'll take the turquoise one and the matching scarf. And E, I'd like those sandals, the black leather ones, too," Heather said excitedly.

"White caftan, red scarf, and brown sandals works for me," Natalie said with smile.

"You have good taste," E said.

In a few minutes, E had haggled a deal for twelve dollars for the caftans, one dollar for the scarves, and five dollars a pair for the sandals. Heather and Natalie paid in American money and walked away satisfied. Once they were inside, they turned to E.

"Where's the ladies restroom? I would like to change," Natalie said.

"There are no restrooms, Miss," E replied.

"No restrooms?" Heather said with an astonished look on her face.

"No, miss. But let me see if there is a place you can use to change." E walked over to a guard who stood in the center of the shrine. After a brief moment, E and the guard were walking toward Chris, Natalie, Heather, and R.O.

"This man will take you to a private bathroom. Just follow him. We'll wait here."

Heather had a worried look on her face.

"Chris, will you go with us?"

"Sure. R.O., stay with E and don't move. Got it?" Chris said sternly.

"Your wish is my command, sire," R.O. said with a smirk on his face.

The guard, Chris, Natalie, and Heather disappeared behind a scarlet curtain next to the wall. E turned toward the burial place of Muhammad Ali and was gazing around. R.O. could see a hundred pigeons in the courtyard and headed that direction. Expecting the pigeons to scatter, he approached them carefully. But they simply moved, leaving him space to walk between them.

"Here, Mr. Pigeon," R.O. said and reached out for a big white one that scurried a few feet away never looking his direction.

Becoming bored with the birds, R.O. looked around at the giant walls of the shrine, the ornate clock built by the French, and the beautiful tile mosaics. But sticking straight up out of the floor of the courtyard was a ceramic barrel of some sort. It had a curved base and was decorated with the same tiles that covered the walls. As he walked over to it, he heard a guide with a group of Taiwanese tourists say that it was called the well of Muhammed. It was an ancient water shaft that led to a room below that was attached to a structure that fed water in from the Nile River. A couple of tourists from an American group walked over to the edge and looked down.

"Bill, that is really dark down there," the tourist said. "Be careful. Hang on to your video camera."

"I know, Orin. I'm hanging on tight," Bill replied to his friend.

R.O. sidled up to the white-haired gentleman and leaned over the side.

"Be careful, son," Bill said.

"I will. Done this a million times," R.O. said and shouted into the well. "Hello," he said and his voice echoed "Hello. Hello. Hello." "Man. Man." "Man, Man." "Heather is an airhead!" "Heather is an airhead, Heather is...."

"Who is an airhead?" Heather said standing right behind him.

Natalie was trying to muffle her laugh.

R.O. turned around quickly and saw Heather standing there with Chris and E.

"Heather, you look great," R.O. said as he eyed his blond-haired sister in the turquoise caftan and black sandals. The matching turquoise scarf was tied around her hair and holding it over her head.

"Thank you. Pretty cute for an airhead, wouldn't you say?" Heather smiled.

Natalie looked even more beautiful because of her age, a mature eighteen.

"And Natalie, what can I say?" R.O. continued.

"Just don't say it," she replied.

"And it really is comfortable and cool," Heather said.

"Where are your clothes?" R.O. asked.

"E took them back out to the taxi. What are you doing?" Heather asked.

"He was examining a water shaft. The shaft is the well of Muhammed and reaches down to the level where the Nile River runs ashore. The water table is very high because of the sandy nature of the soil," E said as he walked up.

"It's really cool, Chris," R.O. said and stepped back. "It makes a great echo chamber. Try it."

Chris walked over and glanced down into the darkness. He looked back, feeling a little foolish. As he leaned over, the gold necklace he had purchased in a little town called Taxco, Mexico, clanged against the side. The tiny echo surprised him.

"That is neat. Hello," he said. "Hello, Hello, Hello," came the echo.

R.O. jumped next to him and started a whole new line of words to echo through the centuries-old chamber. Then he reached into one of his cargo pockets and retrieved a Swiss Army knife that had a red light on the end. He shined it into the hole. The hole was actually a tube that curved down to the next room.

"That is so cool. Look everybody."

All the MacGregors crowded around, staring into the hole. As Heather moved to turn around, R.O. lifted his hand to hoist himself up on the rim, only to hit Heather in the side of the face.

"Thanks, Ryan!" she shouted. She rubbed her face and then felt her ear. "My earring. You knocked off my earring," she said as she felt her earlobe and then down the front of the caftan. Bending to the floor she looked around. Chris did the same and E stepped in to help.

"There it is!" R.O. shouted.

Everyone stood and saw R.O. pointing down the well shaft. As they leaned over the side, R.O. directed the light of his miniature flashlight. The earring had caught on a small seam about six feet down the ceramic-lined tube.

"I'll get it," R.O. said and hopped up on the rim of the shaft.

"No you don't," Chris said and pulled him down.

"But I can get it, Chris. It was my fault it's there," R.O. pleaded.

"I would not advise doing this," E said shaking his head no.

"I would advise that he does get it," Heather said, still miffed about the incident. "I bought these earrings in Grand Cayman and I really do like them."

Natalie stood by quietly not wanting to get into this family quarrel.

"No. I can't let him crawl down there. Mom and Dad wouldn't allow it and I'm not either." Chris stood firm.

R.O. and Heather knew that if they argued too much they would be sent back to Georgia to stay at Aunt Marcia's prison. Everyone knew the arguing was over.

"Let me show you the great Muhammed's burial vault before we go," E said.

The four of them walked through another group of tourists who were speaking French. Approaching the large latticework cage across the front of the crypt, each MacGregor noticed how quiet and respectful everyone was and so they were the same. E didn't even speak. Looking through the lattice work they could see the massive stone sarcophagus a few feet away. After a few minutes, they turned away from the dark crypt and walked through the dense crowds toward the entrance. As they stepped through the massive doors, Chris turned to Heather, Natalie, and E and looked around.

"Where's Ryan?"

"I don't know. He was next to you at the crypt," Heather replied.

"Mr. R.O. must still be inside. I will go see," E said.

"We'll all go. Meet back here if you find him," Chris said. He was not worried. It was commonplace for R.O. to disappear and reappear in places like this.

"Wait," Chris said. They all stopped. "I'll bet you my favorite hunting knife that he went back for the earring. Let's go!"

They pushed against the flow of tourists attempting to leave and hurried back to the courtyard where a hundred pigeons were cooing and looking for food. There was no R.O. present. Chris leaned over the side of the well and looked down to where the earring was hanging. It was gone.

"OK. He went after the earring, got it, and crawled out. Or he went after the earring, got caught up in the excitement and kept on going," Chris said.

"I vote for the second idea," Natalie said shaking her head up and down.

"Me, too," Chris said and put his right foot over the side of the well and then the left. "If I don't come back in ten minutes, E, get help."

"Yes sir, Mr. Chris. I will get help."

Chris slowly lowered himself until his feet touched the curved bottom of the tube. He let go of the rim. He then pushed outward on the sides to steady himself so he could sit down. He looked up and saw Heather, Natalie, and E peering downward.

"You OK, Chris?" "You OK?" "You OK?" Natalie echoed down the hole.

"Yes and don't do that," Chris said.

"Sorry." "Sorry sorry sorry," came Natalie's reply. She put her hands over her mouth.

Chris looked back up and she just raised both hands and waved silently. Looking downward he could see nothing but blackness. He had no flashlight and he didn't have the lighter he always carried in the wilderness for survival. He slowly edged himself down the ceramic tile tube for another ten feet. He could feel the bottom of his shoes begin to slip, so he pushed harder on the sides. As he edged along, he could see that the tile had worn smooth and it was becoming more difficult to hang on. He guessed what had happened to Ryan. R.O. had reached the earring, put it in his pocket, and kept on exploring until he got this far. But R.O.'s arms weren't as long as his were. When he started slipping, knowing R.O., he turned the ceramic tube into a slide.

A cold chill went down Chris' back as he thought about what may lie ahead. He had heard that the tube was connected to the Nile River. Was Ryan down there in the water possibly drowning? He made a quick decision and let go of the sides. He pulled his knees toward his chest and gravity did the rest. His 170 pounds slid down the tube, gaining speed as he went. He thought he would touch bottom momentarily but the slide kept on going. It was black and he couldn't see a thing. Fear crept through his mind. He had been in places like this before. Each time he knew the adrenaline would flow and his heart would race. Suddenly he felt his body fall free of the slide. He was flying through the air. A new fear raced across his mind. Where was the bottom?

And then he felt it as his entire body landed on a wet tile surface and he began to slide again. He lost his breath for a second but the floor was angled down and his impact was light. With the wet surface, he continued to gain speed. Being sensory deprived, no light, no sound, only a wet surface, his mind raced. Then suddenly he began to slow down and he felt his backside begin to heat up from the friction. He quickly pushed his shoes into the dry floor.

"Man," he said as he stopped and slowly got to his feet. An experienced adventurer, he reached over his head and felt around as he stood up so he wouldn't bump his head.

"R.O., if you are OK, you will be in big trouble, buddy," he said softly.

Standing there for a few minutes, his eyes seemed to play tricks on him. He thought he could see a pinhole light ahead somewhere, and then it was gone. Reaching forward he began to walk. He kept walking until the pinhole of light seemed to get larger. His eyes were fully dilated, and he could make out a tunnel ahead. Then he felt his feet become wet. Bending over he moved his hand around in the ankle deep water. He heard a splashing noise and looked up.

"Hey big brother. Is this not cool or what?" R.O. said with a big smile on his face. The tiny knife-light had been replaced by his lighter, which he never left behind.

"Ryan. I am going to kill you when we get back topside. And then Mom will beat you awhile, and then Dad will beat you awhile, and then it will be my turn again."

"Aw come on, Chris. This is an adventure. You love

it, you know it. Follow me. I'll show you what I discovered."

Chris didn't dare fall behind in the blackness as R.O. sloshed down the corridor. The water seemed to get deeper.

"R.O., this water is getting deeper," Chris said.

"Yea, I know. But this is as deep as it gets until you get to the next room." R.O. didn't seem to be worried.

They reached the end of the corridor and entered a large room with high ceilings.

"You were right, R.O. This is awesome." Chris walked around the room.

All the walls were covered with hieroglyphics.

"These are awesome. They look brand new. Not worn out like the ones we've seen in museums or around Cairo on monuments and stuff," Chris observed.

"Yeah, and over here is the door to the Nile," R.O. said and held the lighter up so Chris could see.

"Let me see," Chris said and leaned over his younger brother. "Let me have the lighter."

As Chris held the lighter higher and further into the next room, it lit up a muddy floor with about a foot of water settled into the room. Hieroglyphics covered all the walls. This area under the mosque was nearly six thousand years old and was as much a part of ancient Egypt as the pyramids of Giza.

"OK. It's the Nile. Let's find our way out of here," Chris said.

He stepped away from the room and left R.O. in the dark. R.O. quickly followed him back to the point where they had met. But there were three tunnels to choose from and they couldn't remember which one they came down. The wet floor left no clues for footprints.

"Well, you choose. You got us down here," Chris said. He was a little disgusted.

"Let's take the right one," R.O. said quickly.

"Why?" Chris shot back.

"It feels right!" R.O. replied.

Chris couldn't help but smile knowing the quirky way his brother thought.

They ventured down the right tunnel only to find more hieroglyphics chiseled into the walls. Some of them were still brightly painted with red, gold, blue, and black. A few looked like they were just made a few years ago.

"These are awesome," Chris said as he held the lighter up to the wall.

"How far have we gone?" R.O. asked.

"I would venture only about a hundred feet from the junction."

"I guess Heather and Natalie are getting a little worried. Bet Heather called Mom and Dad by now. They probably have the police getting ready to search for us. At least we can get water. Don't know about food though. How long do you think we can survive without food, Chris?" R.O. asked.

"I don't know. Look at this," Chris said softly.

Both boys looked at each other and raised their eyebrows.

"Do you want to or do you want me to?" Chris asked.

"I'll do it," R.O. replied and moved closer to the wall.

The tension was mounting. Both boys breathed in slowly, not knowing what to expect next. Deep under the shrine of Muhammed Ali in a labyrinth carved out of rock by the ancient Egyptians six thousand years ago, they were about to discover something they thought would never exist in such a place.

R.O. touched the plastic switch with his hand and flipped it up. Suddenly a row of single light bulbs flashed on all the way down the tunnel connected by a single cord hanging from the ceiling.

"Go figure?" Chris shook his head in disbelief.

"A maintenance hallway," R.O. said in astonishment.

As they looked around, they could see brooms, mops, cleaning materials, a floor polishing machine, and buckets. All were just out of reach of the light from the small lighter that Chris had carried down the hallway. It was truly a labyrinth made during the Middle Kingdom of Pharaohs, but now it was a janitors' closet for the massive shrine above. Directly in front of them about thirty feet away was a modern metal door with an exit sign over it with a burned-out lightbulb.

Not saying much to each other but feeling a little embarrassed at their grand thoughts, they opened the door and found a stairway leading upward. Following the steps, about sixty of them, they soon reached another door. Opening it to the bright light of the "upper world" caused them to squint their eyes. Stepping through the doorway, they could see a crowd of people around the tall ceramic opening to Muhammed's Well. As the door closed behind them, they noticed it became part of the enormous wall around the courtyard and only close examination would reveal that it was indeed a door.

As they reached the crowd, they could see that Heather and Natalie were in the center of a group of Japanese tourists. The tourists were snapping their cameras at the two beautiful girls dressed in their new Egyptian attire. E was standing to the side talking to a guard. Working their way closer, Chris got Natalie's attention and she waved. But she didn't move from beside the well where she was posing to the glee of the Japanese photographers. Now within talking distance, Chris spoke first.

"Natalie."

"Hi, Chris. While we were waiting, these nice people started shooting our pictures. I think they believe we belong here or something." Natalie smiled as another flash went off.

"You didn't worry about us?" Chris asked, a little puzzled.

"We did at first. But the guard told E that the tube led down to a janitors' storage area, and you could come back up by the stairs in the wall." Another flash went off as Natalie and Heather struck a pose.

"I see."

"You really smell, Chris," Natalie offered as R.O. walked up beside him.

"And you look disgusting," Heather added directing the comment to her younger brother.

"OK, kids. We're finished for the day. We'll do Saqqara some other time," E said. He turned and thanked the two guards. "As you say in America, we have worn out our welcome, and we better go before the authorities are summoned. This is holy ground and what we have done is not acceptable," E said to them quietly.

Nothing was said as they made their way to the front entrance. In a few minutes they were on the highway toward the bridge and then across the Nile into the tourist and resort district. It was getting late in the afternoon and the citizens of Cairo were back in their cars driving home from work. The light haze of the early morning was now a full blown ozone alert with heavy pollution hanging like a veil across the face of the Egyptian capital.

With Chris and R.O. smelling like the nasty mud of the Nile, the kids didn't have much to say. Heather would intermittently hold her nose and then breathe out the window. She didn't know which was worse, air pollution or the stinky mud on her two brothers.

E was humming a tune that no one recognized. Natalie got Chris's attention and blew him a kiss when R.O. was looking out the window. He smiled back at her hoping for more than an air kiss later. Their relationship in Cayman had developed so quickly over just three days, he really didn't know what to expect. She was eighteen, and he would be eighteen soon. She was a college girl, and he was finishing high school. Girls had always been a mystery to him and this was his first venture at a close relationship.

As the old Mercedes taxi turned into the hotel parking lot, the sun dipped behind the smog-coated clouds and the man-made haze shielded the rays of solar disk, Ra, being pushed across the sky by the Nile beetle. When Ra shed his tears the first time, each tear became a god. But today, Ra's tears would be for something yet to be revealed, but soon it would, in the oracle of the Nile.

9

Princess of the Nile

The MacGregors lined up on the dock almost single file. The exception was that R.O. was standing on a bale of cotton looking through his Leica binoculars across the Nile at two feluccas racing in the wind. The ever flowing south to north current challenged the Nile sailors as the wind always blew from the north, except when the Sahara would raise its fury and change it to blow from the west.

"Look, Dad." R.O. loved to be with his dad who always seemed to be on the run with his career as a scientist. "The feluccas are racing."

Dr. Jack MacGregor hoisted himself up on the massive cotton bale next to his son and took the binoculars.

"Yes. I agree they are racing. Pretty neat if you ask me. Maybe we should try that while we're here. Rent a boat...."

"A felucca," R.O. corrected.

"A felucca and go for a sail."

"That would be tight, Dad," R.O. said as he hopped off the cotton bale and ran over to Mavis.

"Mom. Dad said we could rent a felucca and go sailing on the Nile. Maybe tomorrow, right?"

"Not tomorrow, Ryan. We will be half way to Luxor and Abu Simbel. Maybe when we get back in three days. You know your father has to present a lecture to the board of governors of the International Wildlife Fund tomorrow on the ship. And then there's the conference on the health of the Nile River and Aswan High Dam."

"And then there's the hike we are going to take to the Valley of the Kings, just the family," Jack added as he approached them.

"And me, too," Natalie said. She was standing very close to Chris and gazing into his eyes. Chris's glance was glued to her as well and this time he wasn't blushing.

Their conversation was interrupted when a voice from a loudspeaker on the dock rang out first in Arabic, then English, and finally in French.

"The Princess of the Nile is ready for boarding. Please have your tickets ready and enjoy your cruise," spoke the polite female voice with a slight accent.

The MacGregors, along with about three hundred other passengers, scurried around gathering their bags while being helped by young Egyptian boys hoping for a generous tip in American dollars. The majority of passengers sported bags with wheels that were embroidered or encased in nylon and bore leather luggage tags embossed in gold.

The MacGregors, on the other hand, sorted out their aluminum-braced backpacks, one per person, and their large yellow, red, and green duffels covered with sewn on patches from Grand Cayman Island, Baja California, Colorado, Kenya, and, of course, Texas. Along with the patches of colorful destinations, there were patches for skis, scuba equipment, climbing gear, and any other high tech sporting equipment they had used. The patches would tell any bystander that this bag belonged to someone who traveled the world and lived on the edge!

Mavis was first aboard, then Chris and Natalie,

Heather, R.O., and followed by Jack. As R.O. walked on the deck, he turned around and glanced at the massive smokestacks and the beautiful decks.

"I am going to own this ship for three days!" His eyes sparkled just thinking of all the possibilities. Mavis and Jack looked at each other and let out heavy sighs, knowing just what possibilities that meant with their very energetic and mischievous twelve year old.

Across the dock and from the front seats of a new Peugeot, the two Russians, Sergei Andropov and Alexander Raiken, looked through their binoculars, memorizing every detail about this American family. The network had closed in on the MacGregors. The fast-acting family of Ziyad had located the Visa account of Chris MacGregor. It was tied to an account belonging to one Dr. Jack MacGregor of Texas. The same Jack MacGregor who was staying in the Nassar Convention Center Hotel until two days ago when the family moved to the Cleopatra Resort Hotel. The same Dr. Jack MacGregor who was a world-famous zoologist and much sought-after consultant on environmental affairs. The sleuthing had been complete down to and including the little known fact that the youngest MacGregor son, Ryan, had a penchant for electronics and loved to build things; hence the visit to the Little Shop of Thoth.

Andropov and Raiken had a week to steal the circuit board and get it to Alice Springs, Australia. It would take a full day to fly to Australia and another day to arrive at Alice Springs by private jet. That would give them a small edge but no time to waste. They looked anxiously at each other.

"Do you have a weapon?" Alexander said to Sergei.

"Yes. I am ready. Relax comrade. We have done this thousands of times. This celebrity family is no match for two seasoned KGB operatives." Sergei patted his friend on the shoulder.

"Yes, we are seasoned and ready to retire. I dream about my dacha near St. Petersburg," Alexander said. "Meet me in Luxor. We can fly to Oman. A jet will be waiting there to take us to Australia. If you meet resistance, leave the ship. Use your satellite telephone to reach me. I will pick you up along the way in the small plane. But remember, if you don't get the circuit board, we both will die. The hope of reviving Mother Russia will die."

"I understand, comrade. *Dos ve donya?*" Sergei said and stepped from the Peugeot.

He retrieved a small bag from the backseat and closed the door. He peered into Alexander's eyes and knew the gravity of his task. Looking back toward the MacGregors, who were happily walking across the deck, he felt under his light jacket for his compact Walther 9mm automatic pistol. He carried other weapons in his bag. He knew he would kill the MacGregors if he had to. He nodded to Alexander and walked down the steps toward the dock.

A mere hundred yards away, a tall blond-haired man paid the taxi driver and grabbed his two nylon bags from the backseat of the car. Without a word, Kevin Turner walked quickly across the parking lot until he passed the Peugeot. He trotted down the steps to the dock.

As Turner entered the ticket line, he walked up behind Sergei and didn't utter a word. As far as the two men were concerned, each of them was a single traveler enjoying this exotic cruise up the Nile to the Valley of the Kings. Neither knew that each had the same purpose: to kill the MacGregor family. One had traveled half way around the world to seek revenge and the other to control the world. To each, their causes were equally just, but to others they would be equally evil. Within minutes they were mingling with tourists who were seeking out their cabins.

"Here's our cabin," R.O. said to Chris. "There's Natalie's and Heather's and next door to them Mom and Dad. See ya in three days." R.O. opened the door and stepped inside his cabin. Mavis was right behind him.

Bending over to be at eye level she spoke softly.

"OK, R.O. It is obvious to me you are really going to have a great time. Right?"

"Right," he replied.

"And it is also obvious to me that you want me to kind of stay out of the way. Right?" Mavis said.

"That would be right. Mom, you are way too smart," R.O. said.

"Thank you for the compliment, sweetie. And I think you are way smart, too."

"Thanks, Mom, can I go now?"

"Uh, no. One way to ruin your cruise is to do one thing."

"And what's that Mom?"

"Make me really mad."

"I would never do that, Mom," R. O. said with a serious look on his face.

"That's good. Because, mister, I am going to watch you like the Egyptian god Ra watches everything. And if you so much as get one hair out of place on your head, cause one little ruckus, destroy one piece of property, ours or anyone elses, or not report to me every two hours during this cruise, then I will borrow the handcuffs from one of those big security guards on the top deck and I will handcuff you to the rail of this bed for the entire trip. For your own good, of course. So you won't accidentally fall in the river." Mavis never blinked, raised an eyebrow, or twitched her lips. R.O. took a deep breath.

"I understand, Mom."

"Good. Ryan, I love you and I would be so sad if you got hurt. So check in with me every two hours and stay with Chris, Natalie, or Heather at all times."

"Why do I have to check in if I am with them?"

"So I will know if I need to relieve them of you so they can have a break or something. OK?

"OK, Mom."

Mavis leaned forward and gave him a kiss on the mouth. He quickly took his sleeve and wiped off the kiss complete with the pink lipstick she had planted with the kiss. Mavis looked away but smiled at his quick gesture. Chris had been carrying bags and backpacks into everyone's rooms and had saved his for last. He came in as Mavis was leaving. She gave him a wink.

"R.O. is present and accounted for, Captain." Mavis planted a kiss on him.

"Thanks, Mom," Chris stepped into the cabin.

R.O. had already claimed the top bunk and was pulling out all of his gear and electronic toys. He grabbed a couple of toys he had been working on and stuffed them into the deep pockets of his cargo shorts. He turned to Chris.

"OK. Let's go explore!"

"Hold on. I need to clean up and change my shirt. I told Natalie we would walk the decks to see how big this thing really is. Then it will be time for lunch."

Both boys reached out and grabbed the bunks as the ship swayed a bit as it pulled out from the dock.

"Sea legs. It's all in the legs," Chris said.

"I know. I remember that huge houseboat we lived on in the Gulf of California. You know, when we got to dive with the big manta rays?"

"Yea, that was cool. But this is a river, and I bet there will be lots of traffic."

"All the more reason to report topside, Captain." R.O. opened the door and stepped into the hallway. He looked down the hall both directions at the bustle of passengers moving along. Then suddenly the door directly across from him opened and Natalie stepped out.

She had changed from her shorts and T-shirt into a cute powder blue sundress with spaghetti straps. Her thick auburn hair was pulled back and knotted on top. An exotic looking hair comb she had purchased in Old Cairo was anchored on top. Looking past R.O., she was staring at Chris who had just come into the hall. One look at Natalie and he took a deep sigh.

"Ready for a walk?" she said softly.

"You bet..., I mean, yes." Chris pushed Ryan to the side.

As Chris and Natalie disappeared down the hall into the crowd, Heather stepped into the hallway and stood next to Ryan.

"Guess you're my date, little cutie," Heather said with a wicked smile. She was still wearing her denim capri pants and a cropped Dixie Chicks mini-T-shirt.

"No way," R.O. said and looked back down the hall.

"Well, I heard what Mom said. And I will be more than happy to go get the handcuffs and put them on you myself. I can bring you one meal per day and a bottle. Well, you know what the bottle would be for!" Heather laughed.

"You're sick, Heather. What's the matter, you got your knickers in a twist?"

"Why, you little twirp! Mom said you couldn't talk like that."

"No, she said I couldn't say you've got your panties in a wad. In England, they say knickers in a twist. She's a Brit, so I bet she won't mind," R.O. shot back.

Mavis stuck her head into the hall.

"Ryan O'Keef MacGregor, I do mind. Decent people don't talk like that. That will be one hundred more vocabulary words for the week."

"Aw, Mom," R.O. whined.

"Furthermore Mr. MacGregor, if I hear you say that one more time during our trip, you will be on your way to Georgia before an Egyptian fly can land on your nose. Got it, mister?"

"Yes, Mom," R.O. replied and looked his Mom in the eye before looking down.

Mavis closed the cabin door firmly. Ryan exhaled a heavy sigh.

Heather laughed even more knowing that she had won this skirmish. It was always tough to pay back R.O. when he was dishing it out so fast every day.

"I'm hungry. So let's go see what kind of food this boat is cooking," Heather said and started down the hall. "You're going to need your energy to get all of your homework done." She laughed again even harder.

About twenty feet away she stopped and turned toward R.O. "You are either with me, or with Chris and Natalie, or I take you to Mom and Dad's room for the duration. Your choice. And I am sure that Mom can find even more homework for you, don't you?" She smiled and brushed her long blond hair away from her face and tucked it behind an ear with her right hand.

"Let's eat!" R.O. said as he hurried to catch up with her on the run.

Thirty minutes passed as they tasted food from the buffet in the main dining room and surveyed the crowd. Then they drifted up to the lido deck where music blared across the swimming pool. The smell of grilled onions, hamburgers, and sausages convinced them it was time to stop looking. They noticed Chris and Natalie already eating and walked over.

"Well, here we are," R.O. said. He sat down and started sipping on his soda.

"Isn't this boat huge?" Heather said.

"It's a ship," Chris replied.

"I know, but it is still huge. Why didn't Mom and Dad ever take us on one of those really gigantic cruise ships?" R.O. said.

"Dad always said he wanted to stay on the beach

because it was more accessible to diving," Heather answered.

"And he generally doesn't like to be around tourists. He prefers the adventuresome types we always run into when we're out diving, skiing, or whatever," Chris added. He glanced at Natalie.

Chris and Natalie hadn't been able to spend a lot of time together on Grand Cayman, but the time they did spend bonded them in a way that most young men and women would never understand. They had stared into the face of death in the form of criminals, a man-eating shark, and a hurricane. For these teenagers, it had been an experience they would never forget.

"The Nile River Seminar starts in about thirty minutes and I would like to hear it. Want to go, Natalie?" Chris asked.

"Sure, that's why I came to Cairo."

"I noticed on the marquee in the dining room that an Egyptologist is going to lecture to a special group in the theater. The topic is 'The Lost Mummies of the Pharaohs'. I would like to hear that since Mom has assigned us all those questions about Egypt's Middle Kingdom Pharaohs," Heather said. She always had a intellectual curiosity that helped her earn higher marks than her two brothers.

"Guess I know where I'll be. The Nile River Seminar," R.O. said.

"NO!" was the answer in unison from Chris and Natalie.

"I get the point," R.O. said.

He began eating his hamburger with pickles and ketchup. When they had finished eating, Heather and R.O. headed for the mummy lecture while Chris and Natalie walked toward the Nile River Seminar.

Kevin Turner slowly folded the *London Daily Mirror* and checked the Browning 9mm tucked inside his belt and under the light windbreaker. All fourteen rounds were in the clip, and he was so close. But if he killed the kids now, there would be no time to hunt down the parents and kill them, too. He wanted them all dead. He would have to wait. There would be plenty of time if he had patience. He opened the Daily Mirror and began reading again while sipping on a cup of tea.

Sergei Andropov was looking down on the deck from one level above. He had changed into a pair of shorts, a soft yellow T-shirt, and carried an issue of Time Magazine in his left hand. It was the German edition. He, too, waited his turn. He had to be sure where they were staying, and he needed time to search the cabins. He would only get one chance, and he didn't want to have to kill anyone unnecessarily. It would only make his escape more difficult. He was the pro. A survivor of the cold war.

Kevin Turner, on the other hand, was just a wealthy thug, a mobster, who had no clue that revenge sometimes backfired. But it didn't matter to him. His brother had meant the world to him and his death needed to be avenged. He wanted all of the MacGregors dead. He didn't care how long he had to wait to get this accomplished. And if he could cause some pain in the process, that would be even better.

Chris and Natalie entered the lecture hall, but the guest speaker, Professor Houlette, had been introduced and was ten minutes into his lecture to the hundred or so scholars on the cruise. This brain trust represented environmental scientists from all over the world.

"Everyone present already knows the dilemma we face. The High Aswan Dam and Lake Nassar have brought prosperity to Egypt in the form of cheap and plentiful energy that has fueled a modest economic climb.

"The dam itself has caused irreparable damage to the ecosystem of the river, the Nile Delta, and the Mediterranean Sea. Lake Nassar is now filling up with the rich silt from the Ethiopian highlands. In ancient times, Egyptians benefited from this rich source of nutrients that fed into the streams and estuaries of the Nile creating a nutrient slurry that fed arthropods and other invertebrates. That aided in developing a solid food chain and a nursery for fish larva and associated plankton. Without this rich silt, the southeastern Mediterranean has suffered irreparable damage to its fisheries. So while the economy has improved in some sectors, it has tragic impact in others. Yes, Dr. MacGregor?"

Jack stood to make a comment.

"Professor Houlette, as I understand it, the low level of primary productivity of the phytoplankton of the Levantine Basin, the southeastern Mediterranean, is partly due to the easterly flow of sea water from the Atlantic through the Straits of Gibraltar. It's like a huge underwater bowl that has Israel, Egypt , Libya, Crete, Greece, and Turkey all around the edge.

"I know teams of scientists from my own state of Texas, Texas A & M University, along with other scientists have determined that the lack of silt from the Nile has directly impacted the Nile fisheries. One hundred and ten million tons of silt are captured behind the dam each year. Even your own Department of Oceanography at Alexandria University has come to the same conclusion. The shifting of the sediment has even caused earthquakes."

"Yes, that is true, Dr. MacGregor," Professor Houlette replied. "But the Mediterranean continues to be fickled. She is barren one year and then the very next year, fishing fleets experience record catches. We do not yet understand what is happening. The only thing that is clear is that Lake Nassar continues to fill with silt. Someday that major source of hydropower will be useless and the Mediterranean will be a barren desert devoid of plankton and life."

"And then the radicals among us, the political extremists who want to return Egypt to the dark ages, will have their way. They will have conquered Egypt without firing a bullet or taking one head," an older academic with a white beard said from his seat in the third row.

"Professor Assad. I appreciate your concern," Houlette said. "But what you say can't happen. The governments of the west have a vested interest in the security of a free Egypt. Our neighbor to the east, Israel, cannot afford an aggressive enemy on its southern border."

"But if the radicals gain political control, surely the High Aswan Dam will be destroyed," Professor Assad said and rose to his feet. "It is whispered but one never hears it said publicly. But I will say it for all to hear. A rocket, a bomb, or a missile from a fighter jet or a land based platform could destroy the High Aswan Dam in one second. The ensuing flow of the Nile would create a wall of mud that would flow down the river engulfing one village after the next. It would destroy hundreds of the antiquities that have been moved from the original river valley in 1964.

"The political fallout would remove our president from power. The radicals, with the help of terrorists nations, would rule Egypt. Suez would be closed. War with Israel would surely follow, along with new alliances with Syria, Iraq, and Oman. It would be an Islamic Jihad. But this time, the infidels would not be just the Christians or the Jews. They would also be the conservatives of Islam among us. It would be Arab killing Arab, Jew, and Christian. And it would have all begun because of this river!"

The old professor sat down slowly and looked down at the plush carpet. Jack glanced across the room toward his American colleagues from Texas A & M and the University of Miami. All wore the same worried look as he did. As scientists, they knew that quite often it was major environmental catastrophes that gave rise to political change. But never had any of them been present when it happened or was on the verge of one beginning. He also remembered the comments of the United Nations Secretary General concerning the dam.

All felt the threat of the urgency of what the old professor had commented. There was no melodrama to the lecture and responses. It was all a bitter taste of middle east politics and a major geoglobal ecosystem coming to a crashing halt.

Jack sat down slowly and noticed Chris and Natalie at the back of the room. He forced a soft smile, hoping they would feel more confident that one of their parents was signaling not to worry. It didn't help. Chris leaned over to Natalie.

"Let's go check out the mummies. This is a little too tense right now."

Natalie nodded yes. They left quietly. Once in the hallway, Natalie noticed that they were alone. She stopped abruptly and pulled Chris to a halt. He turned and just as they came face to face, her lips met his quickly. The kiss was long before she slowly pulled away, their lips gently letting go.

"Whew," Chris said. "What was that all about?"

"I needed that. That's all," Natalie said.

"Feel free to need it as much as you want," Chris replied.

"Aye, aye, Captain," she replied.

10

Khensu Eyuf

A few minutes later Chris and Natalie were sitting next to R.O. and Heather in the back row of the little theater. R.O. had managed to find another soda and was eating a greasy plate of French fries and ketchup.

"The first guy just finished. He was pretty boring. But this next guy is going to talk about the mummies," R.O. said. He slurped through a long straw in a Styrofoam cup full of pop.

"Our next speaker is Dr. D. Francis Carpenter, who is presently Professor Emeritus of Egyptology at the University of Chicago. Dr. Carpenter led seventeen expeditions into the Sahara over a forty-five-year career. During that time he has made many discoveries that fill museums around the world. Dr. Carpenter."

"Thank you, Professor Scribner. I was asked to come out of retirement this year," the octogenarian paused and took a drink of water. "I was asked to lead a group of young and energetic scientists on an expedition to the Bahariya Oasis, a few hundred miles southwest of Cairo."

"Bahariya. That's where Dr. Jennifer is working," Heather whispered loudly to her group in the back row.

"We are fortunate, in that we have discovered neo-classical tombs of both Greek and Roman origin. Each of these was buried on the ruins of ancient Egyptian graves dating around 4,000 B.C. It seems that a great Vizier, a mayor we would call him, of the sixth century B.C. had been at war with the Pharaoh Apries. The war was primarily over the gold mines of the mountains to the west of the Nile, but some Egyptologists believe there was even a greater cause for the disagreement." The old professor picked up the glass of water again and slowly took a drink.

"It seems that the mayor, his name was Khensu Eyuf, was always raiding the villages along the Nile south of Memphis and taking the women to be made into wives for his men. Life in the desert was extremely difficult and men far outnumbered women. And the young women along the Nile were easy to abduct." He paused and took another drink of water. He loosened his white shirt by opening the top button.

"They would also travel to the river to steal artifacts and gold. Some of our team believe that they were the ones responsible for raiding many of the Pharaohs' tombs and stealing much of the wealth of several dynasties."

"Where would they take it?" R.O. said loudly.

The room got quiet. Heather, Chris, and Natalie slid down in their seats wanting to become invisible.

"I'm sorry. I couldn't hear you," the professor said.

"Where…did…they…take…the…treasure?" R.O. said, accentuating every word. His siblings and Natalie moved four chairs down from him. He didn't notice.

Adjusting his small wire rim glasses, the old professor strained to see the back row.

"That is a very good question, young man. I don't know." Everyone chuckled.

"But I have a few ideas. Would you like to hear them?" He sipped the water again.

"Yes. Go ahead," R.O. said and also sipped his soda.

Heather, Chris, and Natalie were barely containing their muffled laughter. Heather snorted a couple of times while holding her hand over her mouth.

"Well, you see, the puzzle all begins in Memphis. On the walls of the tombs of the servants to the pharaohs, a story is told about a power that only the gods can have. It isn't said what that power is but it hinted that whoever possesses this power can see the future. A seer, or an oracle, if I may. Some of the tombs have this hieroglyph carved on it." The old professor walked over to a small white board and with a blue marker drew the hieroglyph.

"It is a combination of a cartouche of two Pharaohs and a phrase that we haven't been able to decipher. Oh yes, we can read the hieroglyph and tell you the meaning of each symbol. We can even piece it together as a sentence or phrase. But it is meaningless. It's as if someone would ask you to pass the sugar and you would reply the bread is already sugared. What does that mean? Bread isn't sugared, unless it is a pastry, or a confectionery, or...."

"Cinnamon toast!" R.O. shouted out. Heather almost bolted from the room, but Chris grabbed her by the shirt.

"Yes, of course, young man. My mother used to make cinnamon toast as well. It was very tasty. The hieroglyph is a type of riddle. A riddle we haven't discovered the meaning of," he paused, "so we look for more clues. The clues could be anywhere. We have reason to believe that we will find them in several locations. But we also know the clues could take us to places we haven't yet considered. Also there is one more thing we have to consider."

"What's that?" R.O. said loudly and took a sip on his cup of pop.

"That it is all a hoax. That this mayor was simply playing a joke on the Pharaohs and that the whole scenario of the treasures, the unknown powers, and the hidden box with the treasure in it—it is all a charade."

Chris and Heather sat up in their chairs when they heard the professor mention the hidden box. The gilded box with the mystical treasure inside was indeed the type of lost artifact that had attracted tomb raiders for centuries. The old professor picked up the glass of water. It was nearly touching his lips when the question came.

"Is it the same box that Dr. January is looking for?"

He looked over the top of his glasses and slowly put the water glass down. The audience was looking at Ryan O'Keef MacGregor, once again.

"How did he know that?" Heather whispered.

"I don't know. He was unconscious, we thought," Chris replied.

"This is too weird." Heather looked over at Natalie.

"I see that our youngest member of the audience is very interested in Egyptology. The truth is that we aren't quite sure where the box might be. But it is fun to conjecture where we might find it, isn't it? Well, I am tired. Let's take an hour break and come back after refreshments and a snack. This is a vacation, after all. Isn't it?" The old professor smiled and walked away.

The crowd immediately started buzzing about the lecture and the input of the young man at the back of the room. The old professor made his way toward R.O. in a hurry and stopped next to him. The other kids gathered around.

"Meet me in the lounge in ten minutes, young man. We must talk." The old professor left walking faster than they suspected he could have.

Sitting quietly next to a window, Chris, Natalie, Heather, and R.O. each indulged in another soda, knowing that Mavis would not have approved of so much pop in one day. The old archaeologist drank a glass of sweetened ice tea.

"Sweet ice tea. A habit I acquired when I was attending a seminar at Emory University in Atlanta a few years ago. Tea and candy all mixed together and made cold. Sweet ice tea." He took another sip. "Now, let's talk about Dr. January. How do you know her?" he said.

After Chris gave a brief explanation, the old professor nodded.

"The evidence for the gilded box is very strong. I personally don't believe it to be a myth. I am not sure that the powers that are described are anything but mythology, but the box surely does exist. As a treasure and an artifact it would be priceless."

"How much would it be worth?" Heather asked.

"Young lady, it would rank up there with the funeral mask of King Tutankhamen. A private collector would offer millions of dollars for it, without a doubt."

"And what if the powers were real?" Natalie asked.

"Then the world would be at risk. Wretched men from all the corners of the globe would fight to possess it. To possess it would mean total control of the earth. Alexander the Great, the Caesars of Rome, Genghis Khan, Hitler, Communists like Lenin, Khrushchev, Mao Tse Tung all have tried, but no leader or despot has ever accomplished it.

Without a doubt, there is one evil mind alive today that still believes that he or she can be the first ruler of the world. And if he believed that a power existed that could guarantee that, he would stop at nothing to have it." He sipped his sweet ice tea again. "But then, it may be a myth. The hieroglyph will probably turn out to be a recipe for a cake or maybe even a Pharaoh's tea with sugar in it."

He saluted the crystal glass of sweet ice tea and the kids smiled at the old professor not knowing what to believe. But one thing was for sure. For a moment, their minds fantasized about the glory of ancient Egypt and the majesty of the ruins they would see the next day.

Even if it weren't true, they wanted to believe that they would be the ones who would find the mysterious box, the oracle of the Nile. And when they found it, they would possess the ability to foretell the future.

The evening following the lectures was pretty standard fare for a cruise ship sailing an exotic body of water. Chris and Natalie excused themselves to stroll around the ship and get reacquainted since their adventure in the Cayman Islands.

Heather headed for the source of the live music and found a few other teens who had been forced to cruise with parents and grandparents in this ancient land. Unlike the other teens aboard, however, Heather relished every moment of their global adventure. There was a different land, culture, and people every month. The possibilities were limitless. R.O. was stuck with Mavis and Jack and was ordered to stay involved in his electronics, quit complaining, and be happy, or he knew the alternative year-long vacation. He quickly adjusted and was inventing an electronic spider.

R.O. had mastered the circuitry needed to make large appendages that could support the weight of the small machine and the batteries. His next hurdle was coordinating the movement. For now, it looked like a dying spider with the legs going everywhere and the "techno-arachnid" in a mechanical spasm of sorts. It still made him laugh and that was the point anyway.

Everyone was present and accounted for at 10:00 P.M. sharp, Mavis' rule aboard ship. Each stop of the cruise was well plotted with the MacGregors enjoying their own private tour of the ancient ruins and shrines, compliments of the Egyptian government. They were promised "sights never seen by tourists." But if the desires of four men came true, the MacGregors would never be seen again by anyone.

11

House of Thutmose

As the sun peered above the eastern shore of the Nile, the MacGregors were dressed in their normal adventure gear of khaki cargo shorts, utility belts for any apparatus they might need, lightweight but high-tech Teva hiking sandals to keep their feet comfortable and cool, and colorful T-shirts so Mavis could keep track of everyone. Jack wore his familiar red T-shirt from Cambridge, Natalie wore powder blue, Heather yellow, R.O. green, and Chris wore a new orange OSU basketball T-shirt that Natalie brought him from Oklahoma.

On the floor of the lido deck next to their table were five small lightweight backpacks with assorted gear that they might need. Lights, lighters, ropes, utility hammers, writing instruments, binoculars, water purifying tablets, collapsible water bottles, bug repellent, camera, sunglasses, sunscreen, lip balm, scarves for their necks, desert hats, two compasses, utility knives they bought in Cairo, and R.O.'s electronic spider with spare parts. He had even thrown in the circuit board that he had purchased in Cairo, although he didn't have a clue where it belonged, what it went to, or how it worked. But he liked the patterns and thought he just might figure out how to power it up sooner or later. He might even wire it to the remains of Chris' radio.

Starting off with a light and healthy breakfast appetizer of cereal, granola, raisins, and wheat toast, the MacGregors were served a large platter of fatir, which are Egyptian pancakes stuffed with eggs and apricots. Washing it down with fresh milk, orange juice, and coffee for the adults, everyone sat looking dazed.

"OK guys. We will regret this later in the heat of the day," Mavis said looking around at her stuffed crew. "So, lots of water to flush out the salt and keep the body temps down."

"Right, chief!" Jack said. They all saluted and laughed at the same time.

"Mock me? OK. We'll see who gets the first leg cramps when the temperature hits 110° in the shade."

"Mom, it's not supposed to get that hot until we get past Luxor at Abu Simbel," Chris said softly so as not to get a stern reply.

"We'll see," Mavis said.

Within a few minutes, the MacGregors and Natalie were walking down the ramp from the midship to the pier, which protruded into the Nile so the huge ship could dock. The Princess of the Nile was not a typical deep ocean cruiser but one with a flat bottom made specifically for river travel. It would easily capsize in the waves of the Mediterranean Sea or Atlantic. As Chris, the last of the MacGregor group, stepped onto the pier, the first tourist aboard the ship was just getting up. The temperature was a cool eighty-five degrees and the slight breeze that blew from the north was a relief.

Kevin Turner was looking down from an upper deck. He handed the steward, a boy about fourteen, a crisp hundred dollar bill. It represented a full month's wages for the young man.

"Thanks for waking me up. Keep an eye on them for me, and there will be one of these for you every day,"

Turner said to the boy.

"Thank you, sir. I will sir," the young boy said as he bowed his head and walked away. He was thinking how rich he would be in three days.

Sergei was standing one deck higher and noticed the exchange of money between the man and the steward. He also noticed how the man was staring at the MacGregors and began moving toward the stairs. His KGB mind pictured the scenarios. A counterintelligence agent had discovered the circuit board that was in the possession of the MacGregors. His mission was to acquire it before the Russians or Arabs did. Possibly he was a rogue agent, or maybe even from the United States. The possibilities were limitless.

Sergei had not planned on violence. It was to be a simple theft and then it would be over. But now, the dynamics had changed. Force would come into play and, as in the cold war days, someone was going to die. He would have to kill the agent and maybe even the MacGregors. Whatever this old comrade needed to do, he would accomplish his task and never look back. He regretted killing the children in Chechnya, but he carried out his assignment. He would not hesitate this time either.

"Dr. MacGregor, I am Sami Hasan from the Egyptian Museum," said the nice looking young man in the white cotton pants and shirt.

"Nice to meet you. I'm Jack, this is my wife Mavis, my sons Chris and Ryan, my daughter Heather, and our friend, Natalie Crosswhite."

"Please to meet each of you. I will be your guide today at el-Amarna and then I will accompany you to Abydos, Luxor, and Abu Simbel. The director of the museum said that I should treat the MacGregors as though they were his family."

"How nice," Mavis said.

"Of course, the ship's bursar has been informed that you will be with me all day. We will return here in time for dinner and the evening's lectures."

"I wouldn't want to miss those," Heather whispered sarcastically to Chris.

"I will then travel ahead by motor car and meet you each day at the dock, ready to lead you on a new adventure." Mavis enjoyed hearing Sami Hasan's British English. Her curiosity got the better of her.

"Oxford or Cambridge?" she asked.

"Oxford, class of 95," he replied and smiled. "And yes, I have read your biographical sketches and know of your connection to England and Cambridge. We will have a lot to visit about. My wife is from England. She was raised near Aylesbury. We met at university."

"Oh, how lovely."

"Mom," Heather whispered.

"Oh, yes, hon. Where to first, Sami?"

"Follow me everyone." He led the way to an interesting looking vehicle that was a combination safari bus and truck. It had actually been a truck that had the bed removed and bench seats set in its place. With a canvas canopy overhead, it was the perfect touring vehicle with maximum viewing for everyone. Its rustic beauty was complete with rusting fenders and natural air-conditioning. Within a few minutes, everyone was aboard and the noisy vehicle began to clamber along the dirt road.

Kevin Turner hurriedly paid the lone taxi driver sitting next to the dock a twenty dollar bill and ordered him to follow the truck. Sergei was much more practical. He retrieved his Global Star telephone from his belt clip. After dialing a few numbers, he looked toward the MacGregors as they drove away.

"Yes," Alexander said.

"*Privet tovarish,*" Sergei greeted his friend with a 'hello comrade', common in U.S.S.R. days.

"*Privet.*"

"They just left the ship," Sergei said.

"Good, their first stop is the house of the sculptor

Thutmose," Alexander replied.

"You got the itinerary, I see."

"Yes, hundred dollar bills spend very easily in Cairo, especially in the government and antiquities community. The museum secretaries were very nice and appreciated the extra spending money. I will have to introduce you to them when you return. The MacGregors will go to the Great Temple and then onward to the tomb of Akhenaten. They are scheduled to return about 4:00 P.M.," Alexander said over the noise of the small airplane.

"That should give me plenty of time to bribe the stewards and search their rooms thoroughly. I should have the circuit board before noon. Pick me up at the dock at the river temple," Sergei said.

"Good. The plane is red and white with white pontoons. It is capable of landing on a hard airstrip as well. Be ready to get aboard quickly. We don't need attention."

"A plane will get attention regardless of how swift we are. But don't worry, it will go just fine." Sergei turned off the telephone and replaced it in the holder on his belt. He checked his watch and decided he had time to eat breakfast before he raided their rooms and retrieved what belonged to mother Russia.

The MacGregors reached their first stop rather quickly and were soon wandering through the old mud brick of the ruins of el-Amarna, the Arab name for the ancient Akhetaten, once the capital of Egypt. The Pharaoh, King Akhenaten, built the city on a clear piece of ground that had never been used by any other Pharaoh. R.O. complained for the tenth time he didn't get it why the city was Akhetaten but the Pharaoh was Akhenaten. Chris had given up trying to explain.

"Thutmose was a royal sculptor. Historians believe he is responsible for many of the hieroglyphs of his day. He probably had dozens of workers under his guidance and was favored by the king. As a nobleman, he was given a large house with servants, and a high place in society," Sami said and walked around the ruins pointing at the hieroglyphs.

Turner walked cautiously down the street toward the MacGregor's group. He would not make the same mistake he had made at the Nile River. He opened the duffel bag hanging from his shoulder and retrieved the Browning 9mm pistol. He checked the clip and shoved it back in the bag. He then pulled out a Smith and Wesson 9mm pistol and did the same. He hated the MacGregors.

Growing up in the Cayman Islands, Turner's only brother was his best friend. They had planned to build a small empire with the Spanish gold discovered on the reef. He remembered with great pain waiting for two days to hear from his brother that he had gotten the gold. But instead it was a telephone message from the Royal Cayman Island Police Service telling him his brother had been killed in Hurricane Keely. But he knew better. He knew the MacGregors were at fault and now it was their turn to die.

Turner walked confidently down the street to the house of Thutmose. It was 7:30 A.M. and no tourists were in sight. It was a perfect time for a killing. He held the Smith and Wesson in one hand and the bag in the other. Rounding the corner he could now see the room where the MacGregors were standing. Slowly he moved to the edge of the mud brick wall and peered around the corner. The tour guide's voice sounded off loudly. Turner counted the members of the group but couldn't find the boy. He held the gun high up against his chest, his finger firmly on the trigger. The blond-haired girl was closest to him. He leveled the gun and pointed at the back of her head. She would die first.

"Dad, Mom, a gun, a man with a gun!" R.O. screamed as he walked up behind Turner.

Turner wheeled and fired two quick shots at R.O. as

he dove behind an ancient stele. The bullets left pock marks in the stone surface.

"Run, everyone, run!" shouted Chris as he dragged Heather and Natalie through a doorway into a dark room. Jack, Mavis, and Sami turned to run as Turner fired two bullets in their direction, hitting Sami in the arm and leg. He fell to the ground. Jack reached out to get him, but Mavis yanked him behind a low wall as another bullet ricocheted a foot over their heads.

As Turner pointed to Sami, he remembered that he didn't want to waste any bullets.

"You are one lucky Arab," he said through his teeth and moved toward the doorway where Chris, Natalie, and Heather had ducked.

Jack and Mavis were already running along the back of Thutmose's house searching for a way inside.

"Jack, the kids are in there. I heard Ryan's voice. Where did Chris and the girls go?" she said. They were still running behind the ancient ruins.

"Hang on babe. We'll get to them."

"But we don't have any weapons," Mavis said. Tears welled up in her eyes.

"I know. We just need to get the kids and get back to the truck," Jack replied. "Get down, I hear someone."

Turner was moving very slowly. The pistol was in his right hand. He angrily looked toward Sami, who was moaning in pain. Blood had soaked through his shirt and the right leg of his pants. He looked back toward the dark doorway and tried to see inside.

"Chris, I think he's coming inside," Heather whispered.

"Shhh," Chris whispered back trying to see across the dark room.

Suddenly there was a shadow in the doorway. Chris knew that in another minute the man's eyes would have dilated and he could shoot with accuracy. His moment of surprise was now or never. Bursting into high speed, he sprinted across the room and dove at knee level at the shadow. At the last second, Turner saw the blur of his body and pulled the trigger three times. Each bullet was long, just missing Chris's feet. But the impact was enough to propel both men back into the main part of the house.

Turner's head slammed hard on the rock floor and blood burst from his scalp. The gun flew from his hand and clattered across the rock floor. Natalie and Heather were close behind Chris and in a minute all three were pinning down the semi-conscious Kevin Turner. Jack and Mavis ran back into the room. With Jack now taking control of the weapon and Turner, Mavis hurried over to Sami and pressed hard on the wound on his arm.

"Oh, that hurts," Sami said.

"You are lucky to be alive," Mavis replied. She began wrapping her fashionable rope and copper belt around his left leg. It made a great tourniquet.

"Who is this creep?" R.O. said as he walked in from the courtyard.

Turner was woozy and incoherent.

"Beats me, son. We were lucky. Thanks. What were you doing out there?" Jack asked as he held down the semi-conscious Turner.

"I had to go pee. I knew if I asked Mom, she would make me wait, so I just snuck around the corner and did it. When I was coming back, I saw this guy with the gun pointed at Heather's head."

Heather walked over and kissed R.O. on the cheek. He blushed.

"Chris, come here," Mavis said.

Chris hurried over and knelt down beside Sami.

"He's lost a lot of blood, Mom," Chris said quietly.

"I know. Go get the truck and drive back to the dock. Get the authorities and tell them they need to radio an air ambulance to this location. If they give you any grief, tell them he is the prime minister's son or something," Mavis ordered.

"Got it," Chris said on the run.

Turner was starting to wake up. Jack had already tied his hands with the strap from his duffel bag and secured both guns in his own backpack to turn over to the police. Turner looked around without saying anything. His cunning mind was working. It was better to not let his emotion control this moment. His head throbbed.

In less than ten minutes a siren could be heard. First there were two police vehicles sliding to a stop at the ruins. One was a car, the other a small Japanese pickup. Three policemen ran into the house of Thutmose and Jack began to fill them in. They weren't gentle when they picked up Turner and handcuffed his hands and feet. They tossed him to the side, knocking the wind out of him. He strained to gulp in the air. His head was bleeding again.

The police gently picked up Sami and carried him to the small truck. Mavis stayed with him and climbed into the back. Another police car drove up. Two more policemen took charge of Turner. The MacGregors hopped into the touring truck and followed the police vehicle back toward the dock. The ship's doctor and nurse were waiting for them when they arrived. Mavis stayed next to Sami while the doctor redressed his wounds and released the tourniquets briefly to give the arm and leg some much needed oxygen. The bleeding had stopped and his color was better.

After waiting for nearly an hour, a small blue and white seaplane landed on the Nile and taxied up to the dock. Two nurses hopped out and walked quickly over to where Sami was lying. The police carried him to the air ambulance and in a few minutes he was on his way back to Cairo to a hospital.

Mavis watched as the airplane turned into a small dot in the morning sky. Her hands and shirt were covered with blood. Jack, Chris, Heather, R.O., and

Natalie all stood around her. She turned to Jack and started to cry. Then everyone choked up. The reality finally hit them. They had nearly been murdered. A new friend had nearly died. They didn't understand it.

Sergei worked quickly as he tore through Heather's suitcase and dresser. Natalie's belongings were next. Shirts, socks, underwear, nothing of value. He rushed across the hall. With the key he had paid for, he opened the door to Jack and Mavis' room. He had seen the commotion on the dock and panicked that he been too cavalier about the counterintelligence agent. He should have moved quickly but was lulled into thinking this was not a big deal. He had been wrong. He wondered what had happened on the shore. Why were the police and army present?

He rushed into the last room. Jackpot. He found a bag full of electronic gear. Quickly sorting through it, he heard several people coming down the hall. He zipped up the bag and tucked it under his shirt. Looking down the hall, two stewards stepped into the hallway in front of Jack and Mavis. Sergei moved out of the door and began walking the opposite direction. As he turned to take the stairs down to his cabin, the MacGregors opened the door to their cabin.

Jack and Mavis weren't surprised at the view that greeted them. They stood looking at their clothes scattered around the cabin and then looked back to each other.

"Someone really hates us," Mavis said.

"Ditto that, hon," Jack replied and gave her a peck on the cheek.

From across the hall they could hear the voices of the kids outraged at the latest violation. But it was a tempered outrage. What they had just survived was much more dangerous and ominous than this little attempt at thievery. In about thirty minutes everything was back in order, and Mavis was in the shower washing the dried blood off her body. Likewise the kids, covered with dirt from the house of Thutmose, took turns at showers. Ryan donned a swim suit and hurried up to the pool before Mavis could stop him.

The police came and asked to interview them in the Captain's suite, to which they obliged.

"Who is he?" Mavis said trying to hold her temper.

"Dr. MacGregor, we don't yet know. He was not carrying any identification. We only know that he was on this ship with you and followed you to the shrine," the inspector said politely.

The policeman was dressed much differently from the police in Cairo. He wore a military uniform complete with desert boots and desert camouflage material. He wore the rank of colonel in the army.

"We are very concerned about any attack on tourists, especially a famous family like yourselves. So we will do everything possible to sort this out, provide a fair and speedy trial, and, if found guilty of attempted murder, then we will carry out the sentence quickly. That is usually death by firing squad." The inspector spoke calmly and matter of factly.

"Thank you, sir," Jack said still holding Mavis's hand. "When you find out his identity, we want to know immediately. He may be the same person who tried to kill my family in Cairo."

"We have already been in communication with my counterparts in Cairo. We are working together on this."

The inspector pulled a pack of cigarettes from his pocket and ignited a chrome lighter.

"Please," Mavis interrupted. "I would prefer that you didn't smoke. Thank you. It really will kill you, you know," she added.

The inspector put the tobacco away.

"If that is all," Jack said. "I think we'll be going. Keep us informed."

The inspector rose as the MacGregors walked across the plush carpet of the captain's suite and stepped through the doorway. There were two armed guards present, each holding an automatic rifle.

"Dr. MacGregor, I am sending two armed guards to accompany you at all times until you leave our fair land," the inspector said from the doorway.

"Thank you, Inspector," Jack replied and continued walking.

When the MacGregors had left the hallway to walk down to the passenger level, the inspector pulled his cell phone from his black leather belt holder and pushed the number six. It took nearly a full minute before the ring began. It was answered immediately.

"Yes."

"They have left," the inspector replied.

"Have precautions been taken?"

"Yes, sir," the inspector replied. "I have two of my most trusted men with them. They will do whatever they are told. The MacGregors will be under my watch at all times. When the time is right, I will ensure that they will follow our beloved Pharaohs into the next life."

"Very good. You will be paid handsomely. Retirement is only a few days away for you, my friend."

"My pleasure is to serve you," the inspector replied and pushed the end button on the small black cell phone.

Once back in the room, Mavis made a mental inventory of the day and what they missed. She suggested they return to the shrine. All the kids, minus Ryan, voted no. They wanted to stay on the ship the rest of the day, swimming, sun tanning, and generally enjoying a lot of rest and relaxation. She relented and agreed that the next two days would be long days and the rest would be good. There were plenty more shrines and ruins to see in Egypt.

12

Hawks, Vultures, and Falcons

————————◼️————————

What had been planned as the first of several adventurous excursions from the ship had turned out to be a first rate tourist day of swimming, walking the deck, reading, eating burgers by the pool, and listening to a live band. In short, what would have been considered fun for most families was a little tame for the MacGregors.

Chris and Natalie were enjoying each other's company while Heather spent all afternoon trying to lose R.O. She was attempting to connect with some of the teenagers who had talked their parents and grandparents into letting them stay on the ship rather than walk around the dusty ruins at el-Armana. They were much more interested in socializing with teens than seeing another six thousand year old wall!

Before they knew it, dinner was being served. The group was gathered around the white linen-covered table, replete with real silver flatware, Polish crystal, and fresh cut flowers. A delicate china dish in the middle of the table contained fresh butter.

"It is amazing to me to see the opulence of this ship and then contrast it with the poverty all around us," Natalie said. She sipped her ice water with lime.

"We saw the same thing in East Africa. Poor people who couldn't afford clothes, but big game hunters who paid thousands for the privilege to hunt," Chris added.

"That's true, Son," Jack said. "But one can't compare the two. There will always be people who work, do business, and have money. There will always be people who because of circumstance have little or nothing. That's the reality of life. There are a lot of people around the world who try to feed the hungry but very few who try to help endangered and threatened species. We can only do so much."

"OK, who wants to go with me to hear that old Professor Carpenter tonight?" R.O. said.

Everyone just stared at him. Then they looked at each other in disbelief at what they had just heard.

"Well, I believe I would love to do that," Mavis said.

"I would, too," Chris added.

Natalie squinted her eyes and tried to get his attention. But it was too late. Chris was already mentally at the lecture waiting for the next gem to rush from the mouth of the old Egyptologist.

"I'll go," she added reluctantly.

"Well, I need to go back to the discussion of the High Aswan Dam," Jack said.

"What about you, sweets?" Mavis looked at Heather.

"I'm headed to the teen disco that opens at seven. Wait! That's in ten minutes. Adios, amigos," Heather said and left the table in a hurry.

"Well, all lectures begin in ten minutes so we better get moving, guys." Mavis was having the last word.

Exactly ten minutes later everyone cruised into the lecture rooms or, as in Heather's case, the disco, and became lost in the activities.

The old professor walked to the front. Tonight he was dressed in traditional Egyptian white baggy pants, white short-sleeved shirt with an open collar and slip-on sandals that adorned very tanned feet. He gently brushed his white hair back from his forehead toward the balding part of the back of his head. He seemed in excellent health for such an aged man who had spent the last fifty years digging ancient Egypt out from the Sahara desert.

"Thank you for coming again tonight. We have a real treat. My guest has not arrived but I expect her rather shortly. So to begin, I want to discuss the meaning of the various birds that the ancient Egyptians used in their collection of gods. Each one is as different carved in stone as they are in the feathers adorning them as they fly about the sky. I will go through each briefly, then in more detail after our guest arrives."

Mavis, R.O., Chris, and a reluctant Natalie were perched in the first row this time. R.O. had insisted.

"Seker is a god that is represented as a sparrow-hawk. During the Old Kingdom his job was to guard the next world. Later as the Osiris cult spread throughout Egypt, Seker became guardian of the tomb itself. The Ibis bird represented Thoth. Thoth was the great recorder of all deeds. By writing everything down, he became the source of communication with future Pharaohs so they would know what went on in the past."

"Chris, wasn't that the Little Shop of Thoth where we got all of my stuff? Hey, I didn't see the bag of electronics in the cabin when we checked everything," R.O. whispered. He looked alarmed.

"Come to think of it, I didn't either," Chris replied softly.

"It can wait. Can't cry over spilled milk, me mum used to say," Mavis said and put her hand on Ryan's knee as he was preparing to bolt out of the room.

"Mom," he pleaded in a soft voice.

"Listen. This was your idea," Mavis replied softly but firmly.

"The first falcon, Qebehsenuf, was used for the jar that held the intestines and represented the west. When

I go over the funerary items, I will discuss that in more detail. You must remember that to the Egyptian, death was a journey across the land of 'Nowhere.' It could be tortuous; it could be nothing. But to ensure the safety of the 'ka,' the spirit of the dead, nothing was left to chance. Of course, unless the Devourer ate the 'ka.'"

"Who was the Devourer?" R.O. said finally concentrating on the lecture. Chris and Natalie just tried to sit still and not notice the whole audience staring at them. Mavis smiled with motherly pride.

"Oh, young man, you are back," as if the old Egyptologist could not have noticed. "The Devourer was a wretched beast named Ammut. Ammut was half lion and half alligator. A fairly vicious combination, wouldn't you say?"

"Wow, what an animal!" R.O. said.

"Ammut would patiently wait while Anubis, the Jackal, would weigh the heart of the dead person in a set of scales. In one tray of the scales would be the heart. In the other tray of the scales would be the truth of that person's life. To the Egyptians, the heart was where all intelligent life sprang forth. If Anubis found that the person's life had been free of evil, that is, it balanced with the truth, then the dead person would be granted permission to travel across 'Nowhere' to the next life. All the time, Thoth would be recording this in the book of life for all to see. Thoth was also the god of wisdom. Of course, the Hawk-head supreme god, Osiris, would oversee this trial of truth, as it were." The old man took a drink of water.

"But what if the truth and the heart didn't balance?" R.O. asked loudly. The crowd was very quiet.

"Then, young man, Ammut, half lion, half crocodile would leap from the ground and snatch the heart from the solid gold scales and in one bite devour the heart. The ka would die and not be permitted to cross over to the next life." The room was very quiet.

"Of course, the ka is also represented as a human-headed bird." He continued.

"Awesome and really brutal," R.O. said and pulled a bag of peanuts from one of his cargo pockets.

"Where did you get those?" Mavis whispered.

"On the airplane from Nairobi," R.O. answered. He looked at her as if to ask what the big deal was anyway.

"The other birds I will talk about, after a short intermission, will be the phoenix, which is called the Bennu bird named Ra. This is the famous Ra that becomes associated with the sun disc and worship of Ra, which some call Re, as it evolved.

"Next, a bird that has no enemies in the real world is a good candidate to become a god. It is the vulture. They eat whatever they want. It was only normal that the Egyptians would deify an animal who seemed to have so much power. They called her Nekhebet, the vulture goddess. An entire cult sprang up around Nekhebet and how she would protect upper Egypt.

"And finally, we have another falcon. The falcon, sometimes referred to as a hawk, is tied to Ra, Horus, and, as I mentioned earlier, Seker. The falcon was the god of the sky. Beautiful and majestic, it was the animal that was closest to the sun. The sun represented life and energy, and the falcon took its place with Ra as one of the supreme deities.

"When we return, I will share with you an interesting falcon god that we found at the tomb of Seti I at Abydos. Come back in thirty minutes. Enjoy a refreshment or two."

As people were getting up to leave, the side door of the theater opened and a dark-skinned woman in yellow shorts and a white knit top walked in. Her long auburn haired draped around her smooth-skinned face and sat neatly on top of her shoulders. Chris turned and noticed her immediately. Natalie, following Chris's eyes, spotted her quickly as well. Chris left Mavis, R.O., and

Natalie and walked over to her. When he was about four feet away, he spoke.

"Dr. January."

"Hi, Chris. There's your Mom and my patient."

R.O. had hurried over, Natalie at his heels, wondering who this Arab beauty might be.

"Hey, Doc," R.O. said after recognizing her. Jennifer greeted him with a high five.

Natalie relaxed.

"Hey, Ry...I mean R.O. How goes it? Been feeling fine after the scorpion sting?"

"Doin' great."

"I see that this enterprising young man has no limit of friends. He is acquainted with even the phenomenal Dr. Jennifer January," old Professor Carpenter said.

"Oh yes. We go way back," Jennifer smiled. Her white teeth flashed between burgundy lips and a very dark Sahara tan.

"Hi Dr. MacGregor." Jennifer leaned forward and hugged Mavis.

"Don't we look smashing tonight," Mavis said as she looked over Jennifer's shorts and top. R.O. was agreeing with wide eyes and shaking his head. Chris dared not say or do anything. He smiled, then glanced at Natalie for insurance sake. Jennifer January was a strong woman with an athlete's physique while, at the same time, she could have adorned the cover of any number of fashion magazines.

"Professor Carpenter told me that there was a Nile River conference on the cruise, but I didn't make the connection until this very minute," Jennifer said.

"Are you the guest that Professor Carpenter keeps mentioning?" R.O. asked.

"That's me," Jennifer replied.

"Dr. January and her colleagues have made some very astute observations about recent discoveries in the Sahara that may fit into my little puzzle about Egypt and the nineteenth dynasty. We are going to confer tonight before she flies back to the Bahariya Oasis around ten."

"Did you bring your Jet Ranger?" R.O. asked excitedly.

"Sure did. You mean you didn't hear me land on the heliport, top deck? Man, I must be good or what?" Jennifer smiled.

"I thought I heard something, but I was pretty focused on the lecture," Chris said knowing that this comment wouldn't get him into trouble. "And this is my friend Natalie."

"Pleased to meet you Natalie," Jennifer said.

"Nice to meet you, too," Natalie replied.

In a few minutes, the crowd began to work their way back into the auditorium and soon the lecture was back in full swing. The professor introduced Jennifer. She spoke about the Greco-Roman mummies that had been discovered at the Bahariya Oasis. With a long question and answer session, the old professor never made it back to the podium to finish talking about the birds and gods. It was after ten when they adjourned.

"Jennifer, I truly wish you would stay the night. I am sure the captain can find a cabin. Then we can begin our conferring about Bahariya and Abydos," the old professor said.

"Professor, I've been thinking about it during the evening, and I could use a couple of days off. Being the only female out in the desert gets old. And I get pretty tired of wearing work clothes and boots. So I just talked myself into staying," Jennifer smiled.

"I overheard. I definitely want you to have breakfast with us in the morning. We disembark at Abydos for an all-day excursion. So we can visit then. When we return, we want to host you for dinner," Mavis said. R.O. was eagerly shaking his head up and down.

"I think the professor has plans for me, Dr.

MacGregor," Jennifer replied. "But dinner tomorrow would be good."

"Please call me Mavis."

"OK, Mavis it is," Jennifer said.

Meanwhile, as the passengers returned to their cabins, Natalie grabbed Chris by the arm and coaxed him outside to the veranda deck. The wide deck wrapped around the ship and had lounge chairs literally arm to arm. The moon was at half crescent and the breeze from the Nile placed the temperature at a mild 80 degrees. The sparse vegetation along the Nile appeared dark gray while the Sahara desert was tan. Lights from cooking fires dotted the coastline.

"Chris," Natalie said softly. "This is just too beautiful."

"I agree. It has cooled down some. It doesn't seem possible that the shooting took place this morning. I mean, it seems like it was last week or something," Chris replied.

"No kidding," Natalie said. She leaned up against the rail and looked down at the Nile. The white foam of the wake was visible in the moonlight.

"I'm glad that Sami is going to be all right. Mom said that he had a broken arm from one wound and the bullet in the leg went clean through," Chris said.

"That was so close, Chris. Someone must really hate you guys. Maybe even me, too."

"What makes you think someone would hate you?" Chris asked.

"You know, I noticed something this morning, but in the commotion of the moment, I really didn't think it through. But then the more I thought about it, I think my feelings may be right."

"What?" Chris said, growing impatient at her long explanation.

"I thought I recognized that man. The man with the gun," Natalie said. She turned to look at Chris.

"You did? Where have you seen him?"

Natalie looked him in the eyes. For a moment she forgot what she was going to say and focused instead on his green eyes and the dark brown hair that she adored.

"I can't remember. I just know I've seen him before."

Then she stepped forward and kissed him. After breathing in and out a couple of times, they separated. They heard someone walking down the deck and pushed apart quickly, but only about a foot. Both were breathing deeply as another young couple walked by only glancing at them.

"Where do you go from here? I can't remember what you told me," Natalie said trying to gather her composure.

"It could be anywhere. Dad has been talking about the tiger problem in India, and he and mom have always wanted to see Nepal and the Himalayas. Then there's the habitat encroachment problem for pandas in China. One of Mom's friends from England is in the dinosaur bone trade in Hong Kong, and she wants to visit him. And of course, Australia has tons of wildlife problems mainly from feral species invading habitats of native species. And then Dad has been asked to fly back to Washington, D.C. to testify before Congress on the Arctic National Wilderness and oil drilling. And if that weren't enough, my grandparents, the O'Keefs in London, want us all to come visit and go on one of those haunted castle tours."

"Oh my. You have so much to do. When will you get it all done?" Natalie asked.

"Well, this trip is supposed to last one year. I guess we could do all of those plus a few more," Chris said.

Natalie moved a little closer and kissed him on the cheek. He looked down into her eyes.

"I love your eyes. They're beautiful," he said.

"Thank you. You are too sweet. You seem so much

older than the guys I've dated at the university. I mean, they seem like kids. But you're like all grown up sometimes and then other times you're a kid, too. I can't believe you are just seventeen," Natalie said.

"But I will be eighteen in two days. August 10."

"Chris, I totally forgot. I am so sorry. I remember we talked about it in Cayman the very first time we met. Then I was so consumed with our diving adventure, Hurricane Keely, the Harley, Cayman Brac,...I mean it just slipped my mind," Natalie said in a near panic. Suddenly she leaned forward and kissed him again.

"I will find you a nice birthday present," she said.

"You don't have to do that," Chris said still blushing from the overreaction she had to everything.

"OK. What's an eighteen-year-old world adventurer want for his birthday?" Natalie said stepping back and looking up at his tan chiseled face, which was showing a hint of stubble.

"I would like a new deer rifle. A Browning left hand A-Bolt II Eclipse, so Dad and R.O. and I could go hunting in the Big Bend country back home in Texas. I could give R.O. my Weatherby."

"What else?" Natalie said.

The breeze off the Nile had cooled another two degrees to where it was almost comfortable. They could hear music from the disco on the deck just below them.

"I would like a new sleeping bag. My old one isn't waterproof anymore, and I got wet the last time we camped out near Blue Haven, New Mexico."

"Mr. MacGregor, you are an exciting person. I mean this list is right off the outdoorsman-mountain climber-backpacker home shopping, rather cabin-shopping network," Natalie said. She rolled her eyes and then laughed.

"Hey. There's nothing wrong with a few good tools for the outdoors. And by the way, did anyone tell you that you have a cute laugh?"

"No. Thank you. Don't distract me." She blushed

and continued. "Why don't you ask for wool socks and thermal underwear, too?"

"I could use some new socks and thermal underwear. Do you know how cold it gets hunting elk near Chama, New Mexico? Or hiking the Weimanuche Trail at Wolf Creek Pass, Colorado?"

Natalie was now laughing uncontrollably as both hands covered her mouth. She sat back in one of the plush recliners that lined the deck. Chris just watched and then turned and looked toward the shore across the moon's reflection on the Nile. He saw a Nile crocodile surface and glide by the ship. Natalie realized she might have pushed it just a little too far. She got up and stood next to him so their shoulders touched.

"You know, we have been through a lot together," she said.

He turned and looked at her.

"Yes, and I feel like I have known you all of my life instead of just two months. Natalie, you are the most exciting girl I have ever met, I mean...."

She interrupted him by putting her index finger over his lips. He became quiet.

"I wasn't making fun of you. I like you more than you know."

"Me, too," Chris replied and looked over his shoulder at the six elderly people walking by and smiled at them.

"Now, what do you really want for your eighteenth birthday?" she said.

"I would like to learn how to fly a helicopter."

"No kidding," she answered.

"No kidding. I have been in so many of them that sometimes I just want to take the controls and fly it myself," he said, almost sounding like a kid.

"I think that's neat. I just bet you could almost fly one now. I mean, I know how smart you are."

"Well, I think I could probably hover and some

things, but I'm not that good. I would need to feel the machine in both hands and feel the vibration on both feet. You just don't get in and fly a helicopter. You strap it on like fighter pilots do and then you both fly." He looked down at his watch. It was now 11:00 p.m.

"Time for bed. We have to get up at six again to beat the heat into Abydos. The tomb of Seti I is supposed to be absolutely awesome. It has…"

"I know it must be beautiful, Chris," she interrupted. "Kiss me good night before we head back to the cabins."

He looked into her big green eyes and kissed her quickly before other people walked along. Soon they were knocking on their respective cabin doors. Natalie blew Chris a light kiss as he stepped into his room with R.O. She closed the door.

The room was dimly lit with the light from the bathroom as the only light source. R.O. was already asleep. In a few minutes, Chris was under the covers of the bed in the sixty-eight degree air-conditioned room. The sheets were cold, and he shivered a little. They felt good and they reminded him of winter a long distance away from Egypt.

He closed his eyes and for a moment thought about frost on the windshield of his old jeep and a light snow falling on a horse pasture at his friend's ranch in Santa Rosa. But in New Mexico, the snow always blew sideways and rarely drifted straight down. He envisioned warm mittens, thick socks, and a frosty breath coming with each word he spoke. He flinched in the bed as he dreamed that R.O. was throwing a snowball at him, and Heather fell backwards and made a snow angel. This was something she loved to do since Mom showed them how at age four.

The cold air of the cabin blew on his face; he pulled the covers up to his chin and shivered again. Winter in New Mexico was always fun. His mind drifted until he was in a deep sleep with a cool mountain breeze on his face and the smell of pine trees swirling around his head.

But outside the cabin, the temperature never fell below eighty degrees. When the sun would appear in just a few hours, the temperature would rise to over 100 degrees in just three hours. By noon, every scorpion would be hiding from the sun's rays under a flat rock or piece of debris. Every snake would be curled deep into a den waiting for the evening before it could come out and hunt for food. And every camel would fight the will of its master to avoid any exertion that would make the beast hot and weary.

But for Chris MacGregor, this moment was a snowstorm in the Rocky Mountains of New Mexico, thousands of miles away from the hottest place on earth, the Sahara Desert. Lost in the comforts of the cruise ship cabin, Chris didn't know that by this time tomorrow he, and the ones he loved, would be consumed by the heat and would have little hope of seeing the sun god Ra rise the next day.

13

The Osirieon

By six o'clock the next morning, Jack had already rousted everyone out of bed. Mavis had ordered a special breakfast for her crew from the steward the night before. The group sat at a glass-topped table on the deck overlooking the Nile; two waiters brought out platters of food. On the silver tray there were whole wheat muffins with raisins and almonds, slices of melon, fresh dates and pomegranates, and under a silver-covered dish were a stack of sausages and poached eggs.

"My, my. I guess you will have to call me Queen Hatsheput. This breakfast is fit for a royal family," Mavis said as she dished out the muffins.

"That's King Hatsheput, Mom," R.O. said.

"But Hatsheput was a woman, Ryan," Mavis said. She placed an egg on Jack's plate, followed by a slice of honey dew melon.

"Yes, Mom," Heather joined in. "Hatsheput claimed to have been born of the sun god Ra through the wife of Thutmose I, her earthly father. Thoth, the god of wisdom and records, announced that Ra was the father and when Hatsheput was born, she was indeed divine. She could then lay claim to the throne as King, not Queen."

"Sweets, you get an A for doing your homework." Mavis smiled and leaned down and kissed her on the cheek. "Chris, did you finish the report on Abydos? And Ryan did you read the chapters about Sobek, the crocodile-god of the Fayum?"

"Sure did, boss," Chris shot back. He took a big bite of muffin.

Natalie looked at him and was trying to figure when he did the report because she had been with him the entire time.

"Can I see it?" Mavis asked. She walked over to Chris and looked down expecting to catch him in a ruse about homework.

"Absolutely."

Chris leaned over, opened his pack, and pulled out four papers that were stapled together. They were neatly typed and printed. Mavis took them and glanced over the cover page. She kept looking up at Chris and then back at the paper.

"I'm impressed," Mavis said. She raised an eyebrow and put the paper on the table.

Everyone was eating and trying to wake up. At exactly 6:30 A.M. Jack spoke.

"I've been told that we are going to see some parts of the tombs that are only reserved for professional Egyptologists and high officials. I've also been told that it is very primitive, the ceilings are low, there is lots of water and mud from the digging process, and we shouldn't go if anyone is claustrophobic."

Everyone looked at each other. All were certified scuba divers and had been in very tight areas before.

"OK," Jack continued. "Because once we get in, we are not stopping the tour just to bring someone out. So if you feel a little queasy, you are in for the duration. Understood?"

Jack looked around and made eye contact with everyone.

"Bring basic field gear like we had packed yesterday. We will be supplied with head lanterns if we need them." Jack took a drink of fresh orange juice. "Wear your boots today."

Everyone was getting excited. R.O. ate the sausages and eggs, preferring to have the cereal and milk he ate back home in Texas. He drank a tall glass of orange juice. But for the others, the excitement was impacting their appetite. By 6:45, everyone was standing on the dock. The first of the tourists who needed a little exercise were out walking the decks in their jogging suits. Mavis walked over to R.O. to do a visual check.

"Backpack," she said and held out her hand. She unzipped it and rifled through it noticing that he had packed only the required gear with the exception of a towel from the ship. She carefully pulled out the towel and unrolled it on the dock. Everyone was watching. When it was finally laying flat, she looked up at R.O.

"It's all I've got left, Mom," he said with a sad look on his face. "The thief took my bag of electronics. I was lucky I had my spider and those two circuit boards with me at the ruins. I didn't want to take a chance if he came back so I brought them with me."

Mavis could see a tear welling up in his left eye.

"It's OK, hon. You can bring them along. When we get back, remind me to go down to the ship's store and get a new bag for your spider and stuff. OK.?"

"Thanks, Mom. You're the best," R.O. said and hugged her while she was still kneeling on the dock.

"Good morning everyone," a short man walked up. He was wearing a thobe, the traditional long white shirt of Moslem men. "I am Mosegi. Sami is my friend and colleague at the Egyptian Museum. He sends his regards today. He will be moved to a private room and the doctors say that he will recover nicely."

The short Arab wore a small navy blue fez with gold threaded designs. His shoes were simple leather sandals of a between-the-toe thong design.

"We will have a military escort until we reach the tomb of Seti. From there, we will be just fine and will be on our own. Oh, and by the way, welcome to Abydos. With the tombs of Seti I and Rameses II and a host of other unique shrines, Abydos is by far one of the most unique of all the Pharaohs' properties. It still holds a great deal of mysticism regarding the cult of Osiris, the god of the dead. Egyptologists are baffled by many of the mysteries that have been discovered written on the walls of the tombs in the ancient language. So let us begin."

The short ride to the tomb was taken in three rag-top jeeps. The short caravan was composed of five MacGregors, Natalie, Mosegi, and three Army guards. There was one guard with an automatic rifle in each jeep. Soon they arrived at the massive stone building, nearly one acre in size complete with the traditional lotus flower columns. They were overwhelmed by the magnificence of the temple. R.O. stood up in the back seat of the jeep and held on to the roll bar. Mavis jerked him back down.

"Look at that!" R.O. said.

"I read that Napolean's troops had a similar experience at Luxor. As their ship rounded the bend and they saw the massive temples of Luxor, cheers and applause erupted from the soldiers," Jack observed. "This isn't Luxor, but it is just as impressive."

When the jeeps had stopped, R.O. was first out and into the temple amidst the colossal columns. Chris, Natalie, and Heather were trotting fast behind. They were so excited. The chirping of birds could be heard everywhere.

"Jack," Mavis said as they walked behind the kids, "look at them. If we were with a group of tourists, the kids would be walking along with the adults, just as reserved as the next person. But here, all alone, they are letting their emotions and energy go. Maybe they are feeling what the ancient Egyptians, Greeks, and Romans felt when they approached these shrines and temples thousands of years ago. What do you think?"

"Maybe so," Jack said. "I am just glad they get to see this with us."

Soon they were inside the massive walls surrounded by the colonnades that sported thousands of years of hieroglyphics. Stopping next to the three jeeps was a white Toyota pickup. A soldier and a civilian stepped from the truck and walked over to the three guards. The civilian showed them some papers, and the guards returned to being guards, which meant they just stood around and waited for something bad to happen.

The civilian and the new soldier walked toward the temple of Seti I. Sergei smiled. He had impersonated a soldier, policeman, doctor, lawyer, and many other professions. He was the master of the disguise and foil. He had telephoned Alexander and told him the sack full of electronics gear did not have the circuit board. The kids, he suspected the youngest one, must have it on him. They had only five days to steal it back and get to Australia. He had to find the equipment today!

Murder or kidnapping, it didn't make a difference to him. As he approached the guide, he readied his credentials as a security inspector with the United Nations sent out to ensure that Dr. MacGregor made it back to Cairo safely and that the Egyptian government was fully cooperating.

"Sergei Andropov, U.N. Special Services Division. Here are my credentials." Sergei handed the passport-type identification to Mosegi.

"Mr. Andropov. I wasn't aware that the United Nations was involved in our internal affairs. The Ministry of Antiquities said only our Army would escort us today and tomorrow at Luxor," Mosegi said.

"That was correct yesterday. But I was flown in

overnight," Sergei replied. He replaced his documents in his left front pants pocket. He touched the cell phone in the outside cargo pocket of the khaki pants. "I won't be in the way. I am simply a liaison for the U.N. conference, compliment of the Secretary General."

"I see. How very nice," Mosegi replied. "I was not aware of any Russian members of the security detail in Egypt for the conference."

"I am from Ukraine. Not Russia. Big difference," Sergei shot back trying to perfect the disguise.

"So I've been told," Mosegi replied, still not convinced. But he had no other choice but to go onward. "Will you stay with the guards or travel through the temple?"

"I haven't had the privilege of seeing this great shrine. So if you don't mind?"

"Not at all," Mosegi said. "Shall we go?"

Sergei was quickly introduced but was mostly ignored because of the interest in the great shrine. After all, what was another security officer? The special tour roamed through the massive temple with Mosegi pointing out the major hieroglyphics.

"This is called the kings list. It is one of the rarest of all hieroglyphics in Egypt. It shows the cartouche of each pharaoh for over seventeen hundred years."

"Why did Seti have this and other pharaohs didn't?" Heather asked.

"That is a good question. We can only speculate about that. Possibly Seti wanted to show his royal lineage and how he was superior to the other Pharaohs. His father was Rameses I. And his son became the greatest of all Pharaohs, Rameses II. But Abydos was the original royal cemetery long before the Valley of the Kings became the final burial place for the pharaohs. Seti is not even buried here, even though it is regarded as a burial shrine. Seti was buried within yards of Tutankhamen."

"King Tut. Awesome," R.O. said.

"We'll see that tomorrow," Chris said.

Sergei stood apart from the group. He never took his eyes off of R.O.'s backpack.

"But probably the most significant hieroglyphic to Rameses II, son of Seti, were these. This panel details the opening of the new amethyst and gold mines in the western desert. The ancient Egyptians needed gold for their ceremony and religion. They traded grain with other countries as money. But they kept the gold for themselves to enjoy. When we go down into the Osirieon in a few moments, I have a surprise for you. So don't forget this panel about the gold."

Sergei was paying a little closer attention to Mosegi's lecture. Having spent thirty years as a KGB officer and now a nursemaid to Russian diplomats, he had not accumulated much wealth. A small house on a lake in central Russia, a Russian-built Zil automobile, and an Japanese-made SUV was about it.

He had often wondered why he had been so dedicated when others had filled their pockets with payoffs and graft. He regretted not selling the secrets he had stolen from the American National Security Agency, especially the time he penetrated the famous NSOC and CRITIC cryptography centers at their Washington headquarters. The Americans never suspected anything. But with this last mission, he would earn enough money to retire, even though it would be a meager retirement, indeed.

The group wandered around gazing and talking about the massive temple and the thousands of images carved into the stone pillars and walls. Each represented the painstaking work of art of a person who may have lived only long enough to decorate one wall before he died. Others would pick up the chisel and block and continue the story.

"We will now go to the Osirieon. It is an underground chamber that is dedicated to Osiris as Amun Re, the god of the underworld," Mosegi said and walked along.

"Is it Ra or Re?" Natalie asked. "I have heard both."

"It is both. Re was the first name of the sun god or solar disc. Re was the god who created himself through magic and then created everything else simply by saying its name. Over time, Re became Ra, as the god was given a human and animal shape. There is much discussion among Egyptologists as to which is accurate. It varies with different dynasties. Re is mentioned here. But in the Seti tomb in Luxor, Ra is used."

"How confusing. Just call him the sun god," R.O. observed. "You could sure get a neck ache looking up all the time. There's another owl. How cool."

"The colors of this hallway are just magnificent," Mavis said. She reached out to touch the jackal god, Anubis. His black head and gold necklace seemed as fresh as if they were only a hundred years old instead of nearly four thousand.

"Be careful not to touch, Dr. MacGregor," Mosegi said.

"Oh, yes. I should have known better. My father at the British Museum would have spanked me for sure for doing that," Mavis said.

At the end of the hall, they approached an area that was barricaded from the public with signs in three languages ordering people to stop and go no further. A modern door had been installed in the passageway. Mosegi took a key out of his pocket and unlocked the door.

"There are only electric lights for the first hundred feet or so. I will pass out head lanterns at the bottom of the stairway."

Each person filed in while Mosegi held the door open. Sergei was the last one through before Mosegi locked the door behind them. The normally talkative

MacGregors were very quiet and took each step cautiously, as if they were the first explorers into the underground chamber. When they had reached the bottom of the stairs, Mosegi opened a metal cabinet and passed out headbands that had small battery-operated lights attached.

"Check your lights to be sure the batteries are working. This is the Osirieon. It is a chamber dedicated to Seti as the god Osiris. Osiris was the god responsible for the dead. Obviously Seti believed he was Osiris and built this chamber like a royal tomb."

"What was that noise?" Heather asked. They all became quiet. They heard a clinking noise echoing down the pitch black hallway.

"There are two Egyptologists working here this morning. That was my surprise," Mosegi said.

"Oh, how exciting, kids," Mavis said.

All three were used to their Mom's enthusiasm. Sometimes they just ignored it. They were just glad other people weren't around so they wouldn't be embarrassed again.

Following Mosegi down the dark hallway, hundreds of colorful wall paintings and hieroglyphics jumped into view as the lights suddenly illuminated them. There were plenty of oohs and ahs before they finally saw a dim glow of light ahead. The floor was wet and muddy and the air was stale and musty.

Turning right at a small intersection between two subterranean hallways, they could see two figures kneeling on the floor of the tomb and rubbing a brush on the walls. As they approached, they heard voices and soon they saw faces. One of the people stood up and looked at the eight lanterns pointing at her.

"I tell you what. I just can't escape the MacGregors," Dr. Jennifer January said. Old Professor Carpenter stood up next to her.

"Jennifer," Chris said.

"Hi, Chris. Surprise! The professor asked me to come down here this morning knowing that you all would be along shortly. Isn't this exciting?" Jennifer asked.

"We are absolutely overwhelmed," Jack said. He shook the old professor's hand. "I have seen a lot of natural wonders, but this is incredible."

"I wanted to show all of you something that we have recently discovered," the professor said. Taking his old hand, complete with blue veins and liver spots on the skin, he rubbed it across the neatly cut hieroglyphics.

"Dr. January's team has been researching the new discoveries at the Bahariya Oasis. Before this discovery, we thought the notorious Mayor Khensu Eyuf was simply a Pharaoh hopeful, so to speak. The archaeological evidence at Bahariya has told us that Mayor Khensu Eyuf had carried on a continuing battle with the Pharaoh Apris of the twenty-sixth dynasty."

"But Seti I is a nineteenth dynasty Pharaoh," Jack said.

"What's a dynasty?" R.O. asked politely.

"It is a family group. Father-son-father Pharaohs until a new family becomes Pharaoh," Jennifer said.

"Oh," R.O. said.

"But look everyone," the old professor pointed to the wall where the well-preserved hieroglyphics were carved. "This is a reference to the oracle of Osiris. Highly unusual. But it appears that Seti felt he was Osiris. It tells here that he had the power of not only granting entrance into the afterlife but also telling the dead what was going to happen in the lives of their families they left behind," the old professor said moving his fragile hand across the stone hieroglyphic.

"And Amun Re, the father of the living and the dead, the gods of his own creation, will bring forth the power of the sun and it will give forth light and heat. And from the light and heat will emanate the riches of the land," Jennifer read.

"And then here is another reference to the oracle: the ability to foretell the future. Actually the ancient language says 'to see the future'. Much more powerful than to foretell or prophesy." Old Professor Carpenter had a wide grin on his face. "And then down here light and heat are mentioned once again. It is truly a mystery to us. The Pharaohs claimed to be able to perform a great deal of magic and some of it is recorded in the Judeo-Christian texts. But we have never heard of this dual power. Something that creates light and heat and also can see the future," the professor said.

"This matches the story we found at Bahariya," Jennifer said.

"I remember. The one you told the other night on the ship," Natalie said.

"Exactly. It is the same," the professor interrupted. "There is a link between this inscription in the nineteenth dynasty and the tombs at Bahariya. They are separated not only by two hundred and fifty miles of Sahara desert but over seven hundred years of Egyptian dynasties."

"What do you think, Dr. January?" the professor said and stood up.

"For me, the key is in the reference to the gold mines and that Mayor Khensu Eyuf's tombs reveal the many raids on the Pharaoh's tombs during the sixth century B.C.," Jennifer replied.

"My goodness, this may be the biggest discovery since Lord Carnarvon and Howard Carter discovered the young Tutankhamun. Our mischievous Mayor of Bahariya just might have been responsible for looting the tombs and pyramids of dozens of Pharaohs and stashing the treasures in the desert." The old professor had a smile that went from one wrinkled ear to the other. The twinkle in his eye made him appear twenty years younger.

"The biggest tomb raider of all time," Chris said.

"Look, Professor," Jennifer said and knelt down on one knee in the mud of the ancient tunnel. She pointed to the hieroglyphics. "The sky god reunites the power of light and heat with the solar disc Amun Re. Wait, I've seen this before, the falcon and the solar disc and these hieroglyphics for light and heat. I just didn't make the connection. I've seen it in Bahariya and Farafra, both desert oases."

"Well, I told you, ladies and gentlemen," the old professor was shaking with excitement. "You are witnessing history in the making. Our dear young Dr. January has just put two proverbial pieces of this gigantic jigsaw puzzle together. Most Egyptologists spend a lifetime and never connect two pieces. But at this moment, Dr. January has connected the sky god, the falcon...the falcon of Abydos, we shall call him, to that mad dog Vizier, the mayor of the Bahariya Oasis, Khensu Eyuf." The old professor was so jubilant, he could barely speak. " He was the spoiler of the centuries. Taking from the Pharaohs what very few could, their riches for the afterlife. This is the final clue that we needed."

"So all we have to do is find Khensu Eyuf, and we find all the gold and treasure?" R.O. said plainly.

"Young man. We already know where Khensu Eyuf is buried. We just need to go there and dig up the treasure." Old Professor Carpenter laughed out loud.

Mavis began clapping.

"Awesome," Chris said quietly and looked at the wide-eyed Natalie standing next to him.

"And who else knows of this Mayor Khensu Eyuf, as you call him?" Sergei spoke in his strong Russian accent.

"Who is this man?" asked the professor just noticing Sergei standing at the back of the group.

"I am with the United Nations security detail for the MacGregors," Sergei replied politely not wanting to raise suspicion.

"I see. Well, since you have heard the whole story, you might as well know that the people standing here in this subterranean tunnel, locked away centuries before Khensu Eyuf was mayor, we...we are the only ones who know, or suspect I should say. But my suspicions are 99 percent correct, wouldn't you say, Dr. January?"

"Yes. I would agree," she replied.

"As far as we know, we are the only ones in the world who have connected Seti's Falcon of Abydos, as I have named it, to the ancient gold mines to the east, the rock quarries at Sinai, the raided treasure of the Pharaohs, and the oracle of the Nile," the professor said.

Sergei's mind was racing. Within his grasp was the satellite control circuit board and now, millions, perhaps billions of lost Egyptian treasure.

"And Professor, how is your team going to dig up all of this treasure?" Sergei asked.

"That is not as difficult as it may seem. When Carter was looking for Tutankhamun from 1917 to 1922, he had to dig around a whole mountain to find the first step down into the tomb. We know where the notorious mayor is buried, and his family and his generals and his lost city. I may be simplifying it some, but with our modern technology, the right team could bring the Pharaohs' treasure to the surface within a year." The old professor seemed confident.

"All we need to do is verify the message with the one in Seti's tomb in Luxor and Khensu Eyuf's tomb at Bahariya," the professor said.

"I see. Then I must ask all of you to stand up against the wall," Sergei said.

They looked at him with puzzled expressions on their faces. Suddenly he produced a small short barrel H & K 9mm pistol from his pants pocket.

"Stand up against the wall," Sergei commanded. They moved back. "Now you," he pointed the gun at R.O., "hand me your pack."

R.O. looked at Jack and Jack nodded his head in agreement.

Sergei waved his gun around, emphasizing his control of the moment.

"If you move, I will shoot the little guy first," Sergei said.

He opened the backpack and rifled around inside until he found the ship's towel. Unrolling the towel, he found the electronic spider and the circuit board.

"Finally," he said.

"So you were the scum who raided our cabins," Mavis said with acid in her words.

"That's right, lady, and I will be the scum who shoots your son if you say another word."

Sergei shoved the circuit board inside a hard case and placed it in his pocket. He threw the rest of the items on the muddy floor. R.O. reached out and grabbed his spider and quickly stuffed it in his pocket. Sergei stepped forward and grabbed Heather and pulled her close to him.

"Now tell me, Professor, because if you don't, this young lady won't live two more minutes. What is the key you mentioned about Seti's tomb at Luxor?"

Without hesitation, the professor spoke.

"There is a stele, or stone tablet, on the wall of the antechamber of the tomb. It is shaped like a pyramidion, the capstone for an obelisk. The pyramidion, a small pyramid, tells how to use the oracle to create the heat and light and foretell the future. It holds the secret to finding the lost pharaoh's treasure. Before now, we weren't interpreting it correctly. But it makes perfect sense now. No one knew the connection between Khensu Eyuf and Seti I."

"I see. So if I go to Luxor, read the pyramidion and give the clues to another archaeological team, then I become a wealthy man? That sounds very good to me, Professor. Thank you."

"What are you going to do?" Jack asked.

"I'm not going to kill you, Doctor. I am going to let you die like a Pharaoh, deep in this tomb. A royal tomb for all of you. Some day you may be on display in a museum." Sergei laughed. "But I will need some insurance in case the authorities discover my plot too soon, so I am going to take the blond with me. One move and she dies. Now give her your lanterns."

One by one they took the lanterns from the headbands and handed them to Heather.

"Be strong, sweets," Mavis whispered to Heather as she took her lantern.

"I'm OK, Mom," Heather replied.

"Shut up!" Sergei yelled.

He yanked the lanterns out of her hands and threw them on the wet floor. He stomped on the light bulb of each one. Grabbing Heather's arm, he pushed her away from the others. Pulling open his shirt, he unzipped a wide utility belt that contained extra clips for his gun, money, and a block of C4 explosive. He took the block and pressed it into the wall. He then pushed a thin wire into the block and started stepping backward. The wire unreeled from a spool located inside the utility belt.

"I suggest that you help the old professor to his feet and start running down the tunnel. As soon as Heather and I reach the crossroads to the tunnel, I will perform my best magic. I will bring down a four thousand year-old Pharaoh's shrine in just thirty seconds. And if you are standing too close, you will be crushed or the concussion will rupture every blood vessel in your brain." Sergei kept moving backwards, holding the gun steady.

Jack stood there clinching his fists. Mavis knew what he was thinking.

"No. We are all going to live through this," she whispered.

They looked at each other for a few seconds. He nodded his head in agreement.

"Let's go!" Jack shouted and everyone started running. Jennifer and Natalie grabbed the old professor and dragged him along at high speed. He was churning his legs, but they weren't touching the ground.

Sergei pushed Heather down the hall in the opposite direction.

"Run toward the doors or you will die, too," Sergei said.

"Run honey," Jack said. Heather began to run.

Sergei walked backwards fifty feet to the crossroads in the ancient tunnel. He pulled a small bright yellow ignition box from the utility belt and attached the thin lead wire.

As everyone started running down the tunnel, they could hear Sergei's heinous laugh. They kept running toward the darkness. R.O. tripped and fell but got right back up only to fall into a deep pit. Soon Jack, Mavis, Natalie, Chris, Mosegi, and the professor were falling down all around him. Each yelled or screamed as they hit the bottom six feet below. Chris reacted quickly and pulled out his lighter. Everyone lay crumpled around with old Professor Carpenter having landed on top of Jack and Mavis.

"Quick drop," the professor said.

"Hurry, everyone. Follow me," Jennifer said as she crawled on her knees into a small tunnel.

Jack pushed and shoved until everyone was deep inside the tunnel. Then the bang was heard.

"Cover your ears and close your eyes!" Jack shouted.

Sergei and Heather ducked around the corner of the crossroads and into a false doorway about five feet deep. The concussion rushed by them like a massive wind sucking their breath away and making their heads hurt. Heather screamed. Then there was dust and more noise as the massive stone blocks began to fall. The Russian hovered over Heather until all the noise had stopped.

In a matter of minutes they were racing up the stairway. Sergei took the key that he had taken from Mosegi and opened the door into the temple of Seti. He shoved Heather to the ground and locked the door behind him. He tossed the key through one of the walkways into the sand.

"OK. Here are the rules. You behave and I won't kill you. You even speak when you are not spoken to, and you die. Got it?"

Heather bit her lip telling herself she was not going to cry. She took a deep breath and rose to her feet looking Sergei in the eyes.

"Got it," she said back in his face.

They heard someone running toward them. It was Alexander Raikin.

"Did you get the circuit board?"

"I have it. And my comrade, we have much more. Where is the plane?"

"I landed on the road beside the temple complex," Alexander answered. "Why is she with you?"

"I will explain. But we must first get to the plane and fly to Luxor."

"Luxor? We have only five days to get the circuit board to Australia," Alexander answered, bewildered by the change of plans.

"Comrade. Trust me. When have I let you down? We will go to Luxor and find what I want. Then we will go to Australia and deliver the circuit board. When we return to Egypt, we will be rich, my friend," Sergei said and pointed the gun at Heather.

"Have you gone mad?" Alexander asked.

"You will see just how mad I am," Sergei said. "Now let's hurry."

R.O. leaned against the wall. He could hear voices everywhere. The darkness plays tricks on the mind. Someone far away could be right next to you. He searched his cargo pocket amidst the many things he carried and found his butane lighter. He struck the flint and there was light. Mavis was sitting against Jack. Chris and Jennifer had the old professor on the muddy floor of the cramped tunnel. Natalie was next to them with eyes as wide as saucers. Mosegi was sitting on the floor covered with dust.

"Oh, thank God. Everyone is alive," Mavis said and crawled from person to person. "Let's get out of this tunnel."

Chris pulled his lighter out and so did Jack. Soon there was enough light for them to regroup as they crawled back into the main passageway.

"What now?" Natalie asked.

"Let me think," Jennifer said. "I know there was a team that was reopening some of the old Gunter Dreyer digs next to the temple. Those should be right over our heads. Our hope is that the ancient tombs are connected with the subterranean passageways of the Osirieon cult that Seti built."

Suddenly there was a rumbling noise and everyone froze. No one spoke.

"What's that? Are we going to be crushed to death?" R.O. said what everyone was thinking.

"I hope not, Son," Jack said.

"The blast must have caused more settling in the ancient blocks. I need to see if we are sealed in. Chris, you and Natalie come with me," Jennifer said. She looked at R.O.

"Can I borrow your lighter for a minute?"

"Sure," R.O. replied and handed it to her. "It gets pretty hot. So you have to let it go off every minute or so and blow on it."

"Thanks. We'll be right back."

About five minutes passed before Jennifer, Chris, and Natalie were back.

"It's totally sealed, Dad," Chris said. "I think we're trapped."

14

Entombed

"Professor, are you all right?" Jack asked and held the lighter so he could see the old gentleman's face.

"Oh yes. I have fallen in the best tunnels in the world. Another one isn't going to hurt me. My bones are as strong as some of these Pharaohs whose bones last five thousand years," he replied. "Now help me stand up so I can get this mud off my butt."

R.O. laughed. It was a little comic relief for everyone.

Jack moved the light around illuminating the face of everyone, for a second time, to be sure everyone was OK and nobody was hiding an injury just to appear strong.

"You guys are a mess. That dust and smoke covered all of you. We could make a good cast for a Boris Karloff movie," Jack said.

"Who's Boris Karloff, Dad?" R.O. asked.

"Well, he's…I'll explain later. Right now we need to follow Dr. January and find a way out of here," Jack said. He started walking toward Jennifer who had taken R.O.'s lighter and wandered down the cavernous hallway. In the distance they could see the light but not her form anymore.

"Chris and Natalie, you guys lead. Mavis will walk with Professor Carpenter and Ryan. Mosegi and I will bring up the rear."

Mosegi had yet to say a word.

In a few minutes they had caught up with Jennifer.

"In my opinion we need to keep heading this direction toward the new dig area. Possibly we can find a crossover passageway between the nineteenth dynasty temple area where we are now and the older fifth dynasty digs on the surface."

"I concur, Doctor," Professor Carpenter said. "It seems strange that they are the opposite of what we normally find. The younger dynasty should be over the older. There was an ingenious architect at work in this tunnel. He must have something valuable to hide."

Jennifer led the way. As they wandered through the hallway, the water dried up and the floor was only dirt. The hallway narrowed and soon they were walking bent over at the waist.

"OK, everyone, stop and let the lighters cool. If they get too hot or burn out, we're in trouble," Jack said.

Chris and Natalie sat on the floor next to each other in the dark. Everyone was no more than three feet away. Natalie reached over and found Chris's hand and squeezed it. She then felt up to his face and touched his cheek.

Jack's lighter came back on and everyone stood up again. Mavis jumped up too quickly and bumped her head on the low ceiling.

"Ouch," she said.

"The dirt that accumulates over forty centuries gets as hard as the rock and is difficult to dig out with just a shovel. So we have to burrow around it and make passageways like this one, only four feet high," Jennifer said. She moved ahead.

After about an hour of walking stooped over, Jennifer suddenly stopped.

"Why are we stopping?" Jack asked from the rear.

"Well, we've reached a, how do I say it, a challenging spot in the road," Jennifer replied.

Jack stepped around everyone until he reached the front of the subterranean caravan and was standing next to Jennifer.

"What is it?" he asked anxiously.

"This is where the last team stopped digging," Jennifer said and pointed to the stone blocks that were being chiseled at the end of the small tunnel. "Looks like they made it to this point and then stopped. This block on top is ready to come out. See how they've cut around it. Help me push on it," she said to Jack.

Jack and Jennifer pushed hard. Then Chris joined them and they pushed again harder.

"It moved," Jennifer said. "On the count of three." Natalie and Mavis moved in and now there were eight to ten hands on the block. Each person was shoulder to shoulder trying to move the heavy block.

"It's moving! Don't stop," Jennifer said loudly with determination in her voice.

First it moved only an inch, then two, then five, then suddenly it fell through to the other side. Everyone cheered as it disappeared into a black hole. They never heard it crash to the bottom, and they all looked at each other not quite understanding the significance of that fact.

Jack tried to hoist himself up to the hole but couldn't get the right angle and kept bumping his head and shoulder.

"Ryan, come over here," Jack said.

"Ryan, R.O. I will hold you up to the hole. You will hold the lighter into the next room and tell us what you see. You don't have to worry. We will hold your belt and your feet. Can you do it?"

"That's a roger, Dad."

Chris made a foothold with his hands while Jack

steadied R.O. As R.O. crawled into the two-foot-wide hole, he pushed forward with his desert boots, barely able to bend his knees. He could feel his dad pushing on the bottom of the boots. Once through to the other side, he held the lighter out as far as he could to get a look. At first he couldn't see anything because the lighter was too close to his face. But in a couple of minutes, when his eyes had fully dilated, he could see that the room was a giant hall with ceilings as much as fifty feet high on one side and sloping downward to about ten feet on the other. He looked down and could see that he was about halfway up the wall on one side of the hall.

"Ah!!" R.O. said in fright.

"Ryan. Are you all right?" Jack yelled.

"Yes, Dad. I'm OK," he replied. He looked at the yellow and red painted face of the Pharaoh just inches away from his own. "It is really spooky in here. Let me slide out a little further, Dad," R.O. said as he crawled out a little more.

"Let go of my feet, Dad. I need a little more leverage on my legs," R.O. said.

"OK. Just be careful, Son," Jack said, a cold chill rushing down his arms.

"Oh, Jack," Mavis said as she moved in next to Jack and Chris.

Then suddenly R.O.'s feet disappeared into the darkness. The hole was empty.

"Ryan!" Jack yelled into the hole. "Ryan!"

Everyone rushed up to the hole and peered through, not knowing what to say or to expect.

"Move over. I'm going through," Chris said and quickly climbed up into the hole. His broad shoulders scraped the sides and he barely squeezed through. When his head reached the other side, he couldn't see anything. It was pitch black. He couldn't reach back into the hole to get his lighter from someone in the tunnel.

"Darn it," he said and wiped a drop of sweat from

his right eye. He pulled himself further into the room until he was dangerously balancing on the edge. There was still no sign of R.O. No light. No noise. No movement.

"Ryan!" he shouted.

"Chris, do you see him yet?" Mavis said.

"Ryan!" he shouted again.

"Hey, Chris," came a voice just a foot away as R.O. flipped on his butane lighter.

"What the heck?" Chris said and looked down.

R.O. was standing on a narrow ledge that measured about twelves inches across.

"I found a ledge that leads to some stairs right over here. The stairs go all the way to the floor of this giant room. Here, look what I found."

R.O. held out an ancient torch made of straw and pitch. Chris held it while R.O. lit it with his lighter. It had been dry for four thousand years and blazed instantly. Chris crawled out onto the ledge. The torch lit up the entire room like a ballroom at Christmas. There was furniture strewn everywhere. The walls were brightly painted in the most colorful combinations.

"Chris!" Mavis called again.

"I found him. He's all right," Chris shouted back through the hole. Looking back through the hole he could see Natalie staring at him.

"Come on in. You aren't going to believe this!" Chris said.

She hiked up into the hole. One by one they all made it into the next room with Jennifer and Jack pushing the aged professor across the smooth stone through the hole. With everyone finally standing on the floor of the giant hall, the bold and dramatic art of ancient Egypt all around them, no one said a word for a minute. Then the professor spoke.

"An unblemished tomb. Never in my life did I think I would ever be one of the first to witness this," the old man said. He walked around. He took the torch from Chris and held it up against one wall and over a piece of furniture and then against another wall. He walked around the room quickly.

"Who does it belong to, Professor?" Jennifer asked. "We were in the nineteenth dynasty in the tunnel. The fifth dynasty is on the surface above. Who would hide a tomb between two dynasties?"

"A very smart Pharaoh," Mavis said. "Jack, we've got to hurry. Heather."

"I feel the same, honey. But we've got to figure out how to get out of here," he replied.

"Look over here," Jennifer pointed as she lit another torch from the royal stash of torches. "You realize that every time we light one of these, a $5,000 artifact goes up in smoke."

"Unbelievable! Five thousand dollars for a torch?" R.O. said in amazement.

"She means a four-thousand-year-old torch that belonged to a Pharaoh," Chris said and lit another one. "I can smell the money burning," he teased.

"See this pile of sand in the corner. This must be seeping in from above where the excavations are taking place. Chris, let me stand on your shoulders," Jennifer said.

As Chris knelt down, the attractive brunette climbed on his back and then put each boot on his shoulders. Chris stood up. Jennifer reached high and touched an ancient cedar beam that reached across the room.

"Man," she said cautiously. "That is barely hanging in there. A little nudge and down it comes, and who knows what's on top of this wall," Jennifer said.

"I've got an idea," Mavis said, her mind working to get to Heather. "Let's move all of this old furniture into the next room. The small room that R.O. found. Then we'll cram ourselves in there and pull the beam down and see what happens."

Everyone stood quietly looking at her.

"Mom, that's nuts," R.O. said what everyone was thinking.

"Ryan," Jack said firmly. "Maybe we should think this through."

"Dr. Mavis is right," the old professor came out of his trance from looking at the new discovery. "That is going to be our only hope. The antechamber next to this room is very well constructed. The stone supports look like they were just dropped into place. If this room doesn't fill with sand and bury us, then there is a very good chance we will find a way to the surface. The cedar beam is the key."

"Then let's do it," Mavis said, never ceasing to think about Heather. "Jack, we either make it and find Heather or we die and she dies anyway. That's the grim reality as I see it."

"I agree. It is our only hope," Mosegi said.

"How do we pull the beam down?" Natalie asked.

"With this," Chris said and pointed to a chair. "The leather strapping is not brittle. We unwind it and tie it to the beam. Then we pull it from the antechamber. Boom, down it comes."

"Then let's get moving the furniture. Chris, you unwind the leather and you and Jennifer tie it to the beam. Go, go, we're running out of time for Heather," Jack ordered. Everyone started moving.

Within twenty minutes the ancient furniture, pots, and images of the gods were carefully stored in the small room. R.O. was fascinated with the small replicas of the pantheon of the gods that were carved out of solid gold. He lined them up perfectly on a small dresser made of a lightweight wood and painted bright yellow. The yellow had barely faded.

Jennifer was standing on Chris's shoulders again, trying to find a way to attach the leather straps.

"There just isn't a splinter or hole or anything,"

Jennifer said. She was perplexed at the situation.

"Try this." Chris reached into his pocket and pulled out his knife. He unfolded it carefully and handed it up, butt first, to Dr. January. "Now push the blade through the leather and into the wood," he said.

"Got it. Am doing it right now," Jennifer said and pushed hard. The beam moved. "Oh gosh." Her heart felt like it was in her throat. "We almost died on that one."

"Jennifer, you don't have a choice," Jack said, now standing next to Chris. Push the blade in hard or it won't hold when we tug on it."

"OK. I'll try it again."

Jennifer pushed harder, holding the beam with one hand and pushing with the other. Suddenly the steel blade sank into the ancient wood.

"I think I've got it. Coming down," she said.

"Great. Now everyone into the antechamber," Jack ordered.

Mavis was coughing from all the smoke that was filling the room.

"If we aren't crushed to death, we'll probably suffocate," R.O. said and leaned up against his dad.

Jennifer and Chris were the last ones into the small room.

"Do you want the honors, Doctor?" Chris said and handed the end of the long leather rope to Jennifer.

"Well, I suppose. At least you won't be alive to hate me if this fails," she replied.

"That's a pleasant thought," Natalie said under her breath.

"On three. One, two, three…."

Jennifer gave the leather rope a firm tug. The knife popped loose and clattered to the ground at their feet. Chris bent over and picked it up. The blade wasn't even chipped. Everyone looked disappointed even though sudden death had been a possibility.

"We'll try it again," Chris said. He stepped from the small room with Jennifer right behind him. As they neared the corner, they both felt sand falling around them and looked up.

"Oh my gosh, it's coming down!" Jennifer yelled.

They began to run the short distance to the room as the cedar beam crashed to the floor next to them. Two huge blocks of stone bounced to the middle of the room just brushing against Chris' right leg as he dove for the safety of the antechamber behind Jennifer. Jack grabbed his arms and dragged him in.

"Cover your mouths!" Jack yelled as dust rushed into the small room, creating a miniature dirt storm.

No one panicked as the sand poured through the doorway and crawled up their legs first to their ankles and then to their knees. R.O. kept climbing on top of the sand until he was face to face with Mavis. Then he got bogged down and couldn't climb anymore. Soon the passageway to the room was sealed off and the torches were dead. Darkness fell upon them again and with it their optimism about surviving.

"I think the sand has stopped moving," Jennifer said.

Jack flipped on his butane lighter and shown it around the room.

"R.O., Chris, Natalie, Mavis, Jennifer, and Mosegi... where's the professor?"

"Oh my," Mavis said and started feeling around in the sand.

"I've got him," Chris said and pulled the old man to the top of the sand and dusted the sand off of his face. He coughed a couple of times. He looked like a thousand-year-old mummy encrusted with the dirt on his white hair and beard.

"Professor," Jennifer said anxiously.

"I'm OK. Been holding my breath. Just like the time we had a little cave in at Senswosret II in Luxor. Just a matter of timing," he said.

"Wait, the sand is moving again," Jack said and pointed at the door.

The fine grains of sand were running, one on top of the next like an army racing to a conquest and led by gravity. It shifted and then moved again. Everyone was amazed as they watched the uncanny movement as if the sand were alive. Then suddenly it started moving away from them toward the opposite wall over the top of the furniture. A rumbling could be heard.

"Do you hear it?" Jack looked at Jennifer.

"I do, the walls are vibrating. The pressure of the sand was too much. We may be in for a ride. Good luck, everybody," Jennifer said looking upward in the corner.

The instant she finished her sentence the far wall began to move away from them and more sand from the desert above began to pour in. It started piling up in front of them.

"Climb! Let's climb!" Mavis shouted and everyone got the idea quickly.

Chris grabbed the old professor and yanked hard until his legs were free. He felt the old Egyptologist's back pop.

"I'm OK, son. Let's keep going," Professor Carpenter said to Chris.

As the sand moved into the room, everyone was scurrying in the darkness trying to stay on top. Soon they were pressed up against the ceiling and bent over in half.

"Something has got to give or this is it," Natalie said. She found herself stuck in the corner.

Jack ignited his lighter and noted that all had made it. Ryan was hanging onto his belt. Then the rumble began again and he could feel the vibration of the wall next to them and the ceiling. Suddenly the seam in the corner began to separate and more sand began pouring in on Natalie.

"Chris! Help me!" she screamed.

Chris lunged through the sand and started pulling her away from the ever-widening seam. Sand was pouring in so fast her legs were becoming buried. Then the walls began to move.

"The whole temple area has grown unstable!" Jennifer shouted and held onto the old professor.

"Wait, there's light," R.O. said. He started digging toward it. As the sand poured in, he pushed his way past and through the seam in the ceiling, which was now two feet wide. Choking on a face full of sand, he pushed onward and soon disappeared through the seam. More sand poured through.

"Follow Ryan, everyone!" Jack yelled. "Hurry! The seam will close soon!"

Natalie was pushed through the sand with muffled screams. Chris was shoving her and pulling at his Mom behind him. Next the professor was shoved upward by Jennifer and Jack. Mosegi, who had never said a word, and Jennifer were next. Jack was last.

As Jack pushed one last time on the bottom of Jennifer's boot, the sand got up his nose. He sneezed and coughed and tried to catch a breath. He could see the light flickering between the avalanches of sand. His ears became clogged and the screams and rumbling became muted.

Jack crawled with all his strength against the weight of the moving sand. It invaded his eyes, rubbing under the eyelids. He spit and pulled, but he didn't seem to be making any headway. He tried to cry out for help, but his mouth filled with more sand. He choked and coughed again. Sand was pouring into his shirt and shorts and boots. He would dig but slip back down rubbing against the ancient stone of the shrine. His lungs were struggling to expand, and he began gasping for air under the weight of the sand.

For the first time in his adult life, Jack MacGregor

felt fear racing through his body. At any moment, he knew he would pass out and there would be no way for his family to dig him out in time. He would surely die. Then suddenly he felt hands grabbing his arms and shirt. He could hear muffled noises. There was a burst of sunlight. As he was pulled from the grip of the living sand, he coughed hard and fresh air filled his lungs.

"Dad, Dad." R.O. said and knelt down beside him.

"Dad. Breathe deep. We made it," Chris looked down at him.

Jennifer rushed up to Jack with a canteen of water she had retrieved from the jeeps. He felt the cool water splash across his face and eyes. He saw Jennifer going from person to person pouring the water on everyone.

Jack looked around through his scratchy eyes and saw the casualties. They were perched on the side of a dune in a small valley next to Seti's tomb. Everyone was sitting or lying with the exception of Chris and Jennifer, who were up evaluating the situation. Jack rose to his knees and sand drained from his shirt and shorts. He looked back to where they had crawled out of the subterranean ruins. The hole was gone and a four-foot dune was still swirling over the spot.

"We can't rest too long, Dad," Chris said.

As they all rose to their feet, Jennifer was walking toward the parking area next to Seti's temple where the three police jeeps were still parked next to a green truck with a canvas-covered bed. Two of the policemen met her half way.

Mavis walked over and stood next to Jack. She shook her head.

"Do you think they'll hurt Heather?" She asked.

"I hope not. I don't know. He tried to kill us, again, I think. I really don't know what this is all about," Jack said.

They all walked over to where Jennifer was talking to the police. They dusted the sand off as they went, creating their own little dirt storm behind them.

"These policemen said that when Sergei and Heather came out, another man was waiting for them. They left in a small plane. Where? They don't know."

At that moment, another military jeep drove up and the police inspector got out and rushed over to them.

"One of my men just radioed me that you had been assaulted again. I am so sorry," he said.

"He took our daughter," Mavis said.

"I will notify the others along the way. How long has it been?"

"About two hours," Jack replied and dusted more sand out of his hair.

"Give me a minute. I need to talk to everyone," Jennifer said and gathered everyone around her away from the policemen.

The inspector walked away a few yards. He opened his cell phone and made a call.

"Professor," Jennifer said. "The Russian has a two-hour jump on us. I think he will go to Luxor and try to solve the riddle of the pyramidion design on the wall in Seti's tomb. All he has to do is negotiate an agreement with an archaeology team and no one would reveal what he has learned. They would save it for themselves.

"Luxor is only two hours by desert road across the mountains. They should be arriving right about now." Jennifer checked her watch. "Add one hour to arrive at the tomb site, an hour back, and the scores of tourists to maneuver around. And where would they stash Heather? They have some real logistics problems."

"Yes, Jennifer. It would be my guess that he would also try to destroy the message on the pyramidion so that no one else would know the connection between Khensu Eyuf and the lost treasure of the Pharaohs," the professor replied.

"What are you both saying?" Mavis said with a frantic look on her face. "Will they hurt Heather?"

"I doubt it. Not right away. They could use her as a bargaining chip, just in case we did survive. Or they could sell her for a profit to the white slave market on their way to Australia," Jennifer said.

"Now, I'm really mad," Mavis said.

"Dr. January. Do you remember the Italian team led by Anthony Stancampiano? They were the team who was digging in the ancient quarries in Sinai," the professor said.

"Yes, I do. I know what you are thinking. The obelisk in the Red Sea," Jennifer replied.

"An obelisk in the Red Sea. Under water?" R.O. asked, now joining the group.

"The Italian team discovered a broken obelisk that was being transported to this location. The top of the obelisk, the pyramidion, had the hieroglyphics of both Seti and Rameses II. On one side, it is an exact duplicate to the one on the stele in Seti's tomb at Luxor. Egyptologists have always known they were a match, but we didn't understand the full meaning of the translation until today. If we had the information from the obelisk, we could complete the puzzle," Professor Carpenter said. "We would know exactly where to look in the palace of Khensu Eyuf."

"But that's in Sinai," Jack said.

"And I can be there in one hour in my helicopter. One hour there, one hour back. I can fly directly to the oasis. By my calculations, if we leave now, we will get there before the Russians do. Unless they have a twin engine aircraft, they won't beat us there," Jennifer said with confidence.

"May I assist you?" the police inspector said politely as he interrupted.

"Yes, you can take us back to the ship," Mavis said.

"And I want to borrow one of your jeeps," Jennifer said.

"Very well," the inspector said. He gave the orders

in Arabic to the two soldiers.

"Chris, you and Natalie come with me. I will need some help once I get to Sinai," Jennifer said.

"Got it," Chris replied as he took Natalie's hand and hurried behind Jennifer.

Mavis, Jack, Ryan, Mosegi, and Professor Carpenter were helped up into the back of the canvas-covered truck. The soldier started the diesel engine and pointed the truck toward the main road that led toward the palm-covered docks. As the jeep and the truck drove away, the inspector dialed another number on his cell phone.

"I couldn't stop January. She and the two oldest kids are flying to Ras Mohammad to check the hieroglyphic on the submerged obelisk. Yes, I tried to detain them. But I can't murder them in broad daylight. My men will dispose of the parents, the young boy, the archaeologist, and the old man in the desert. But you need to have someone waiting on January when they arrive. Yes, sir, I will take care of the Russians," the inspector said. He closed the call on the tiny cell phone.

"Mom, the truck is headed the wrong way," R.O. said as he looked out the back of the truck.

Mavis and Jack hurried to the back of the truck and peered through the canvas flap, getting a blast of hot air in their faces.

"He's right. We're being driven into the desert. Looks like an old Bedouin track. The river is over there," Jack pointed to the thin green ribbon of vegetation about four miles away and getting further in the distance. "Everyone out. Now hurry!"

Jack grabbed R.O.'s arm and helped him jump to the soft sand beside the track. He and Mavis lowered the old professor over the side, expecting the worse as he rolled twice. Then they both sprang out the back over the gate. Mosegi was the last to bail out. The two soldiers never noticed their escape.

"We're about five miles from the river. It's ten in the morning. If we get moving, we won't die today," Jack said. "How are you, professor?"

"I think I injured my shoulder, but I can still walk. I walk three miles every day on my treadmill back home," he said proudly. "I must say, you people know how to make life interesting." He smiled.

Jennifer, Chris, and Natalie arrived at the Bell Jet Ranger and quickly jumped aboard.

"Thank goodness I flew it off the ship this morning before dawn," Jennifer said.

As she fired it up and got the rotors turning, Natalie dug through the ice chest and found cold bottles of water and passed them around. Soon they were airborne and turning east toward the Red Sea. Like the god of the sky, the falcon, the helicopter chased the shadow of the noon sun across the Nile River valley. By the time they reached the Red Sea, with the sun at twelve noon, Jack, Mavis, R.O., Mosegi, and the professor were climbing the last dune looking down on the Princess of the Nile as she pulled from the dock. Still a mile away, there was no way they could stop the big lumbering ship.

"Jack, I am too tired to cry," Mavis said as she plopped down on the sand.

A small aircraft flew overhead and circled around them. It flew back and this time came in very low. R.O. waved and waved as it went by. The desert sojourners struggled down the last dune as the small craft descended for a landing on the road next to a cotton field that was in bloom. Too tired to know what to expect, they walked over to the plane as a tall Arab stepped out.

"R.O., what's up dude?"

"E!"

15

Ras Mohammed

The noonday sun reflecting off the blue waters of the Red Sea was a magnificent sight. Delicate white reefs lined the Egyptian coast as a few clouds drifted overhead. The air was so dry, the chance of seeing just one cloud was slim. Today they were lucky. There must have been a half dozen clouds.

"Hey, Bryan," Jennifer spoke into her Global Starr telephone she had patched into her radio headset.

"This is the gorgeous Dr. January, I presume? This must be my lucky day," the voice from the other end said in an Aussie accent.

"Hi Bryan. This is all business today, mate," Jennifer replied with a smile on her face.

"What? You mean you aren't calling to ask me if you can stay at my condo at Sharm el Sheikh? Or use my jet skis down by the resort? Or marry me on the beach tonight?"

Natalie was smiling. She and Chris could hear the conversation through their headsets too.

"No, sweetheart. I need a big favor." Jennifer cringed waiting for the reply.

"I love for you to owe me, Jenn. Name it. I'll do it!"

"I will be landing at the dock in front of the Royal Desert Resort. I need three sets of diving gear, masks, fins, everything. I also need a fast boat to get to the round top reef in less than twenty minutes. I want a Nikonos underwater camera with fast film I can use without a flash. No, make that two cameras. I need a back up. And I want a basket of food to be put in my chopper before I take off. Clothes, three T-shirts, two mediums and one extra large. Two beach shorts, women's size two, and" glancing back to Natalie, "make that two size two shorts. A pair of male beach shorts, medium. And don't forget three swimsuits. And one more thing. Two size six ladies beach sandals and one size eleven men's." She guessed at Chris's shoe size.

"Is that all, sweetheart? You know you're my favorite Sheila in the whole world," Bryan replied.

"Yes, Bryan. I know that. You tell me every time I fly to Ras Mohammed," Jennifer replied.

"All righty then. I'll have my people get on it straight away. Count yourself lucky I own the boutique, dive shop, and the restaurant. Ciao!" Bryan hung up on the other end.

"Bryan's a great guy. He has asked me to marry him every time I fly over here to dive or hang out."

"Why don't you?" Natalie asked.

"It would ruin a great friendship," Jennifer said. "But then again, don't you have to be friends first before you get married?"

Chris blushed as Jennifer looked back at him.

"Look down right now," Jennifer said quickly. "Down there, you can see a wreck sitting in sixty feet of water. It is so clear. That's the Dunraven. It was a spy ship for T.E. Lawrence."

"Lawrence of Arabia," Chris said.

"Right on. It's a great dive, but you have to be a master diver because of the currents."

They were thirty-three minutes from the tip of Sinai and thirty-three centuries further in time than the object they came to see.

★★★★★★★

The 1963 maroon Mercedes, replete with little fins and a rusted left front fender, sped along the dirt and gravel road with a blue cloud of oil and diesel fumes spewing from the rear exhaust. The heat from the desert blew from the north between the twin peaks of Katherina and Sinai.

The short man at the steering wheel, wearing only khaki pants and a solid white business shirt, dabbed the perspiration from his face with a green bandanna and chewed vigorously on the butt of a very bad cigar. Precancerous sores had already begun to form on his lips. The spittle seeped from the corners of his mouth and ran down his face with an occasional drop falling to rest on the white shirt, leaving a brown stain.

His beard was about two days old in length with course gray hairs standing watch over fewer black ones. A new leather briefcase lay on the floor of the passenger side. As the rough gravel road intersected with the coastal highway, he slowed to a crawl and watched a tourist bus from Cairo pass at a speed just over sixty miles per hour. He spit out the window, shifted the Mercedes into second, and jumped onto the asphalt road about a kilometer behind the tan and silver bus.

Shifting quickly into third and then fourth, the old German car belched what seemed to be another quart of oil out the rear exhaust pipe as he moved to a half kilometer behind the bus. Dabbing his face again with the green bandanna, he leaned over and pulled the briefcase into the front seat. Not quite paying attention, he swerved the car back onto the road to avoid the disaster of a quick plunge into the Red Sea two hundred feet below the road. The road sign noted that Ras Mohammed was twelve kilometers from the junction.

The bus turned to the right and was followed by the Mercedes. The short man in the stained white shirt spit out the window again. The spit blew through the open back window and landed on the cracked leather seat, seeping into the exposed yellow foam. As the road narrowed and climbed around the cliff, it was nothing less than a breathtaking view of the coral reefs of the Red Sea. The Mercedes closed the distance from the bus.

As the Arab reached a fork in the road leading down to the hotel, he wheeled the old Mercedes up onto the mountain road and downshifted into third, then second, for the hard climb. A rush of wind filled with the smell of salt and fish blew off the Red Sea through the open windows of the Mercedes. Smoke billowed from the exhaust as the old car reached the plateau and turned into a parking lot, half filled with cars and one minibus that was painted orange and white. It was marked "Sinai Safaris" in bold English letters with Arabic letters underneath.

The Arab glanced around quickly and located the car he wanted. It was a new black Jaguar with leather seats that smelled like a lady's handbag just off the rack at Harrod's in Piccadilly Circus. Leaning against the left front fender was a tall man in a white suit and a neatly trimmed beard. His short black hair and deeply tanned skin were a striking contrast to the suit. The Mercedes came to a halt. The old Arab handed the new briefcase out the window without a word.

The man in the white suit motioned for him to park the car. The old Arab spit on the ground and threw the briefcase back into the front floorboard in disgust. He was merely a messenger and only wanted his money and nothing more. When the Mercedes came to a stop, the old man sprang out of the door and started talking angrily in Arabic. The white-suited man said nothing but walked up to the car with a firm look on his face.

When he reached the back of the car, he told the old

man to open the trunk. He refused until the man in the white suit pulled a CZ75 automatic pistol from a shoulder holster on his left side. The Czech 9mm gleamed in the sun from the chrome finish accented with a gold action release, hammer, and safety. The old Arab stared at the gun and, as ordered, he pushed the button that opened the trunk. As the trunk reached half its open height, the old man reached for a rusted tire iron only to hear the soft pop of the pistol. The pain was under his left arm in the side of his chest. Before he could touch it, somehow to futilely soothe it, the CZ popped again, and all of his pain was gone. The old Arab's bloody head preceded his body into the depth of the trunk.

The tall man in the white suit glanced around the parking lot as he lifted the old Arab's feet into the trunk and closed it quickly. He walked to the passenger side, opened the door, and picked up the new leather briefcase. He tucked the CZ75 into a soft leather holster under his white jacket. With the briefcase in hand, the man walked across the parking area toward the stone wall. Once at the wall he could see the dozen or more tourists milling around taking pictures and enjoying the view of Ras Mohammed.

Jennifer set the sleek red and white helicopter down on the soft white beach in front of the resorts. Kids began running toward the chopper while lifeguards tried to herd them back to a safety zone. Once the rotors stopped, a tall man with blond hair dressed in colorful shorts and a white muscle shirt walked up to the helicopter.

"Bryan," Jennifer said as she stepped out of pilot's door.

"Dr. January. You definitely need to fire your hairdresser. I mean, unless you are going to the Halloween Ball dressed as a desert rat," Bryan said.

"Thanks. Good to see you, too," Jennifer said and kissed him on the cheek.

Chris and Natalie had already walked over to the beach shower and with their clothes on started rinsing the sand out of their hair.

"Swim suits and gear," Jennifer said.

Bryan clapped his hands and two young girls ran up to them. Bryan spoke in Arabic and the girls ran over to Chris and Natalie carrying a basket of beachwear. Natalie first stepped behind the outside change curtain and shed her clothes. She slipped on the swim suit. Then it was Chris' turn. Soon Jennifer was there and they were all rubbing the sand out of their hair.

"OK. No time to waste. Where's the boat?"

"Follow me," Bryan said.

At the end of the dock, they boarded a nineteen-foot ski rig with twin Mercury outboards. It was painted yellow with a purple lightening bolt down the side.

"Aren't you going to tell me what this is all about, Jennifer?" Bryan asked.

"Someday over the dinner I owe you," she said. She backed the boat away from the dock.

"You can tell me on our honeymoon!" Bryan shouted back.

As the high-powered ski rig made a quick turn about, Jennifer kicked it into high gear and water sprayed all over the dock. Bryan dodged the spray and waved. Chris secured the dive gear in the back while Natalie enjoyed not having sand in her clothes anymore.

"Now, as I told you during the flight over, the nineteenth dynasty quarry was located on the tip of Sinai. The Arabs later named this Ras Mohammed, which means the head of Mohammed. When the Egyptian stonecutters were shipping the obelisk to stand at the Rameses II temple at Abydos, the ship met with a storm and capsized. The obelisk fell to the bottom and broke in half. Wasn't worth salvaging.

"Today the obelisk sits on the edge of the world's largest perfectly circular reef. It is truly a natural wonder," Jennifer yelled over the sound of the big Mercury engines.

"Who are those people?" Natalie asked. She pointed at a dozen or so boats.

"Divers. The Red Sea is one of the top five diving locations in the world," Jennifer replied.

"I knew that," Natalie said and slapped her head mockingly.

"Gear up," Jennifer said.

Chris and Natalie, expert divers, quickly pulled on the buoyancy compensators, weight belts, tanks, and regulators. Chris found a dive computer in the bottom of the bag. Turning it on, it read "low battery." He tossed it back in the bag. He knew he would have to rely on his Rolex Submariner dive watch and experience. Both attached a knife to their left legs.

"I'll steer," Chris said as he awkwardly leaned against the console fully equipped.

Jennifer quickly put on her gear and took back the wheel.

"Look in that cloth bag. Should be two cameras," she said.

Chris quickly found the cameras and checked the film and power. Both were ready to go. Jennifer began cutting back the power.

"Has the reef overgrown the obelisk?" Natalie asked.

"Yes, it did. But when the archeology team found it, they were able to clear off the top section. That's all we want. Just the small pyramid at the top. The pyramidion with the clue about Seti," Jennifer replied.

"Drop the anchor, Chris."

Chris dropped the anchor to the sandy bottom. It hooked quickly.

"Well, let's go. The reef is about one hundred feet that way."

"How far out are we?" Natalie asked looking back at the row of luxury resorts.

"Just about a quarter of a mile. Too far for beach tourists. Only experienced master divers dive out here. You'll find a few brave snorkelers and wind surfers."

Jennifer put her regulator in her mouth, pulled her mask down and stepped over the gunnel into the crystal clear sea. The surface water temperature was near 78 degrees. Natalie and Chris looked at each other again.

"Can you believe this?" Natalie said.

"Barely. Well. Heather's waiting," Chris replied.

Natalie leaned forward and kissed him on the mouth.

"For luck," she said.

"For luck." Chris stepped over the side and dove to ten feet quickly.

He grabbed his nose to equalize and instantly heard his ears pop. With that over, he could concentrate on the dive. He made an adjustment to his mask and buoyancy compensator. When he reached Jennifer, she handed him the other Nikonos camera.

Natalie swam up behind them. Kicking at an even pace, considering the exercise that had already been required that day, they were at the reef in about three minutes. Jennifer pointed toward the obelisk, where it had been resting for over four thousand years. Chris shook his head in awe. Soon they were next to it and Jennifer was checking out the hieroglyphics. Natalie and Chris appreciated the opportunity to just touch it.

A large sergeant major fish zoomed by Natalie. Chris pointed at a small manta ray swimming next to the reef. It appeared to be flying. They heard a clicking noise and looked over to see Jennifer waving at them. When they reached her side, she was pointing at something on the bottom side of the obelisk. Then she pointed toward the surface. They all followed their smallest bubbles thirty feet to the surface. As they broke the water, Jennifer started talking.

"The part of the pyramidion that I need is on the bottom side. I need a macro lens to get that close. I will take the boat back to the dock. It shouldn't take me ten minutes to get it and be back. Do you want to wait here or ride back?"

"Wait here," Chris and Natalie said at the same time.

As soon as Jennifer fired up the boat and pulled up the anchor, Chris and Natalie were back down under enjoying, the best they could, being together in the ocean once again.

Nearing the lookout point, the Arab in the white suit stopped and rested the briefcase on the wall. Below, the aquamarine of the Red Sea rendered a breathtaking sight, a view that he had seen many times since his first visit when he was only three years old. But then there were no gravel or paved roads, no luxury hotels, no cars. His family came here on his uncle's horses and his father's camels. They came because it was a holy place, the "cape of the prophet."

But now he squinted his eyes in disgust at the Europeans, Americans, and Japanese who wandered around the holy mountain. To him they represented repression, imperialism, and depravity. They were the infidels. And to these Arab brothers who brought them here, truly death would be too easy an atonement for their sin. Beneath the cliff were the luxury hotels facing toward the perfectly circular reef. Fair-skinned tourists swam and snorkeled and occasionally he could see the exhaust bubbles of a scuba diver.

But the greatest natural wonder of Ras Mohammed was the deep blue wall of the ocean that dropped off a short distance from the round reef. It was partly this beauty that brought the man in the white suit his only smile of the day. In the depths, he could easily see dozens, maybe even hundreds, of hammerhead sharks. Nature had somehow created its own heaven and hell a few meters apart.

Opening the briefcase, he picked up the cell phone with a new untraceable number. It was resting flat against a folder labeled "Suissebanc, Zurich." Punching in a series of numbers, he was quickly connected to the thirty-two-foot Bertram yacht that sat lazily in the swells about a half mile from the circular reef. Someone answered his call.

"Yes?"

"Begin, they are here. I have your money. Twenty thousand dollars U.S."

There was a click on the other end. The big Bertram yacht fired up its twin inboard motors and headed for the wall and the hammerhead sharks. As it reached the first group of sharks, two young boys threw the butchered carcass of a goat over the gunwales. On the second pass, the swarming hammerheads were beginning to frenzy as they moved closer to the reef. With each pass, the boat's crew tossed a butchered goat into the clear aquamarine sea.

The hungry hammerheads followed the bloody path in the sea closer and closer to the reef until the Bertram, ramming an underwater coral head, turned back to the open sea, dumping its last butchered goat into the water on top of three scuba divers.

The voracious sharks moved into the reef. The tourists at the lookout moved quickly to the wall and another screamed as a hammerhead pulled a snorkeler under in one swift pass.

Down on the beach at the hotels, a never-before-used shark horn blew loudly as awestruck tourists scrambled from their lounge chairs and from beneath the palm-thatched umbrellas. A brave group of swimmers had reached the top of the reef and with the help of four divers attempted to fight off the marauding sharks. It was really not a fight, but just a matter of out lasting the predators, one victim at a time.

In the distance the whipping of a Sikorsky helicopter could be heard. The Arab smiled as the sharks moved in quicker for the kill. The white-suited killer could now see his comrades in the Sikorsky climbing from the ocean surface to the top of the overlook, just a few hundred feet away. He jumped to the top of the stone wall as the helicopter moved in slowly and dropped a rope ladder. Grabbing the briefcase, he jumped to the ladder dangling over the hundred-foot drop. Holding on tightly, he shouted in Arabic for the helicopter to get moving.

As it turned toward the sea, his instincts made him look back. He looked down on the reef to the now pink water. He yelled out a cry of both joy and rage and again felt the success of purging the earth of its human debris. Jihad had begun! Soon he was pulled into the helicopter; the door closed, and he could feel the chill of the air-conditioner. It had been a good day.

Chris could see the sharks moving quickly across the reef. He grabbed Natalie and pointed. They went deeper and watched the slaughter from below. Sliding under the obelisk, they cringed every time a hammerhead took a lunge toward a diver. Sometimes it was a miss, but most of the time it was the trail of red in the water that told them of the hit. The attack lingered into ten minutes, then fifteen. Then Natalie pointed up.

Through the crystal clear water they could see the red and white Jet Ranger hovering over the obelisk. Frantically looking around, they noticed the sharks were concentrated in the middle of the reef about a hundred feet away. It was now or never.

Quickly they began to ascend. Careful not to explode their brains from a small bubble, they knew that death by shark was a greater and more likely risk. As they broke the surface, they could see Jennifer in her dive suit waving them aboard. The landing strut of the helicopter was just barely touching the water.

"Lose the gear," Chris shouted.

Natalie pulled the emergency release and slid out of the buoyancy compensator and tank. It fell free to the top of the reef. She yanked hard at the quick release of the weight belt and dropped it, too. Chris pushed her from behind as she climbed into the open side door of the helicopter. Once she was in, she turned to reach for Chris.

"Throw me the lens!" he yelled.

"Chris! The sharks!" Natalie replied.

"No, I'm not going without the pictures. Throw me the lens."

Natalie leaned forward and took the lens from Jennifer. Taking aim, she tossed it to him. He caught it in his outstretched left hand. With one fast twist he attached the lens, put his regulator back in his mouth and headed back down. Jennifer lifted the helicopter higher into the air to hover. As Chris neared the obelisk, a hammerhead, with blood seeping from his gills, headed straight for him.

Chris quickly ducked under the ancient shrine. The shark kept swimming by, obviously already full of tourist meat. Chris lay flat on his back up against a brain coral formation with the lens only a foot from the side of the pyramidion. He adjusted the light setting and started shooting. Moving around to get the whole structure, he soon ran out of film.

Suddenly he felt something yank at his fin. The shark jerked wildly and pulled the fin off of his foot and swallowed it in one bite. The big hammerhead then charged back toward Chris and bit at his shoulder. Chris wedged himself further under the obelisk and the left eye of the hammerhead pushed up against his face as the teeth scissored away at the brain coral under him. Chris hit the eye with the camera and the shark pulled away for a minute.

Chris peeked out and could see Jennifer bringing the helicopter back down to hover. With the sun directly overhead, it created a perfect shadow. He thought quickly. Then the shark came back in for another attack. Chris retreated under the ancient shrine once again and kicked the side of the shark with his bare foot. What a stupid thing to do, he thought. After a couple attempts at biting, the shark moved on to easier prey, still swimming around the reef.

Chris could see the shadow of the helicopter again. He thought about Heather. He knew that this moment might save her or cause her to die. He had to make his move.

Quickly he unfastened his weight belt and dropped it. He unfastened the B.C. vest and pulled the tank around in front of him like a shield. He wrapped the strap of the Nikonos camera around his wrist; he was ready.

Moving out from under the obelisk, he saw it was clear. He kicked with his only fin toward the surface. He didn't see the hammerhead coming from the other side of the reef behind him. He glanced over his shoulder in time to see the jaw dropping and the rows of teeth being pushed forward to crush his head. He shoved the tank toward the massive hammerhead and it bit down on the valves and regulator hoses. It began to jerk violently right and left. Chris let go and started a free ascent to the surface. It was his only hope to survive. He opened his mouth and blew hard as the rush of bubbles raced from his lungs and expanded with every foot he rose.

The surface was rushing toward him as he suddenly ran out of air. Water flooded into his mouth and throat. Then he felt the air on his face. Throwing his mask back he sucked in all the air he could handle. He coughed violently. The saltwater burned his eyes and nose.

"Grab hold! Chris, grab hold!" Natalie was yelling.

Chris looked back and saw the shark charging toward him. He grabbed the landing strut, and Jennifer pushed forward quickly on the collective causing the helicopter to jump out of the water. The shark lunged forward with mouth open and teeth exposed. Chris yanked his feet out of the water but he wasn't fast enough. Two of the sharks teeth dug into his calf. The helicopter pulled Chris away from the shark but not before a ten-inch gash was raked down the back of his leg.

"Ahg!" Chris yelled.

Natalie screamed and then leaned over and tried to pull Chris in. He was too heavy and he was barely hanging on. Jennifer urgently flew the chopper toward the beach. In a minute she was setting down. Chris fell free to the sand. Once the rotors had slowed down, Natalie jumped out. Jennifer grabbed her medical kit and hurried over to Chris.

"Got the pics, Doc," Chris said.

"Good, let's get you patched up and on our way back to the Sahara," Jennifer said as she opened the red metal box.

Within a few minutes, after an injection of Bupivacaine, four quick stitches, and wrapping the wound with a sterile bandage, they were off. The shiny red and white helicopter rushed westward against the clock.

The hurdles that were left to jump were very high, but these three adventurers had done it before. Develop the film, solve the puzzle, fly to the oasis ahead of the Russians, free Heather, find the treasure, and lastly discover what is the oracle of the Nile. If Jennifer, Chris, and Natalie were Isis, Nephtsis, and Sobek, it would still be a monumental task. Even if they were gods!

16

114 Degrees

———————◯————————

Alexander landed the Cessna 180 on the small commercial airstrip at Luxor. With the specially fitted El Dorado Floats, it could land on the Nile or cruise into a landing strip with the hidden landing gear. Heather stared out the window from the second row passenger seat. Her hands were cramping from the duct tape that was wrapped around her wrists. Her fingertips were blue.

"My fingers are going to break off if you don't loosen this tape," she complained.

Sergei turned around and looked down to where her hands were resting in her lap. Her fingers were indeed blue. He took a small knife out of his pocket and cut the tape, freeing her hands. Heather just stared at him.

"Aren't you going to say thank you or something?" Sergei asked in a mocking tone.

"Eat dirt, scum bag!" Heather said calmly.

"Oh, we have a temper, do we? Maybe I should tape the mouth also?" Sergei said.

Heather just stared back. The wheels touched down

just as a Lear Jet was taxiing to take off. The airport was primarily for private and smaller commercial aircraft.

"Where is this wall with the hieroglyphics about the gold?" Alexander asked as he taxied toward a small hanger.

"It is in the tomb of Seti I. It is just past noon. The shrines and tombs close at 5:00 P.M. We have plenty of time. I brought my camera to take the photos we need. You will stay with the girl in the hangar while I am gone. I will be back in two hours or less," Sergei said. He opened the door of the Cessna as it rolled to a stop. The prop was still spinning. He hurried across the tarmac. Alexander pulled the small H & K pistol from a holster on his waist.

"You are much too pretty to kill. We could get, maybe, $25,000 for you. If the sheik were rich, maybe even $50,000. You would make a good wife and have a dozen babies." He grinned.

"You're sick. Your friend is sick. And when my family catches up with you, you will wish that you had become a victim of the cold war instead of ending up here in Egypt!" Heather replied with venom in her voice.

"We will see who ends up the victim," Alexander said. He pulled back the hammer on the automatic pistol. "Keeping you alive is Sergei's idea. Not mine. Just remember that."

Heather turned and looked out the window. The heat was creeping into the cabin. A trickle of sweat rolled down her back. When she wiggled the toes in her boots, she could feel the sand. She could feel it in her shorts. Her lips were dry and her mouth was parched. It hurt to blink.

"When we step out of the airplane, I will hold your arm until we get inside the hangar. If you try to run, I will kill you instantly. Is that clear?"

"I hear you."

"Now get out slowly as I open the door."

Sergei had found a camel for hire and was well on his way past major shrines to the Valley of the Kings and the tomb of Seti I.

"E. What are you doing here?" R.O. said. He slapped him a high five.

"That's a long story, R.O., Dr. MacGregor, Dr. MacGregor, Professor Carpenter, and you are..."

"I'm Mosegi. I was the guide for the temples at Abydos. I work for the Egyptian Museum in Cairo."

E opened his thobe and reached inside the front pocket of his khaki pants. He retrieved a thin leather billfold and opened it. Under the clear plastic lens was an identification card with his photo I.D. and a small badge.

el Serapis bin Khety Qakare Merenamum
bin Babu al Sadat
Egyptian Secret Service
#664749299
Special Services for the President of Egypt

"We have been tailing the Russians since they came into the country five days ago. They are known assassins suspected of killing the leaders of seven nations, most recently in Chechnya. We lost them when they split up two days ago. We knew Sergei Andropov was aboard the Princess of the Nile. But we couldn't locate Alexander Raikin until he rented an aircraft this morning using an old alias. Bad habits never die. I was late getting to the airport so I have been about two hours behind him all day. I was assigned to the Secretary General when I met you. Tell me what happened. The American CIA lost him as well. These two former KGB agents are very clever."

"KGB!" Mavis said with a surprise. "Oh my. Heather. We've got to find her."

"They have Heather?" E asked.

"Yes. We believe they are going to Luxor. There they will, more or less, read an ancient clue that will tell them where to go next," Jack said.

"Dr. January, Chris, and Natalie went after the same clue," R.O. said.

"They are in Luxor?" E said.

"No, they flew to Ras Mohammed," R.O. said. "The clue is on an obelisk on the bottom of the Red Sea."

"The Red Sea?" E asked.

"Then they are going to fly to the oasis and find the lost treasure of the Pharaohs before the Russians get there," Mosegi said.

"Hold it. Hold it. Hold it. E is a smart detective, but you have me very confused. I want to know where Heather is. Heather is first."

"She is in Luxor by now," Mavis answered.

"Good. I will call my people in Luxor and have them find the Russians and detain them," E replied.

"That's too easy," Mavis said. "Trust me. It won't happen like that."

"We shall see," E said. He pulled out his cell phone. In a few minutes he was talking to another agent in Luxor.

"Andropov and Raiken are there now. Small plane. Yes. They have a girl. Fourteen-year-old blond. American. Name is Heather MacGregor. M...a...c, you know how to spell it. I have to take care of these people first. They look like they need water and shade pretty soon. Yes. Maybe two hours at the earliest. I don't know. Keep this line free. I will call you back. Yes. Good-bye." E closed the small cell phone and dropped it into his baggy pants pocket. It clinked up against a Walter PPK .380 caliber pistol.

"My friend will look for her now. But he is alone and we have reason to believe that the local police inspector cannot be trusted. He is also an officer in the

Army," E said.

"Police, Army…who runs this country?" Jack said in disgust.

E shook his head. "There are many evil forces who want to rule Egypt. My president is working to keep control. Not all Arabs are bad."

"Fly us to Luxor," Mavis said.

"The professor needs water badly. We all need water," Mosegi said.

"Honey, he's right. We've got to get the professor to safety and get some fluids in us. If we get sick now, then we won't be much good to Heather." Jack looked into her blue eyes.

"I know. I'm weary. If she is with these two agents, then maybe she has a chance. Hopefully they are too smart to hurt her," Mavis tried to reason in her mind.

"There is a string of hotels about twenty miles up river. Let me take you there. Then you can try to contact Chris. My agent in Luxor can take a look there. We can get the professor out of the sun and heat."

"OK. Let's do it. Daylight's burning," Jack said.

In less than ten minutes, all five were crammed into the small four-passenger plane. As the aircraft hummed down the road next to the cotton field, E pulled back on the stick and pushed the throttle to maximum. Setting the flaps, he was ready to take off. It was a heavy load. Everyone was hot and tired but they recognized a problem when they saw one. The palm trees, dead ahead, didn't seem to get any shorter. The plane drew closer and closer. The wheels left the ground. E spoke to the plane in Arabic, but you could tell he was pleading for it to fly higher. Finally as they approached the row of palms, the wind lifted the plane just above the top branches and out over the Nile River.

"Whew. That was close," E said.

The comment didn't make anyone very happy. All wondered if the landing was going to be any different.

"Dave."

"Hi, Jennifer. What's up kid?"

"Dave, I need a big favor," Jennifer spoke into her radio headset. "I'm flying in from Bryan's at Ras Mohammed with a camera full of film that I need developed yesterday."

"Sounds like the Dr. January I know. Got a hot mummy on it or something?" Dave laughed on the other end.

"Sort a, kind of…anyway, can you do it?" Jennifer asked.

"Sure, when?"

"Now. I am ten minutes away. I will put the chopper down at the commercial fuel dock on the river two miles south of Asyut. Can you meet me there?"

"You know I can. How's Bryan? Is he ever going to leave that desolate peninsula for civilization?"

"Look who's talking. I wouldn't exactly call Asyut a thriving metropolis. See you in ten minutes." Jennifer turned off the cell phone and the radio hookup.

"Who's Dave?" Natalie asked out of curiosity.

"Dave is a retired Navy Seal from California. Hated the rat race and civilian life in the states. He owns a film laboratory at Asyut where he develops all the half-day service film for the cruise ships going up and down the Nile. He owns a couple of cigarette boats that pick up and deliver the pics for the tourists. Of course, if you develop here, you pay big. He doesn't do it for the money though. I think it's because he is free. He drives an old Chevy truck and goes into Cairo when his band is playing blue grass music at the Longhorn Cafe."

Jennifer saw their raised eyebrows.

"Yup, even Egypt has a Longhorn Cafe!"

"The Nile, dead ahead," Jennifer said.

As the helicopter crossed over the barren waste of the eastern banks, Jennifer circled north and followed the river to the town of Asyut, the home of an ancient cemetery and two tombs belonging to sons of Rameses II. As Jennifer swung again to the northeast, Chris could see the ancient caravan route across the desert toward the el-Kharga Oasis. He thought for a second that this might be the route they would follow to intercept the Russians and Heather. He hoped it would.

"Fuel dock dead ahead," Jennifer said. She brought the Bell Jet Ranger in for a soft landing.

"You two stay with the helicopter. I have a Colt .45 automatic in my medical kit in case anyone messes with the helicopter. Use it if you have to. If someone shows a gun around here, they usually try to use it on you, so be careful."

"I will. Heather's life is at stake," Chris said.

Jennifer stepped out into the heat and felt the wind like a blast furnace on her face. It was hard to blink, and the hot wind made her wheeze briefly. She ran across the dock with the Nikonos camera in her hand. She climbed up the thirty-plus steps to where Dave was waiting and gave him a hug. He was a middle-aged man with gray hair and a neatly-trimmed goatee. He wore a Hawaiian print shirt, tan shorts, and leather slip-on sandals.

"Let's go," Jennifer said. She hopped into his 1965 Chevy pickup.

In about ten minutes they were at the film lab located on the south edge of modern Asyut. Dave and a technician opened the camera and the processing began.

"I'm still thirsty. How's your leg?" Natalie looked down at the blood-soaked bandage on Chris' leg.

"As long as I keep the Bupivacaine injections going, I don't feel a thing. It's very numb," he replied. "I'm thirsty, too."

Natalie opened the ice chest that Bryan had brought them and found several flavors of fruit drinks and

sodas. Sealed in waterproof bags were cheese sandwiches and slices of oranges.

"Bryan's a pretty handy friend to have," Natalie
said as she opened a sandwich and took a bite. "I don't
usually like cheese sandwiches but this one is wonderful."

Chris downed a fruit drink and was halfway through
a second one when he heard doors shut. They looked to
the top of the dock and saw four Army soldiers with
automatic rifles running their way.

"This doesn't look good," Chris said. He jumped
over the collective into the pilot's chair. "Buckle up,
we're leaving."

Without arguing, Natalie leaned back and snapped
the belt on quickly. Before the first soldier had reached
the stairs leading down to the dock, Chris had flipped
all the right switches and the rotor was beginning to
spin.

"Hurry! They're running!" Natalie shouted.

As if he had done it a hundred times, Chris pressed
both feet into the pedals to control the rear rotor. He
increased the speed of the rotors with the throttle and,
when the dials told him the rotational speed was correct, he pushed on the collective. The helicopter jumped
into the air and went straight up. Chris calmly pushed
the cyclic forward and the chopper moved over the river
quickly, leaving the soldiers behind. Either frustrated or
surprised, they pointed their rifles but didn't fire them.

"Chris," Natalie said. He couldn't hear her. She
pulled her headset on. She leaned forward and put a
headset on Chris.

"Chris."

"What?" he said quickly.

His knuckles were white and his breathing was fast.

"Do you know how to fly this thing?" Natalie said
with her fingers crossed.

"Yes. I think. I've watched pilots hundreds of times

since I was ten. I paid attention to every detail."

Suddenly the helicopter started moving sideways.

"Chris!" Natalie screamed.

"Calm down. I just have to adjust the pedals. There, we're straight again. Start looking for the blue Chevy pickup. We've got to find Jennifer." Chris was trying to remain calm.

He felt something warm on his foot and then his foot went numb. He looked down and noticed a pool of blood on the Plexiglas window below him. He had broken open the shark bite when he jumped into the seat.

"There it is. On the asphalt street. The main road. Do you see it?" Natalie said through her headset.

"Yes. Look. She is going out to the truck."

Jennifer January looked up when she heard the Bell Jet Ranger.

"Oh my gosh!" Her mouth hung open as she saw Chris whiz by just above tree top level.

"Where can he land around here?" she yelled at Dave.

"Get in. They can follow us,"

Dave fired up the 1965 Chevy with dual chrome mufflers and revved the engine. It sounded like a hot rod. Shoving it into first, he left rubber coming out of the parking lot onto the main road.

"They're on the road. There, Chris." Natalie pointed at the pickup.

"I've got'em. Come on, Jennifer, find a place where I can set this down."

His right foot was totally numb now and the chopper started flying sideways again.

"Chris, straighten it out," Natalie shouted.

"I'm trying. My foot is numb."

Natalie looked over his shoulder and saw the pool of blood. She put her hands over her mouth.

"Hurry, Dave. I've got a bad feeling about this,"

Jennifer said over the road noise and the rush of the hot wind through the window.

"Here's a spot," Dave said. He pulled down a road between two barren fields.

The Jet Ranger whirred overhead as Chris pulled back on the collective and backed off on the throttle. The chopper spun around a couple of times before he got it under control. It was leaning too far forward. The rotor nearly clipped the ground. Leveling it out, he finally set in on the hard ground with a bounce.

"Thank God," Natalie whispered.

Jennifer hugged Dave.

"I owe you big time, Dave!" she yelled as she sprinted toward the chopper.

"Anytime, Darlin!" he yelled back.

Kicking the sand off of her beach sandals, Jennifer opened the door and helped Chris get out. He crawled into the back. She saw the blood-soaked bandages and the pool of blood on the Plexiglas bottom window.

"I'll find out what happened later. Natalie. New dressing. Rub the antibiotic salve into it first. We've got to get out of here."

Jennifer quickly got the rotors going back to full speed and waved to Dave as she lifted off. Dave hopped into his truck and drove back onto the main road into traffic just as the three police jeeps pulled into the field and watched Jennifer disappear into the distance.

"Man. That was close. How's the patient?" Jennifer said.

"He'll live."

Jennifer's cell phone rang.

"Mavis. Where are you?" Jennifer said.

Mavis MacGregor was standing in the kiddie pool of the King's Inn near Abydos. She was fully clothed. When she had walked into the lobby, where Jack and Mosegi had retrieved a bottle of water for Professor Carpenter, she spotted the pool. Without taking off her boots or clothes, she just stepped in and sat down. A pool of brown silt formed around her from the dirt and sand in her clothes and two little girls quickly evacuated the pool. A mother chastised Mavis for dirtying up the children's area. Mavis just smiled at her. She leaned back and dunked her long auburn hair in the water. The sand still stuck to her scalp.

"I'm in a kiddie pool. I borrowed a cell phone and I found your card. The one you gave us the night R.O. was stung by the scorpion."

"Five days ago," Jennifer said.

"Just five days ago. You're right."

"We have the photos and now that I know where you are, I am on my way to pick you up. How is the professor?"

"He's very tired but he can still read the clues for us. By the way, they tried to take us out to the desert to die. But we were rescued by the Egyptian Secret Service."

"Mavis, this is getting way too complicated, even for me," Jennifer said.

"How far away are you?" Mavis asked as she lowered to shoulder level in the pool.

"ETA is thirty-eight minutes. Be ready to head to the desert. My guess is that the Russians are just now leaving Luxor, and we have a two hundred-mile advantage. That would put us at the oasis about forty-five minutes ahead of them if they are in light aircraft."

"I hope you are right, dear," Mavis said. "Are Chris and Natalie all right?"

"They're great," Jennifer said and wished she could cross her fingers for the little exaggeration she just told. No need for Mavis to worry any more than she already was worrying.

"Hang on. Be there before you know it." Jennifer switched off.

Mavis leaned over and handed the cell phone back to the pool manager and thanked him with an American twenty dollar bill she dug from her pocket. The young man took the already wet money and dipped it into the pool to get the dirt and mud off of it. He then dried it on his pants leg and smiled.

"Wet or dry. It will still spend," he said.

Jack and R.O. walked out and found Mavis. R.O. dumped his techno-spider on the side of the pool and performed a cannonball next to his mother.

"OK. Thank you, Ryan," she said without chastising him.

He walked through the shallow water and sat next to his mother.

"Well, Mom. Here we are. Looking for Heather again. At least Chris is OK. And I am sure that Heather is OK, too. Africa made her tough!"

As Alexander Raiken looked across the hangar and then out toward the plane, Heather knew it was now or never. Lunging forward she grabbed the gun in her hand and bit down hard on Alexander's hand. He wouldn't let go of the gun. He screamed and yelled at her. She bit harder. He tried to hit her with his free hand, but he knew if he let go she would have the gun.

Suddenly Heather swung sideways and kicked him twice in the back of the knee. They both fell to the ground and her blond sandy hair fell in his face spilling fine grains of sand into his eyes.

"Ah, you little witch!" he yelled.

Hanging on to his gun hand, she shoved a knee into his gut and bit his arm as hard as she could. She caught her lip in the bite and felt the sting. The warm blood dripped on her chin. They rolled again and this time Heather made it to her feet. Her strong swimmer's arms and shoulders were paying off. Alexander Raikin looked up. He yelled at her in Russian. She stepped forward and kicked him in the jaw. His head jerked back and he let go of the gun. He was out cold.

Not believing what she had just done, she stepped back and looked around. "Oh my gosh," she said.

She shook her stinging hands and wiped the blood off of her chin. It was a pretty wide cut. Then she took off in a run. She made it just to the hangar door when she saw Sergei approaching. She turned and sprinted back toward Alexander, who began to moan. He raised his head and reached for the gun. Heather kicked him in the back of the head and kept running by. He was out again. She sprinted as hard as she could until she reached the other side of the hangar.

The door was open only eighteen inches, but she lunged with all of her strength and dove for the opening. As she slid through, the metal edge caught the back of her shirt and tore it from the collar to her belt. She felt the pain on her back as the metal dug into her flesh. The flap on her right rear pocket caught and was ripped off. But she was on the other side.

Without stopping, she ran toward the main terminal. The hot wind buffeted her face. She didn't notice the wound on her lip was now bleeding freely. Blood was running down the front of her shirt. Her legs muscles ached from the climbing at Abydos, but she didn't care. She knew her life depended on her endurance and resolve to escape. She swung her arms like a sprinter and with each long step chanted to herself, "Pull, Pull, Pull," as her swim coach used to yell at her. "Pull," she said it again.

Heather heard a pop and a whiz and knew that Sergei was shooting at her. She took a fast step sideways, like a soccer drill and then back. A bullet creased the tarmac at her feet. She ran faster, stepping right and then left. She heard the motor of a car and didn't look back. She was afraid of what she might see. She pulled her arms harder and heard another pop and a ricochet. Suddenly an arm was around her.

"No! No!" Heather yelled and flailed at her pursuer.

Then two more arms grabbed her and pulled her up and into the bed of the little Toyota truck. She fell on her back and looked up in terror. She started kicking and hitting.

"No! Kill me now!" she screamed.

"Heather. We aren't going to kill you,"

"No!" she swung hard with her fists and connected on the cheek of one of the men and knocked him back. She felt the pain in her hand.

Suddenly she felt a body fall over her and she could smell someone's breath in her face. She couldn't move anymore. Her energy was drained from her.

"Heather. We are your friends. Jack and Mavis sent us," the man said calmly.

She looked up and focused on the face of the young Arab lying across her. She began to cry. He pulled away from her as the truck entered the main road and mingled into traffic. The heat of the afternoon was immense and dried her tears as they left her powder blue eyes. Her cheeks felt like clay from the mingling of the sand and the tears.

"We are friends of the one you call E. We are Egyptian Secret Service. We came to rescue you."

Heather leaned forward and put her arms around his neck. Blood from her mouth and face soaked into his white shirt.

"Thank you," she said between sobs. "Thank you."

E sprinted through the open air lobby of the hotel out to the pool area where Mavis, R.O., and now Jack were sitting fully clothed in the kiddie pool. He looked up as he saw Dr. Jennifer January hovering above them in the spirited red and white Bell Jet Ranger. Old Professor Carpenter hobbled out to the pool and stepped in up to his waist.

"Great news. My people in Luxor have rescued Heather. She is safe!" E exclaimed.

Pandemonium broke out among the MacGregors. Mavis started crying. Tears welled up in Jack's eyes. R.O. performed another cannonball, this time drenching two fully dressed tourists.

"Oh, Jack." Mavis kissed him.

"I know. How we get into these messes is beyond me. But we do."

"May I interrupt this joyous moment for an observation," the old professor said as he poured muddy water out of his shoes into the now murky pool.

"Praises be, your daughter is safe. By all estimates, the youngsters above us have the photo we need to solve the puzzle of the Oracle of the Nile and the lost treasure of the Pharaohs. Now, do you really want those Russians to find all of that after what they have done to you...and me?" The old professor gave them a sly look and then put his shoe back on.

Mavis looked up at Chris, Jennifer, and Natalie hovering over the pool about two hundred feet high. She looked at Jack and then at R.O.

"It's time to get back in their face. I say we go after it. The professor's right," Mavis said as she gritted the sand between her teeth.

"If that's what you want. But if it gets dicey, we back off. Deal?" Jack bargained.

"Deal."

E spoke into his cell phone to Jennifer in the helicopter.

"That's a roger. We'll set down in the parking lot. Call a fuel truck from the dock to bring me some juice, will ya? We've got a long ride into the Sahara and I don't want to walk!"

17

Sign of the Falcon

It was a near euphoric mood in the passenger cabin of the helicopter. But the fatigue lines on the face of Dr. Jennifer January were running very deep. Still clad in her pink beach shorts, white tank top, and turquoise beach sandals, she had on her favorite pair of sunglasses. Her hair was tied up in a knot on the top of her head, and gold earrings dangled from her earlobes.

Chris sat in the back with his leg up. Mavis had already inspected the wound and pronounced that twelve stitches would have to be taken and Chris was lucky to even have a leg. R.O. said he wanted the scar but could do without the shark bite. He even asked Chris if he could take a picture of it on his new digital camera so he could email pictures to his friend Drew Nevius back home in Texas.

The professor was not to be left behind. Having taken a fully-clothed bath in the kiddie pool, he was refreshed and said that even if he died today, it would still be the happiest day of his career. He was busy studying the underwater photos of the pyramidion and trying to decipher the hieroglyphics. Jack was listening.

"It appears to me that the mysterious Oracle of the Nile was in the possession of Rameses I, the father of Seti I. Seti," he said, looking at Jack, "Seti I was considered to be a bright young man with great vision. He had plans to build magnificent cities out of the desert on the banks of the Nile. It was this inspiration that he passed on to his son Rameses II, who actually did what Seti had set out to do. That was a tongue twister, Doctor," the old professor said and smiled.

"It is my belief that this mysterious box was passed down from Pharaoh to Pharaoh until Apries had it. Then Mayor Khensu Eyuf came and took it away from him. Here is the missing piece of the puzzle." He pointed to the photograph of the obelisk.

"This is the sign of the ka, the winged spirit flying from the Pharaoh's body. The ka is going to the afterlife to be united with the Pharaoh. See this spot here," the professor said. Natalie leaned over next to Jack and looked.

"The power of heat and light belongs to Ra. As Anubis devours the unfaithful, only the faithful will receive a blessing. It appears that this statement was not only an oracle but the power of the mysterious box. The source—whatever it is—had this power.

"Wait, the words mean vision. The Nile beetle is in the wrong place. That's the key. When the Nile beetle follows the sign of Ra rather than precedes it, it changes the meaning. Why didn't I see this before?" the professor asked himself.

Jennifer had been listening over the headset.

"Bingo, Professor. I think you have it," she said. She rubbed her right thigh, which was aching. "Natalie, look in the medical kit and hand me a Tylenol™. There should be a whole bottle of it there."

Natalie rummaged through the kit, noticing the Colt .45 automatic pistol and moved it to get to the bottle of Tylenol. She opened the bottle and took out a capsule and handed it to Jennifer. The helicopter buzzed along with a tailwind at 120 mph at a 500-foot altitude. To the passengers it seemed like they were right on top of the dunes. The rising heat from the sand combined with the air. It expanded quickly and was buffeting the aircraft.

"Look, Mom, two camels," R.O. said and pointed below. "They look like the one we rode the other day, Bedouin camels."

The heat on the inside of the helicopter began to build up until it was nearly eighty-five degrees. Everyone was perspiring, their shirts soaked through. Mavis passed around the last of Bryan's water bottles. Old Professor Carpenter kept looking at the photos over and over again and mumbling to himself.

He stroked his white beard and repeated, "I can't believe I didn't see that before. And to think it was the falcon at Seti's shrine that was the key to all of this. Those Egyptian priests and scribes were clever. They knew, young man," he looked at R.O., "that the best place to hide something was in plain view."

Alexander and Sergei were cruising at fifteen hundred feet when Sergei spoke out.

"There it is. Bahariya Oasis. The city is on the east. What we are looking for is the archaeological dig on the northwest."

"Right, comrade." Alexander banked the plane to the west and leveled at five hundred feet.

After circling the northwest quadrant of the oasis, Sergei became frustrated.

"I do not see it."

"Let's make a wider arc," Alexander replied and banked further to the west. The Cessna droned along riding on the rising heat much better than Dr. January's Jet Ranger.

"Look, past those dunes. Due west. The camp!" Sergei pointed down.

"I see it. Now we must find a place to land."

"There will be a road. There is always a road," Sergei replied.

Alexander found the road that connected the dig to the main village and oasis. It was straight as an arrow for about a quarter mile, all the distance he needed.

"How far from Bahariya?" Jack asked Jennifer through the headset intercom.

"ETA is twenty minutes," she replied.

"Good, this heat is getting unbearable," Mavis said. She tied a scarf around her forehead to keep her hair out of her face.

"It is nearly four o'clock. We still have two hours of heat before the desert gets relief from the sun," Chris said as he stepped back up front next to Jennifer.

"How's the leg?" Jennifer asked.

"Natalie and Mom put three butterfly bandages on it to hold the wound together. Then they redressed it with the antibiotic salve. It's getting pretty sore though," he said and looked down through the plexiglass window below his feet.

"I want to hold back on the painkillers for awhile," Jennifer said.

"That's OK. I can deal with it," Chris replied.

The helicopter approached the massive village and oasis from the south but veered directly toward the archaeological dig in the desert. Jennifer had been working there for over a year and living in a house in Bahariya.

Like other desert oasis towns, Bahariya was very quaint with the lake and underground stream as the focal point of the community. There was a small inn, a school, and a mosque. A store much like an old frontier trading post was next to the police and fire station, both very primitive. The roads were dirt and sand, the streets were dirt, the yards were dirt. The only thing green were the trees near the small three-acre lake. Not much had changed in twenty-five hundred years since Mayor Khensu Eyuf ruled like a king. But his royal palace and tombs were a mile away into the Sahara.

"Look," Jennifer said. "The dig."

Everyone looked out the left side of the aircraft at the vast complex that had been dug out of the desert. The massive pylons of the temple were standing tall, connected to the four-foot thick wall that quickly disappeared into the dunes on both sides.

"Dad. Look at this," R.O. said.

"Wait until you see inside. You will think you were back at Abydos inside Seti's shrine and mock tomb site," Jennifer replied. "Funny, I don't see any jeeps or trucks. Maybe everyone went into the oasis to beat the heat," she murmured to herself.

She lowered the helicopter to within fifty feet of the front two pylons, the massive front walls of Eyuf's palace. The red and white sleek aircraft looked like a giant winged god that adorned one of the great temple reliefs along the Nile.

When the rotor had stopped turning, everyone stepped into the Sahara. The hot air felt like heat from an oven on their faces. Their wet shirts immediately dried and their eyes burned. It still hurt to blink. A wind gust sent sand into their mouths and noses, the substance they had been living in for twelve hours.

"We live in a time warp," Mavis said. "Jack, can you believe this place? Right out here in the middle of nowhere."

"No, Madam," old Professor Carpenter said. "'Nowhere' is where you go when Anubis says you have lived a life of truth." He smiled.

"That's right. I'm learning," Mavis said. She watched R.O. run up to the gateway that opened next to the left pylon. He disappeared behind the wall.

"Ryan O'Keef MacGregor. You are going to be the death of me yet," she said with disgust. "We can barely walk and here he is running in 110-degree heat."

"One hundred and fourteen degrees," Jennifer said as she looked at the thermostat on the outside of the helicopter. "Had to install that so I would know when the hoses might blow. We better let this baby have a rest for a few hours. We have everything we need until dark. When it cools off, we'll fly back to Cairo."

"Now, show me the wall of the palace where the puzzle fits together, Doctor," Professor Carpenter said. He started walking toward the palace. He wobbled and weaved a bit. Mavis caught up with him and grabbed his arm.

"I'm fine, young lady, but I will let any beautiful woman provide an escort." They both smiled.

Jack fell back to walk with Chris and Natalie. Chris was limping a little but other than that seemed to do quite well. In five minutes they were all standing inside the main courtyard behind the first massive pylon. The red, yellow, and purple of the hieroglyphics were magnificent. The dry climate had protected them for nearly twenty-five centuries.

"These are absolutely breathtaking," Natalie said. She walked over and touched the wall of color and stone.

"Where's R.O.?" Jack said.

"Looks like his tracks lead inside the palace," Chris replied. He followed the tracks through the heavy sand.

"We can bring a bulldozer out here and shove this aside and then one week later, it's back. I believe sand is really a life form," Jennifer said as she followed along behind Chris. The old professor was right behind them, keeping stride. His excitement was at the highest level. You would have thought he was forty instead of eighty years old.

"R.O.!" Chris yelled as he walked up the stone and marble steps.

"Where did the marble come from?" Natalie asked,

aware it was not a natural stone for this part of Africa.

"We believe that Mayor Khensu Eyuf imported it from Greece or Rome. We could never figure out how he became so wealthy. Now we may have the answer to that. He was history's greatest thief!" Jennifer said. She leaned over and brushed the sand away, revealing a beautiful marble and stone mosaic on the floor.

"R.O.!" Chris shouted as everyone else entered the palace. The afternoon sun shone through the massive door opening.

"We have a tool closet over here with flashlights. I'll get them," Jennifer said. She walked across the giant room. In a few minutes she returned with four large flashlights in black metal casings. "The wall where I saw the falcon is in the next room."

"R.O." Chris yelled again.

"I'm right here," he said as he walked in from the next room.

Mavis walked over to him and explained some new rules about staying together.

"OK. Mom. I'm getting hungry."

"Dinner will be late, so adjust!" she said firmly.

Mavis, Jack, Chris, Natalie, Jennifer, and the professor entered the next room.

"Why is there black on the walls?" Jack asked.

"We believe there was a fire. Some hieroglyphs we discovered at the Farafra Oasis told of a great battle between the Pharaoh Apries and Mayor Eyuf. If you read the account on Apries's tomb, you would believe he won. If you read the account on Eyuf's tomb, you would think he won," Jennifer said.

"I think that our maverick mayor won," Professor Carpenter said and smiled.

"We'll soon see," Jack added.

"The wall is over here," Jennifer said.

She held her light up high and pointed it toward the wall, which ended in a pile of sand.

"This is a doorway and we have no clue what is behind it or under the sand. Just haven't gotten that far yet. This is it."

She shined the light on the wall that was covered ceiling to floor with hieroglyphics, paintings, and several cartouche. They all were awestruck at the same time.

"I still can't believe I didn't see it before. It is the cartouche of Senswosret III. It reads 'Re lives forever'. See the sign of Ra, the eye, then the Nile beetle preceding the sign of ka, the up-stretched arms. It is enclosed with the oval that signifies a royal seal or cartouche. But if you read the signs just before the cartouche, you can see clearly that the cartouche is totally out of place."

The professor held up the enlarged photograph of the pyramidion of the obelisk at Ras Mohammad.

"In context it reads, 'the god of the sky, the falcon, becomes one with Amun Re and with his great power rules the world and sees the future."

"The oracle, the falcon…it was all right here in front of us all the time," Jennifer said and looked around the room.

"R.O., don't do that," Jack said. Ryan was feeling around the cartouche and touching everything he possibly could. He took his techno-spider out of his pocket and unscrewed the butt of one of the flashlights. The others were talking and didn't see him do it. He then pushed the battery into the battery holder in the back of the spider and the eight red eyes lit up. The legs started moving but this time in synchronous motion.

"I just needed a more powerful battery," R.O. said to himself.

He then placed the spider, with it claw-like feet, on the wall of hieroglyphs and let go. It began crawling up the wall.

"Ryan O'Keef MacGregor! Just what are you doing?" Mavis said as she walked over to him.

"Mom, look at it climb. It just needed a stronger power source. I had it wired correctly all along."

Pretty soon everyone was entertained by watching the electronic spider glide across the surface of the ancient stone wall while almost slipping and crashing to its death several times. Finally it reached the edge and stopped. Its legs turned and turned but it wouldn't go anywhere.

"I think your spider is stuck," Chris said softly. "Here, hop up on my shoulders and get it."

Jack lifted R.O. up and he stood on Chris' shoulders. Chris shifted his weight to his good leg. R.O. reached up and grabbed the spider. As he pulled the wedged arachnid from the wall, sand trickled from the corner and created a small pile on the floor. Some of it fell into Jennifer's face.

"That's great. I just can't get enough of the Sahara anymore. She stepped back and poured some water in her eyes from the water bottle she had carried along.

"Wait. How did sand get that high?"

"My question precisely, young lady," Professor Carpenter said. He walked toward the corner.

"Anyone have a knife?" Jennifer asked.

All the MacGregors reached into their pockets, Jack was the first to produce one and handed it to Jennifer. She took the shiny blade and pushed it into the corner. Then she dragged it down about a foot as it inserted slowly.

"There is a seam that runs from ceiling to floor."

Everyone could hear the metal scraping against the stone walls as sand began to seep through. She turned and pulled the knife out of the seam. Stepping to her right a couple of feet, she felt around the stone that had the cartouche carved on it. She pushed the knife into the seam and the soft sand gave way instantly. Pushing harder she worked some sand out of one side. Chris quickly produced his knife and pushed on the other side. Within minutes they had the block completely outlined.

"It worked once in Seti's. It might work again. Let's push," she said and looked around.

Immediately six hands were on the block and everyone was shoulder to shoulder.

"Three, two, one, now," she said and the bodies leaned into the wall. The stone gave about an inch.

"Again, three, two, one, now," everyone grunted and moaned and the stone moved another inch and stopped.

Suddenly the wall began to move on its center axis as a carousel spins around.

"It's moving! Get back! Get back," Jack yelled.

Everyone jumped back quickly with R.O. tripping over the pile of sand and landing on his back. When it had moved about five feet, it ground to a halt as the stone dug into the pile of sand.

"Incredible," Mavis said.

"Well, we found a door. Let's go in," the professor said. "Someone might be at home."

Old Professor Carpenter held his flashlight in front of him and slipped through the two-foot opening. Others followed one by one with Jack entering last. The next room was very small and sand covered the floor about two feet deep. There was an arched doorway across the ten-foot room. No one said a word as Jennifer stepped by the professor and walked through the doorway.

"Cut through solid stone," Jack said once inside the hallway.

"Watch your step. We're going down at a steep angle," Jennifer said and led onward.

"Ryan, you will walk by me," Mavis said in a tone that meant business.

"Roger, Captain," R.O. grinned and saluted.

The winding stairway went on for quite some time.

"It is getting cooler down here. How far are we

below the surface?" Natalie said to Chris.

"Maybe two hundred, three hundred feet. I can't tell. I like the temperature though. Must be seventy-five degrees down here," Chris replied.

"Seventy-one exactly," Jack said looking at his watch.

Having reached the last step, they were now in a narrow rock tunnel. Old Professor Carpenter was still leading the way. Everyone followed feeling refreshed with the cool moist air of the subterranean passageway.

"Jack, I can't believe I am doing this again," Mavis said.

"It'll be OK, babe. Trust me," Jack replied.

Mavis turned and gave him a cold stare.

As they walked through the tunnel, they began to hear a rushing noise. It got louder and louder the further down they went.

"Ah, curly hair once again," Mavis said as she ran her hands through her sand-matted hair. "What I wouldn't do for a shampoo right now."

"Me, too," Natalie said.

The roar was getting to the point of being deafening when they emerged from the tunnel to a ledge overlooking an underground river in a large cavern. They stood in awe looking down on the rushing water before them. Their flashlights lit up the giant cavern and revealed a swiftly moving river rushing out of the stone face of the rock and traveling two hundred feet before disappearing into an underground tunnel.

"Obviously this is the source of the oasis," the professor said and rubbed his bearded chin. "Maybe for the entire eastern Sahara. A great discovery by itself. But, alas a dead end for us."

"Not yet, Professor," Chris said. He pointed to a small opening in the wall of the cave to their right. "Let's see where that goes," he said and limped into the opening and disappeared.

Jack was right behind him. "Y'all stay here."

Jack caught up to Chris inside another tunnel. They reached another stairway going down. Carefully following the steps down, they reached the bottom. They shined their lights across the tunnel. Water was standing about a foot deep. The noise was deafening.

"We must be under the river," yelled Jack.

"I think you're right," Chris shouted back about a foot from Jack's face. "The cold water makes my leg feel better."

Jack stepped around him and found a set of steps going upward. He began climbing. Chris followed. They reached the top of the steps and were now on the other side of the cave. As they emerged from the tunnel, they could see the others still waiting with their flashlights pointing in all directions. Jennifer saw them and waved her light side-to-side. Chris responded by doing the same.

"They found a way across. Let's go," Jennifer said. "Are you up to it, Professor?"

"Wouldn't miss it for the world," he replied.

Within minutes they were down the steps and wading through the icy cold water.

"Man, is this cold!" R.O. said.

"It feels wonderful," Natalie replied.

Jennifer held onto the professor as they began the climb up the wet steps. They were all soaking wet for the fourth time that day. But this time they weren't hot.

"There is another opening up here," Jack shouted over the rushing noise of the river.

"Look, there," the professor shown his flashlight on the wall of the cave. "It is the sign of the sky god, the falcon. And next to it, the cartouche of Senswosret III, which we now know was just a trick. That sly Mayor Eyuf. No wonder he thought he should be Pharaoh."

They walked toward the opening and stepped through.

18

Oracle of the Nile

"It appears this has been under water several times. There are watermarks all the way to the top of the cave," Mavis observed with her professional scientific eye.

"I concur," Professor Carpenter said. "I noticed in the tunnel below the river how the formation had been displaced and flooded, probably several times. I would conjecture that through the centuries the availability of upstream water would dictate that this cave would flood periodically. Earthquakes could be a cause as the sand shifts on the surface."

"Are we going in or not?" R.O. asked impatiently.

"Let's go," Chris said as he peered into darkness.

He shown his light straight ahead and squeezed through the passageway. At one time it had been a square cut door. On the inside he found a small room with plaster walls. Faint patterns of ancient Egyptian paintings were everywhere. But gone were the bold colors and shapes that were evident in the palace above. By the time everyone had crowded into the room, they were literally shoulder to shoulder. R.O. was ready to venture into the next one, but Mavis had him by the neck of his T-shirt.

"This reminds me too much of earlier today, minus the heat and sand," Natalie said as she wrung some of the water from her dirty auburn hair.

"Me, too, dear," Mavis agreed.

"R.O. managed to wriggle free. He stepped backwards and tripped on Chris's foot. As he fell, his backpack rubbed against the wall.

"Sorry, Chris. I didn't get your shark bite, did I? I don't want to mess it up until I get a good picture to send back home," R.O. said with concern in his voice.

"Thanks for the warm feelings, little brother," Chris said. He noticed the wall where R.O. had fallen. "Move over a bit," Chris said.

He directed his flashlight on the wall and knelt down. He reached out and touched it.

"Look everybody," he said.

The professor and Jennifer were there first. Both were rubbing the wall. Then Jennifer took out a pocket knife and scraped it. She looked at the professor.

"Pure gold. The walls are lined with gold," she said.

Mavis gasped. Everyone had goose bumps on their arms and necks.

"We must proceed." The professor stood up. He looked like he had just taken a ten-hour nap and was ready to run a race.

Jennifer led the way into the other rooms, which were empty except for an old stone that was rather plain by Egyptian standards.

"I think we have found all we are going to find," the old professor said.

"Not so fast," Jack said. "Look straight up."

Everyone looked to where he was shining his flashlight. There was a hole in the ceiling about three feet across. The shadows and the remains of darkly painted hieroglyphics had hidden it from them.

"OK, R.O. It's time to do your thing again," Jack said with complete confidence.

He reached over and, with Chris on the other arm, lifted R.O. straight up. R.O. grabbed the rock ledge and pulled himself higher. Finally he was standing up in the hole about waist high. R.O. felt around in his deep cargo pocket and pulled out his lighter. He pressed down on the thumb trigger and nothing happened. He tried it three more times before he gave up and tucked it back into his pocket. Next he pulled out his Swiss Army knife and pressed down on the insignia on the side of the knife. The red L.E.D. light came on. It was just enough light to illuminate a couple of feet around him.

"I think there is another room up here. It's worth checking out. Throw me a big flashlight," R.O. said and put the knife back into his pocket. He was now balanced on the outstretched arms of Chris and Jack.

"Sure, Son, coming right up," Jack said and nodded to Mavis.

Mavis took her best aim and threw the flashlight through the hole up to Ryan.

"Got it. Thanks, Dad," he replied.

"You're welcome, Son." Beads of sweat were beginning to pop onto his forehead.

R.O. laid the flashlight down and hoisted himself up through the hole. Everyone looked at each other. They had been through this once before today. But now, they were too weary to even discuss it. Fighting back fatigue, muscle cramps and hunger, the weary adventurers waited patiently while their little mole searched out the room above them. Jack looked at his Rolex Explorer watch. Only three minutes had passed. It had seemed more like ten.

"Dad, catch," R.O. hollered from above.

Not knowing what was coming down from the hole, everyone stepped back. Suddenly a long pole began a descent through the hole. Chris and Jack reached out and nabbed it in midair before it reached the ground. They both held on tightly for a moment. A normal reaction. Then Chris let go and Jack handed it to the professor.

The old professor held it close to his face for his old eyes to investigate. Jennifer shined her light on the pole. She was already smiling.

"My, my. I am holding in my hands a walking stick that is from the New Kingdom. There are three cartouche on it, so it must have been passed down from father to son to son. Ah yes, Rameses I, Seti I, Rameses II."

The professor didn't speak another word. A lump formed in his throat and his eyes began to water.

"It is all so plain now. Why didn't I see it earlier?" he said again and handed the cane to Jennifer. "If I am not mistaken, this is pure gold inlaid around ivory. This Pharaoh's cane is worth at least one million dollars on the open market. Much much more than the gold plaster we found in the room."

"R.O.!" Jack hollered.

"What, Dad?" R.O. hollered back.

"Is there anymore of this up there?"

"I counted just two rooms and another stairway going up, Dad. And they are all full of this old stuff," R.O. yelled back down.

"I'm going up," Jennifer said excitedly.

Soon they were all lining up to go. Jennifer went first, then Chris and Jack pushed the professor up as Jennifer pulled. He hadn't fallen apart yet, but they worried every time they tugged on him. Then it was Natalie, Mavis, and Chris. Chris leaned back through the hole and caught Jack's hand when Jack took a running jump. Then Mavis and Jennifer helped pull him up.

The first room was large but not gigantic like Seti's hidden room. Everyone scattered out into the two rooms. They were filled with wooden furniture and carvings. But no gold or ceremonial objects of Egyptian religion.

"Well, looks like we have a short climb left," the professor said.

"Professor, how do you do it? I'm exhausted," Mavis said.

"Well, I don't know. If I had known I was going to live this long, I probably would have eaten better."

They were all in the tunnel and climbing up the stairs when Jennifer suddenly stopped. Jack and Chris moved up next to her.

"Looks like the earthquake shook up the staircase a little," Jack observed.

"Yes, but if we are careful we can step on the rubble and make it. It's only ten feet to that doorway," Jennifer replied.

"What's this?" Chris said and knelt down. He directed the beam of his flashlight on a shiny object and picked it up. "A bracelet."

Jennifer took it and read the inscription that was written in the ancient Egyptian language.

"For Ona, a daughter of Isis, and the beauty of the desert."

"How sweet," Mavis said and took the delicate gold bracelet. "Somebody got upset when they lost this. I assure you I would."

"I don't know, Mom. Not if they were trying to escape the earthquake that caused this mess," Chris said.

"Professor, do you feel up to one last challenge?" Jennifer said.

"Well. If I make it, then I will have fulfilled a lifetime of discovery. If I don't make it, then I won't know about it. So let's go."

Carefully walking over the rubble that had settled evenly over three thousand years, they were all safely across and standing in another room in this lost and forgotten underground palace.

"Mom, I thought I heard something back there," R.O. said as he sided up to Mavis and pointed his light in her face.

"Ryan. Take the light out of my face, please. And no, you didn't hear anything," she said firmly. Fatigue and hunger was beginning to wear on everyone.

But what they were about to see would leave them all numb and devoid of feeling for a brief moment. Oohs and aahs could be heard by everyone as the riches of the cache belonging to Mayor Khensu Eyuf was illumined with each flashlight. As the light would hit the gold, the rays would sparkle across the room in a light show. With six flashlights, it looked like a laser show on New Year's Eve.

"Everyone, gather round please," the old professor said calmly.

Within a minute the adventurers were all gathered around him. Their eyes were as wide as saucers. R.O. had a funeral necklace around his neck that covered his whole chest. It was laced with a mosaic of rare stones, gold, turquoise, and obsidian. He was also holding a battle spear in his right hand.

"What we have here is the biggest collection of royal funeral treasure in the entire world. Universities and art museums around the world, all together, do not have what is in these three rooms and what we found below. It seems that our beloved Mayor Eyuf was quite a bandit. Be careful not to touch anything. The humidity is pretty high in here, and I noticed some of the fabrics were molding and the furniture was brittle. Of course, the gold is unharmed."

Everyone laughed.

"And we are glad it is unharmed," Sergei said as he stepped into the room.

"Oh my gosh," Mavis said.

"In your enthusiasm, you missed our airplane neatly camouflaged outside the west wall. Then we simply followed you to the palace and watched you figure out the puzzle. Quite clever. We wouldn't have been able to do it. Quite impressive, too," Sergei said as he shifted the gun to his other hand. Alexander held the light. He had a white bandage around his head and a bloody spot on the side.

"Bet Heather gave him the headache," R.O. said.

"Yes, but of course she did. Feisty young daughter you have there. She would have fetched $50,000 on the white slave market," Alexander said.

"Animals. Both of you are animals," Mavis said.

"Now for the treasure. Seems we have hit the jackpot, comrade. We have enough time to secure the gold, fly back to Cairo tonight, rent some trucks, and come back here tomorrow. We should be able to clean out all of the gold in one day, don't you think?" Sergei said.

"Maybe a half day," replied Alexander. "It depends on how many archaeologists we have to kill tomorrow."

"You slime," Jennifer said.

"It's time to say good-bye, MacGregors," Sergei said and took aim at Jack first.

Two loud thuds could be heard as the bullets whizzed through the air from the silenced gun and impacted on the body. Then there were two more thuds.

Sergei and Alexander fell to the floor dead. A voice from the doorway could be heard. Mavis leapt into Jack's arms.

"Oh Jack," Mavis said.

"I just couldn't let that happen," the voice said.

"Nor I," said another.

Kevin Turner stepped into the light with Ziyad by his side.

"I owe it to my brother to be the one who kills the MacGregor family," Turner said.

"You. How did you get here? You were arrested," Chris said firmly.

"A good show, didn't you think. It seems my dear friend here has a cousin who was the police inspector who picked me up. And it is with him I have been collaborating to find you. Funny how our paths crossed.

The Little Shop of Thoth, the Nile River flying episode, then the House of Thutmose. I had no intention of becoming a billionaire or interfering with the espionage of these late KGB agents against the United States. That was just...dumb luck. Lucky for me I didn't kill you sooner. I wouldn't have fallen into such wealth."

"Enough talk; move into the next room please," Ziyad said and waved his CZ 75 automatic pistol.

Jack took the lead and walked through the wide arched doorway into a large room. As each of the flashlights entered the room, it became brighter. The air was drier and the heat of the desert permeated the air. One wall was covered with a mound of sand from ceiling to floor. The group was forced up against the sand.

"A nice place for a firing squad," Turner said.

R.O. was backing up and fell into the mound of sand. His hand touched a hard surface. He shuffled the sand and felt a table top. Turner was still talking and Ziyad was telling him to hurry and get it over. R.O. then noticed a faint light in the sand. He brushed aside more sand and the glow got brighter. He leaned toward it and it brightened even more. He looked up. No one had noticed. He reached out and touched Chris on the back. He cautiously turned around.

R.O. pointed down. Chris watched as R.O. leaned into the sand and something glowed underneath. Chris moved to his left to cover him more and pulled Natalie with him. She saw what was happening. They heard Jack talking to Turner.

R.O. began to dig quickly until he felt the cover of a gilded box. The light was brighter. He laid his flashlight next to it to camouflage the light. But it began to glow brighter. He hurried and finally had the box free. It was glowing intensely.

"Hey, what are you kids doing? Shoot them first," Ziyad ordered Turner. "If you don't, I will line them up and shoot them all with one bullet from my pistol. I will steal your vengeance."

R.O. opened the lid and the light burst out like a spotlight. He closed it quickly but it was too late. It had illuminated half of the room before growing dark again. They heard Mavis speak softly.

"On three, lights out. Do it, Chris," she whispered through the shouting of Turner and Ziyad as to who would kill the MacGregors. Chris got the message.

"One, two, three!"

Everyone switched out their flashlights. Only Turner and Ziyad's were on. Chris turned and grabbed the ancient gilded box and opened the lid. The light erupted like a wind from the box, blinding everyone. Everyone gasped from the pain of the beam. Chris heaved the box toward Turner and Ziyad. Everyone scattered among the ancient furniture as the guns started blasting. It was all over in a minute.

There was silence and the gilded box lay in the middle of the room glowing like the noonday sun. They could see that the room was brightly painted and carved with ornate hieroglyphics. Turner and Ziyad lay motionless on the floor.

Jack ran over and picked up the guns and knelt down next to them. While he checked the big Arab, Jennifer checked Turner for a pulse.

"This one's gone," Jennifer said.

"Mine, too. But I don't see any bullet wounds," Jack replied.

"Me either." Jennifer raised her eyebrows.

The old professor walked over, holding one hand over his left arm, where blood had soiled his shirt.

"Professor. You were hit!" Jennifer jumped up and helped him to the floor.

"Chris, Natalie, Mavis, R.O. Everyone OK?" Jack said.

"Check, Dad," Chris said.

"Negative, Dr. MacGregor. Chris is bleeding from his ear," Natalie said.

Mavis hurried over and dabbed it with the sleeve of her shirt. A bullet had sliced through his earlobe.

"You'll be fine," she said.

"I know, Mom. That's what I said," Chris replied. "I did feel the bullet whiz by."

Mavis kissed him on the cheek.

"Hey, look at this," R.O. said. He leaned toward the box and the light got brighter. The room was on fire with the light. "Wow, it hurts my eyes," he said.

"I believe the young man has discovered the Oracle of the Nile," the old professor said. "Light and heat and to see the future."

"Can you see the future, little brother?" Chris asked.

"Give me a minute. I have it. Mom and Dad are going to buy an electronics store and give it to me." R.O. smiled.

"We just might do that," Mavis said and rose to her feet. "But for now, I want to leave this room of death behind us. Let's go."

In a moment they were all walking back through the rooms, down the rubble and stairway toward the hole in the floor that led to the river area. To their surprise, they found a ladder that had been left by one of the intruders.

"Must have been the big Arab," R.O. said.

"It's one of our ladders from the dig outside the wall. Who knows why they knew to bring it. I'm just glad they did," Jennifer said and climbed down.

After the twenty-minute walk and climb, they entered the palace of Khensu Eyuf. The sun was slipping behind the dunes to the west.

R.O. walked over and sat on the steps of the palace and looked toward the dark sky in the east. Then Chris and Natalie joined him. Soon Jack, Mavis, Jennifer and the professor were all sitting on the steps. Lights from cars and trucks could be seen on the desert road from Cairo. The modern caravan was about two miles away.

"The cavalry is coming to the rescue," Jack said with a tired voice.

Mavis leaned up against him.

"Bet it's E," R.O. said and took his spider out of his pocket. He brushed some of the caked-on dirt off his knee and set the spider on it.

Everyone was simply too exhausted to talk. But old Professor Carpenter looked like he was twenty again. A twinkle was in his eye and a smile spread across his wrinkled face.

"I can't believe I didn't see it before," he said for the hundredth time.

"But you did this time. And that's all that matters," Mavis said.

The caravan of cars and trucks stopped and dozens of people exited on the run. In the front of the pack was a fourteen-year-old blond from Texas with a very swollen lip.

"Heather!" Mavis shouted. "It's Heather!"

Mavis stood and nearly stumbled from her tired and sore legs, but she still managed to walk quickly. Heather nearly knocked her down as they collided.

"Heather," was all that Mavis could say. "You're going to have to stop doing this to me, lass," Mavis kissed her on her swollen lip.

"Ouch," Heather said. Tears rolled down her cheeks.

Soon the family was gathered around. A gust of wind signaled the coming of the night as the sand was lifted and swirled around the palace. Medics and nurses began checking everyone as E led a team of police and scientists from the Egyptian Museum into the palace and down to the subterranean treasure trove.

"Jack," Mavis said as a nurse checked her over.

"What honey?"

"I'm ready for a real vacation. And this time, you aren't going to any zoology, ecology, or environmental conference. Got that?"

"I got it," Jack replied and kissed her.

Epilogue

On the Mediterranean Sea Coast
Near Alexandria, Egypt

E walked across the expansive deck. He was dressed in a light blue silk shirt and white linen pants that were neatly pressed. The Italian loafers he wore, without socks, had small tassels on the top. His beard was neatly trimmed and his hair was combed.

"Hey E. Need a date?" Heather said as she got up out of the lounge chair in her yellow swim suit.

"I'm impressed, too," Mavis said joining them from inside the condo. "How about some lemonade and chocolate chip cookies with nuts?"

"Sure. Sounds great."

Chris was hobbling down the beach with Natalie by his side. They could see everyone on the deck and started walking back toward the group. A flock of gulls hovered overhead. Chris had been throwing peanuts up to them.

"Chris, where do we go from here?" Natalie said.

They stopped walking.

"I don't know. Where do you want to go? I mean, I've had the wildest times of my life when you're around," Chris said and laughed.

"That's my line, buster," Natalie said.

"Well. I'm eighteen. You're eighteen. What more could you want? You're not dating a younger man anymore," Chris smiled again and squeezed her hand.

Natalie wasn't smiling. She was trying to be serious.

"I have to go back to Cairo for a few days to complete my internship. They won't believe what I've been doing. Then it's back to Oklahoma next month to OSU. Classes, sorority, football games, late nights studying...you know. Pretty tame stuff compared to the way the MacGregors live," Natalie said.

"But very important stuff. I wish I could do all of that. But I am glad I get to do this too. This year will be over before we know it and I have to go to college somewhere. Maybe I'll come to Stillwater."

"Or Oxford or Cambridge or some place like that," Natalie tried to smile. Tears were forming in her eyes. "I am going to miss you so much, Chris MacGregor. But I know that we have plenty of time ahead of us."

"Natalie," Chris was looking deep into her eyes. "If there is a fire there, it will still be burning next week, next month, or even next year. It will be tough on me too, but time is on our side."

Natalie leaned forward and kissed him tenderly.

"Hey Chris! E is here!" R.O. yelled from the deck of the condo about fifty yards away.

Natalie and Chris blushed when they realized someone was watching. They walked the rest of the way up the beach and climbed the whitewashed wooden steps of the expansive deck.

"E was just telling about the investigation," Mavis said. She set down a tray with a pitcher of lemonade and glasses on the table.

"I want to hear, too," Dr. Jennifer January said as she stepped out of the condo and onto the deck.

"We didn't hear you land," Jack said.

"I didn't. I had to drive. The helicopter is in the shop

for a major overhaul. Seems I sucked up just a little too much Sahara the other day. The mechanic said he was surprised I was able to fly back to Cairo from the oasis."

"We're glad you're safe," Jack said. "Go ahead E."

"First let me give this to R.O. We found this with the Russians."

He handed a circuit board to R.O. and then a sack of electronics gear,"

"Hot dog," R.O. said as he jumped across to get it. He immediately moved to the deck and dumped it all out and began sorting through it.

"Turner was the brother of James T. Turner of Georgetown, Grand Cayman Island."

"I told you I recognized that guy," Natalie said. She looked at Chris.

"Yes, we remember that Turner well," Mavis said.

"He had hired Ziyad to find you and to, shall we say, eliminate you. He didn't know that Ziyad was involved with the Russians. We have arrested Ziyad dozens of times, but he was always able to get off. His crime family runs and owns everything in Cairo. He had connections to several terrorist organizations. So right after the Russians called Ziyad, Turner was bought out of jail. Ziyad had made the connection. He knew from then on that Turner and the Russians were after you. All he had to do was sit back and find out what was so important about it. Then he would move in."

E turned toward Jennifer.

"Your mechanic called us yesterday with some interesting news. We had suspected that Ziyad was a step ahead of all of us during the whole episode. So I told your mechanic to go over the helicopter with a fine tooth comb when you took it to get repaired. He found four listening devices.

Remember, Ziyad has been in the espionage business for nearly fifty years. He was no fool until this time he let greed kill him. He knew our plan. He knew about the trip to Ras Mohammed. He had his son waiting there for you using a secure cell phone and a faked shark attack to cover it up. He knew about the puzzle on the wall of Seti's tomb. He knew about the flight to Bahariya five hours before we did. He and Turner met in Cairo and simply drove to the desert and ditched the car. They walked into the palace and hid until the Russians arrived. The Russians, being expert at things covert, threw a camouflage net over the plane and you never spotted it," E said.

"We were way too excited to get into the palace," Chris said and sat down slowly.

"How are the leg and the ear?" E asked.

"Dr. January cleaned up the bite and put in three more stitches. It's pretty sore but I'll be good in few days. The ear will have a little dent in it, I'm afraid."

"A cute dent," Natalie said.

"Well, the professor briefed me this morning before I left the Egyptian Museum. They have been able to identify twelve different dynasties from the loot that the Mayor of Bahariya had raided from the Pharaohs. There is no estimated value. It was simply too high to calculate. It would be worth more than the entire net worth of Egypt if it were all sold on legitimate or black market venues."

"I'm stunned," Jennifer said.

"You'll be famous," R.O. piped up as he attached the circuit board to his electronic spider with a soldering iron and silver solder. He then wired the remains of Chris' radio into it. It was looking more like a deformed spider. So he connected the transmitter and amplifier and spliced in the satellite dish's cable. He wasn't sure what he was doing, but it was fun just the same. Everyone ignored him as he moved about the deck.

"That's right," Jack said.

"The professor said that the Egyptian Museum will financially support any archaeological study you want and will fund the hospital at Bahariya in the amount of ten million dollars," E said looking at Jennifer. Tears welled up in her eyes and she covered her face with her hands.

"Oh dear," Mavis said and moved over to her.

Jennifer looked up. "I've got to thank someone right now, so thank you all for making this happen. I can't believe it."

"It was fate or something I guess," Natalie said.

"It was Isis, or Anubis, or Sobek. Don't forget about them. The devourer will eat your heart," R.O. said and attached a battery power cable to the spider. Everyone ignored his remark.

"The professor will tell you more, I am sure. It is way out of my league," E said. "Well, anyway, the Egyptian government thanks you. We have made forty-three arrests in Ziyad's family and the Russian contacts in Egypt in three days. Professor Carpenter did say that they examined the mysterious box and the only conclusion they could arrive at is that it was full of rocks called molybdenum in quartz, apetite, diopside, and scheelite," E said reading from a list he had taken out of his pocket.

"He said they belong to a family of rocks that glow brightly when exposed to ultraviolet rays. They found that the funeral necklace that R.O. was wearing had some low level radioactive materials in it. Not enough to hurt you unless you wore the necklace for twenty years. But possibly enough to cause the rocks to react as you described. They still aren't sure. They'll probably test it for years."

"Then how did Turner and Ziyad die?" Jennifer asked.

"The autopsy revealed a brain aneurysm in both men. A blood vessel blew up on them," E replied.

"How weird is that?" Heather said.

Everyone revealed the same feeling by the expressions on their faces. Nobody spoke for a few seconds.

"So the Oracle of the Nile was nothing more than a box of ultraviolet radiation-sensitive rocks," Jennifer said.

"But don't forget. Two men died and no one can explain to me how they got a brain aneurysm at the same moment," Mavis said.

"More curses of the Pharaoh stuff, Mom?" Chris said and smiled. "Maybe we do need to go on that ghost castle tour in England you keep pushing."

Everyone laughed including Mavis, who was always a good sport. Well, almost always.

Suddenly the fifteen-foot diameter television satellite dish began to move. Everyone looked down at R.O. He was holding his spider with one hand and Jack's laptop computer was on the deck next to him.

"R.O.," Jack said.

"Look. I hooked up the spider to the satellite cable and the battery cable. Remember I built my spider out of Heather's radio and Chris' and all the neat stuff we got at the Little Shop of Thoth."

"You little creep. I've been looking for that radio and you had it the entire time?" Heather pushed out her swollen blue lip into an impressive pout.

"Then I found this new CD in the stuff E gave me and popped it into the laptop. When I attached the modem to the circuit board and back to the laptop, I started getting this funny picture of the earth on the screen."

Everyone crowded around the laptop LED. It was a map of the earth with orbit lines drawn all over it."

"That looks like satellite tracking," Jack said quickly.

The satellite dish suddenly stopped and the spider was going crazy. The circuit board was beginning to smoke as various connections were melted. Finally, the spider stopped moving and the laptop went dead. Jack looked at R.O.

"I think you killed both the spider and my computer," Jack said in a matter-of-fact tone.

As a father he knew that with the events of the last days, a few pieces of hardware weren't very important on the whole scale of things.

"Yea, I think you're right, Dad. Bummer. I really liked Spike," R.O. said.

Chris and Heather looked at each other and tried not to laugh. They had learned their lesson once before about R.O.'s penchant for naming things.

"Was Spike your spider, honey?" Mavis asked.

"Yup. And a good techno-arachnid he was," R.O. said and stood up. "Got any lemonade and cookies left?"

"Sure do, pal," Jack said and handed him a glass.

"Well, I must go, but I can't leave until I ask this last question," E said looking at Jack, Mavis, R.O., Chris, Heather, and Natalie individually. "Where do you go next?"

"Personally, I really do want to go visit my Mum in England and take a castle tour," Mavis said.

"I think going to the outback in Australia would be fun," Heather said.

"I have to go to Washington next week for three days to testify before Congress on the Arctic National Wilderness and oil drilling, so who knows?"

"I've always wanted to walk on the Great Wall of China and to visit the bamboo forests of the giant Pandas," Chris said.

"And I think we ought to go to Nepal so I can climb K2!" R.O. exclaimed. "Then we can go take photos of the Bengal tigers in India."

Jack's Globalstar telephone rang. He picked it up and answered.

"Dr. Jack MacGregor here. Yes, we are winding up our stay in Egypt. Yes, the Nile conference was good. It will take time but I am sure progress will be made at Aswan. I think the Nile crocodile and the waterfowl are safe, for now. Yes, that's correct. I agree. That is a most serious situation. Yes, I would like to help, but…yes, I do agree…that would be a good first step. Do you have funding for that? Excellent…yes. I could ask my family. They are accompanying me everywhere this year as I write my book. I understand. Five weeks." Jack looked at Mavis who gave him a scowl. "I could be there in say, two months." He winked at Mavis and she smiled.

"I understand. That would be dangerous, but do-able. No, I've taken risks before. Sometimes you have to in this business. OK. I agree. We'll come. Yes, I'm excited too. Yes, and I am sure they will be excited as well. Thank you. I'll look for the details in my email. Give me a couple of days to get a new computer. Mine just got fried. Oh it was just a simple accident. Very good. You, too. Good-bye."

Jack turned off the Globalstar telephone and set it on the table. All eyes were glued on him.

"What?" he said firmly.

"Well, Hon. I believe the children and I are waiting to hear about our next stop. You know, this book you are writing and what not," Mavis said in her best British accent sounding very aristocratic and nothing like the Texas-Brit mom she was back home.

Chris, Heather, R.O., Natalie, Jennifer and even E were sitting on the edge of their chairs.

"You'll be so excited to hear," Jack said. He took a sip of lemonade and smiled.

• • • • •

NASA Uplink Terminal
Alice Springs, Northern Territory
Australia

"Hey, Jeffrey. Did you see that?"
"Sure did, mate. The whole screen lit up like the Olympics in Sydney."

"Every satellite link came on-line for a least ten seconds. We need to notify HQ and call Houston on a secure line. Let them know that someone someplace on mother earth just hacked into the world's most secure satellite communication system."

"That's weird. The signal came from somewhere along the Mediterranean coast, possibly Egypt or Libya."

"Probably Libyan terrorists up to something again. Better notify the National Security Administration and the CIA, too. They may want to turn their eyes on that beach, yep, there it is, near Alexandria, Egypt. They'll get a good look the next time one of their 'big brother' satellites flies over."

"Looks like that'll be in about eleven minutes. As for me, I brought two corned beef and Swiss on rye. Do you want hot or mild mustard on yours?"

****

"OK. Dad, we're dying to know," Heather said. "Please?"

"Well, this family has been beat up pretty badly the last three months, and I did promise your mother a real vacation. I do need to do more library research so we need to go where I can spend some time with books, confer with colleagues via the internet, and basically gather my thoughts. I've decided we should go to Naples, Italy, for about two months. A colleague has a large villa we can use for free. It is close to several universities and libraries. Then around November or December, we'll continue our journey. I've mapped out wildlife projects in China, India, Australia, South America, and Antarctica. But our next stop, I should say adventure, will be ..."

They all hung on the edge of their chairs.

"ALASKA!"

Coming Soon from Pelican Publishing Company:

Czar of Alaska: The Cross of Charlemagne

Look for the next book in the *MacGregor Family Adventure Series* as they continue their epic journey around the earth!

Arctic National Wildlife Refuge, oil drilling, environmental terrorists, caribou migrations, giant grizzlies, whales, sled dogs, sea otters, and a host of exciting characters are all wrapped up in a modern adventure about Alaska.

Disclaimer and Warning to All Readers

Electricity can injure and kill. Kids should never play with electronics or electricity. They should only be involved in electronic "type" projects under the supervision of their parents or legal guardian.

SCUBA diving should not be attempted without prior training and certification by a professional dive master. Diving without professional instruction can kill or injure.

The exploration of caves should be left to professional explorers. Caving is a dangerous sport.

Minors should never use firearms without professional training and supervision of their parents or legal guardians. Responsible use of any firearm, by any person, is of the utmost importance. Shooting sports and hunting should only be attempted after proper supervision by a professionally trained person or organization and within the statutes of the jurisdiction where you live.

Hang-gliding is a unique but very dangerous sport and should only be attempted after professional training and under the supervision of parents or legal guardian.

The MacGregor family kids are involved in dangerous and life-threatening endeavors in all of their adventures. Children should be warned that this is a work of fiction and in real life only trained professionals are involved in these activities. At the age of adulthood, with professional training and safety precautions, many of these activities may be safely duplicated.

Richard E. Trout and Langmarc Publishing

NOTES

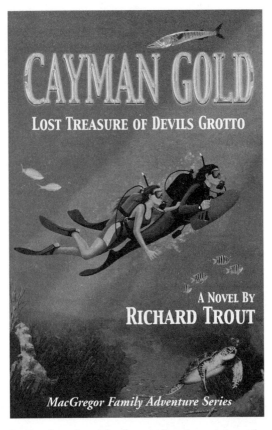

CAYMAN GOLD

LOST TREASURE OF DEVILS GROTTO

A NOVEL BY
RICHARD TROUT

MacGregor Family Adventure Series

Suddenly faced with the task of saving a lost Spanish treasure embedded in protected coral reef, the MacGregor teens rely on their courage and scuba-diving skills to explore and investigate the waters and beaches of the Cayman Islands. This first novel in the techno-thriller *MacGregor Family Adventure Series* involves sinister pirate forces, strange sea creatures, and hospitable natives, as well as issues of endangered species and environmental management. Meticulously detailed yet quick-paced, this novel is an introduction to the enterprising MacGregor clan, who have just entered what will be a full year of worldwide escapades. As with each Richard Trout book, the themes of family and wildlife conservation are apparent throughout each adventure.

ELEPHANT TEARS
Mask of the Elephant

A NOVEL BY
RICHARD TROUT

MacGregor Family Adventure Series

In this second novel in the *MacGregor Family Adventure Series*, zoologist Dr. Jack MacGregor again strives to protect the earth's dwindling resources and endangered animals, pursuing an international cartel that is exploiting elephants in East Africa. The family's three teenagers, Chris, Heather, and Ryan, become part of the action and team up with native Africans and a seasoned American aviator to save the animals and bring the exploiters to justice. Traversing the landscape of Serengeti, Amboseli, Masai Mara, and Mount Kilimanjaro, the MacGregor teens learn about African culture and wildlife through the eyes of their new friend, native Kikuyu Samburua. This is another stimulating, action-packed journey that will appeal to all ages with its contemporary perspective of culture, environmental management, and solid family values.

NOTES

NOTES